AFTER THE FIRST DEATH THERE IS NO OTHER

The Iowa School of Letters Award for Short Fiction

AFTER THE FIRST DEATH THERE IS NO OTHER

Natalie L. M. Petesch

University of Iowa Press, Iowa City

The previously published stories in this collection appear by permission:

"A Brief Biography of Ellie Brume," *Kansas Quarterly* 6 (Winter, 1973–74).

"L'il Britches," *Texas Observer* 56 (December, 1964).

"Nails," *Second Wave* 2 (Summer, 1972).

"Selma," *South Dakota Review* 10 (Spring, 1972).

"The Girl Who Was Afraid of Snow," *Moving Out* 2 (February, 1972).

"The End of the World," *University of Portland Review* 23 (Spring, 1971).

Library of Congress Cataloging in Publication Data

Petesch, Natalie L   M   1924–
    After the first death there is no other.

        CONTENTS: The grievance adjuster.—A brief biography
    of Ellie Brume.—My crystal. [etc.]
        I. Title.
    PZ4.P4877Af [PS3566.E772]   813'.5'4   74–8851
    ISBN 0–87745–050–1

University of Iowa Press, Iowa City 52242
© 1974 by The University of Iowa. All rights reserved
Printed in the United States of America

. . . for the lovers, their arms
Round the griefs of the ages . . . .

—Dylan Thomas

Contents

The Grievance Adjuster

work for an insurance company. We are not really big, though we have been around a long time. Not your Hancock, Hartford, Prudential kind of thing. No Lloyds of London. We're old but reputable, and—in spite of occasional rumblings in the stock market—solvent. You've heard of Vita, doubtless. You've wondered, exactly what we insure.

We insure, not your life, but your beliefs. Those others who insure your life, can bring your widow or children a monthly check after you die. But who has the hardihood (or the charity) as we do, to indemnify for despair? In every policy issued by us there is a special Fealty Clause which offers full compensation for loss: of Faith, of Love, of Belief in the Several Varieties of Western Religion, or of Interest in Your Work. Along with this is included (under Section II B) a low-priced but comprehensive coverage for the parents of war-deserters (both those residing abroad and those in U.S. prisons). We also have a popular low-premium "B" policy for Bitterness and/or Boredom. All policies are non-cancellable.

You can see now—our policies are rather different. Not something everyone would think of. Yet most of my friends—just ordinary clerks, managers, salesmen, teachers, parents—are insured by my Company. I myself am what is known as "insurance poor." I keep my beliefs under constant surveillance. As soon as my optimism flags, I increase my insurance coverage. Just as you would, if you noticed a twinge of arthritis. "Old age," you might think to yourself. "Better up my coverage, just in case." In this way I keep myself insured against every contingency. My highest premium is paid to the Company against loss of faith in the Company. If this seems absurd, just think about it a moment. It's my livelihood, isn't it? And don't pianists insure their hands? dancers their legs? Thus I am heavily insured against Catastrophic Despair, the first sign of which, as you may have observed, is unbelief. Since joining the Company I have tried to handle all claims equitably: I am a professional, not one who single-mindedly, and with obvious self-interest, bucks for the Company.

Therefore I approach today's assignment, L—— Apartments, with something like ceremony. I am dressed for the occasion—dark suit, clean, white buttoned-down shirt; both are in that simple style which is no longer fashionable but which has the advantage of never being flashy. I try always to look the same—calm, ministerial: after all, freedom from pain is a kind of sacrament.

Now I notice that L—— Apartments are vaguely familiar to me. I have probably been here before. That is good: that probably means that, recently at least, there has not been much despair here. It will be a routine day, an easy day. There are some days when I feel I owe it to myself to have easy days. Like the cancer specialist who looks solidly at his list of "recoveries": how long since there has been any new growth? Despair, I've noticed, tends to be recidivistic.

Yes, I have been here before. About two years ago. Not much has changed. What was their claim? I check my casebook: I see that it was a marriage which had been abruptly destroyed. After twenty-three years the wife had committed suicide; the husband, Mr. Sardis, naturally demanded payment for the destruction of his faith: a triple indemnity case. He claimed no longer to believe in love, marriage, or even the resurrection of the dead: a very bad case. We were obliged, initially, to pay him a large sum of money, since obviously the death of his wife constituted irreversible damage. Fortunately, however, his

2

daughter was at that time of a marriageable age, and we were able to persuade him to invest the remainder of his claim in his daughter's future. This investment turned out to be a success: his daughter quickly married a nice young man from Skyros, and Mr. Sardis was soon looking forward to being a grandfather. Since that time he has received only minimal payment for the loss of the wife. If Mr. Sardis should remarry, then according to Section VI Paragraph 2(b) of his policy, the Company would no longer be obliged to make these payments, as to all intents and purposes, Mr. Sardis would have entered into a period of renewed optimism.

I now remembered the case very well. I had been just a beginner with Vita Company and Mr. Sardis's claim had been the largest settled by the Company that year. At the time I had been troubled by thoughts of my own inadequacy in handling the suit, but the Vice President, Mr. Cormoran, assured me personally that no Grievance Adjuster could have done better. Now, two years since that visit, I noticed that the walls of L—— Apartments were still limned with water stains which had oozed down the dun-colored paint in oddly obscene designs: they had not painted the place after all (I made a note of it). I began to climb slowly up the stairs as the elevator was still not working (I made a note of it).

I must confess I felt slightly annoyed by these physical liabilities. How was I to do my job without cooperation from the authorities? They had promised they would repair the elevator shortly after receiving a minor adjustment claim from the fifth floor. The tenant, Mrs. Kovic, suffered from a heart ailment, and when she had made the claim (she sued on a Bitterness and/or Boredom Policy, a policy in which—really—the Company just breaks even, they are thinking of discontinuing it). We had granted her immediate cash payment as it seemed a matter easily taken care of and not likely to repeat itself. After all, it was merely a question of repairing the elevator. Claims for invisible losses are much harder to adjust and inevitably more expensive: that is where all my professional skill comes in. Skill, not guile. Vita Company does not need to misrepresent anything or anyone. "A Grievance Adjuster is a moral bookkeeper—he is neither crook, casuist nor clown," I sometimes remind my wife, Moira, who likes to hear me say so.

With this phrase in mind I knock, not tentatively but with confidence at Mrs. Williams' door. I refuse to notice that her door is colored with pizza sauce, pink popsicle juice and the imprint of fists—all blending into an unrecognizable blur as if brought about by some grotesque struggle between hunger and brute force. But I refuse to be distracted by these signs of conflict. A sign is not a *conclusion*, I tell myself in most professional manner. I now enter and refuse again to take in the odor in which it seems the whole apartment is enveloped. I will tell Moira tonight: "The whole apartment was like an *enchilada* stuffed with its own odor."

This pleasant image dissolves, however, as I glance at Mrs. Williams' face. She has not risen to greet me but remains seated at the small table in the combination living-room-kitchen. Though she does not rise to greet me, I feel my visit is not hopeless, because I sense here, not despair but anger. Anger is easier to handle, there are outlets. With despair one is operating in a vacuum: nothing can be evoked, not even rage. We pay incredible indemnity rates for despair.

Mrs. Williams and I understand each other at once, no need for amenities. She knows why I am here. She is "Furious."

"They got me this job cleanin' up at the hospital," she says. "What I need a job for? I got two chillrun here, don't I? And the baby don't even *walk* yet by hisself. I need *money*, that's all I need. I don't need no job where I don't learn nothin' except what I already know." She paused, sucked in her breath angrily, readying it to blast out again: "Now they want me to go cleanin' up after sick people, people *dyin'*. They just usin' us to help break up the hospital strike, what *I* think, but I ain't political no way. Politics don't interest me, but buyin' groceries *do* interest me. And they don't want to even pay me enough to buy groceries with. Then I supposed to come back here and do all my *own* work."

From where I stood I could see that the apartment was badly in need of cleaning, that where supper should have been cooking there steamed a metal pail. Diapers, I observed to myself. She wouldn't be cooking in that thing (I made a note of it). She was now demanding full payment. She said she was "madder than a bull," that she was "fit to be tied," that she was "ready to go down to Welfare and picket," etc., etc. But I was quick to notice that in spite of her rage there were overtones of "Idealism" —that in spite of her wrath she referred frequently, with tenderness and dedication, to her children. My experience as a Grievance Adjuster indicates that "Anger" combined with "Idealism" will give you a fair prognosis. It will nearly always turn out to be far less costly than, say, "Depression" or even sometimes less expensive than "Boredom." Because in cases of "Depression," you will frequently find the client calling back several weeks later to be indemnified for "Self-loathing," "Despair" or even "Attempted Suicide"—all included under our Catastrophic Coverage, of course, but very expensive for the Company to settle. Therefore Mrs. Williams' anger was a good sign.

But as I suggested before, I am not one of these Grievance Adjusters who is interested only in avoiding Company responsibility. If Mrs. Williams could really benefit by maximum compensation for "Rage," I was prepared to fill out the necessary forms for her prompt reimbursement. But would she so benefit? After anger, what? We at Vita Company have learned that a generous investment in the pacification of "Rage" will bring you back a return of 33⅓ per cent on every insurance dollar. For instance, suppose Mrs. Williams *should* go amok and badly batter one or both of her children? Later someday we at Vita Company would have to compensate the children at triple the present rates. Also we have statistical evidence that battered children are not amenable to reinvestment in the Company—no matter what future incentives are offered them. So then, it is clearly a question of restoring Mrs. Williams' belief in happiness so that some day her children will not be arbitrarily rejected for one of our noncancellable Fealty Policies. So it is a very delicate moral decision which I must now make.

I decide, therefore, that it is one of those occasions for Gifts and Prizes. Gifts and Prizes are what we give occasionally instead of cash when the situation is frankly "Economic." These clients are (quite simply) the product of a third or even fourth generation "Poverty-Syndrome," and it is best to temper their outbursts with Prizes. We have these programmed far in advance. So I now show Mrs. Williams our Illustrated Catalogue of Gifts and Prizes, rewards which she is guaranteed by the Company to enjoy once she has adjusted to her present powerlessness: a color TV (Mrs. Williams' eyes widened at once, and I knew I was on the right track); a trip to Disneyland; a lifetime gift certificate to Sheffburger's where she and her children could enjoy a Superburger Supper (with Coke) once a week anywhere in the United States or Europe; a retirement condominium near a simulated lake in Turkey, Arizona (it was to be in a development which the Company had not yet built but we were programmed for just such clients as Mrs. Williams: it was an imaginative plan which, in effect, created a ruralization of the ghetto —and twenty years from now, according to our Vice President, Mr. Cormoran, Mrs. Williams would be able to have the very same or similar neighbors she presently enjoyed in L—— Building right beside her in Turkey, Arizona). We also included among our more immediate Gifts and Prizes an arrangement whereby Mrs. Williams' children would be bussed to a school (on a strictly volunteer basis, of course) to receive Quality Education.*

I could see at a glance that my first assignment for the day was working out perfectly. Mrs. Williams not only ceased to be "Angry" but she began to cry. That was perfect. She was now ready for joy, and I left her a bottle of our best quality Möet, which, if she should feel slightly depressed later, she might enjoy at her leisure: and it would also help her sleep.

My success with Mrs. Williams had created in me a euphoria, a satisfaction with my work which most employees rarely experience: not everyone is privileged to deflect anger and create

---

* I hasten to add in the event Vita Company should through any oversight of mine be accused of conscious or unconscious racism that the Company has not nor has it ever had any written record of Mrs. Williams' racial or ethnic background. My record book, for example, does not indicate whether Mrs. Williams was black, Puerto-Rican, or Oriental. I can testify that Mrs. Williams' deprivations were purely "Economic" and did not constitute discrimination on the basis of race, age, sex, or national origin by Vita Company.

happiness. The illusion of happiness, you will say. But I affirm that there is not any difference.

Take the case, a most difficult one, of the artist-fellow who lives on the fifth floor of L—— Building (the top one—he shares the bathroom with Mrs. Kovic). His name is Bill Corbie, but he signs his paintings Twa Corbies because, he explains, he had an identical twin who died in infancy and he has always felt a double responsibility to live and work: in short, he claims to be *both* Corbies. An odd idea, you will admit. Corbie was a fairly good artist, though that is really not relevant here. He had called me in to state his claim: "Self-Loathing." Maintaining that professional decorum which is so necessary if one is employed by Vita Company, I managed to refrain from remarking: *"Both selves, Mr. Corbie?"* It was fortunate that I made no such remark, because I soon realized that it was a very serious matter to him. He had discovered himself to be in a desperate and ironic situation. He could not even commit suicide: first, because he felt he owed one life, so to speak, to his deceased brother; second, because the pleasure his brain experienced at the sight of a World he could not stop painting made it impossible for him to destroy the consciousness wherein that brain resided. Finally —and I believe this to have been his real crux—his craving for an audience for his Art was so insatiable that he could not face Death without first having satisfied that craving. In a word: Death itself was meaningless to him unless he could share his paintings first. At least so he explained it, as he issued his complaint.

So, in spite of this "Loathing" for himself, Corbie continued painting, despising himself more every day for not having the ferocity to finish it off with one final *hari-kari*. And he drank a lot: always a bad sign. When he finally telephoned Vita Company, our Vice President, Mr. Cormoran, greatly feared we would have to indemnify Corbie to the fullest. When I first arrived at L—— Building in answer to Corbie's call (I made several visits that month, by the way, which I seldom do), I was inclined to agree with Mr. Cormoran. Corbie joked and laughed with fearful desperation, and every joke was aimed at himself. These self-flagellant bouts of merriment were followed by a horrible digust.

I felt that what he wished most of all was that some obliging visitor (myself) would strike him across the face, expressing that disdain and contempt for the identity of Bill Corbie which he himself so whole-heartedly shared. If I had done so, I felt certain he would have looked at me, tears of self-loathing welling in his eyes, and he would have murmured: "I deserve it. I deserve it. You are right to punish me: I've wasted my life. . . ." Or some such nonsense. To indulge such fellows would put Vita Company in danger of bankruptcy every time some self-professed genius turned his hand to a brush.

I should perhaps mention with regard to Corbie's case that it was nearing the end of the year and we had had several claims similar to his, which Vita Company (rather quixotically, I think), had paid in full. Vita's bookkeepers were at that very time working on our annual budget, trying to balance our accounts. If we were not to pay out an exorbitant sum—made even more prohibitive by the fact that Corbie had succeeded years ago in persuading the Company to expand his Fealty Policy to include his deceased twin, it was necessary for the Company to take strong practical measures.

Mr. Cormoran advised "Fireproofing." "Fireproofing" had been very useful in the past with artists and sculptors, and has even been successful with those women who practice the antique arts—embroidery, quilting, needlepoint, lacemaking, etc. Women, we have found, are equally fanatical about their "Art," although the usefulness of their product spares the Company some of the pretensions of your Corbie-type artist. We of course understood what Mr. Cormoran intended. Our Fireproofers were sent out during the evening while Corbie was out having his usual drink in a neighborhood bar. Two Vita Company Fireproofers climbed to the roof of L—— Building and carefully— and of course without being seen—set fire to Corbie's apartment through the window facing the courtyard. It was easy to do; the curtains were paper thin and the yellow window shades were as dry as onion skin. The Proofers had opened the gas jets for a few minutes and a gust of wind from the courtyard made the whole place immediately combustible. But Vita Company has perfected the technique over the years, and the Proofers knew precisely at what moment to send a man over to the neighborhood bar to inform Corbie that L—— Building was on fire.

Immediately Corbie rushed across the street to L—— Building, up the five flights of stairs (the elevator was not working), and without a thought for his own safety hurled himself into the blazing apartment to rescue his paintings (the Proofers had set the fire in the living room so that nearly all Corbie's paintings stored in the back bedroom were unharmed by the heat). Corbie rescued as many as he could, at tremendous risk to himself. In the process of doing so, his left hand was so badly burned that several fingers later became gangrenous and were removed. Yet we were not surprised to hear that upon being discharged from the hospital Corbie recalled his claim. In his own eyes, you understand, he was some kind of hero: he had risked all to save what he valued more than life itself. Even the loss of the fingers on his left hand spurred him to rejoice that nothing worse had happened, that for instance, it had not been his *right* hand which had been injured in the fire. To this day Bill Corbie works every day with absolute dedication and has even begun something new which he calls "Scripturing." Using a mixture of gilt and oils which creates the burnished glow of *egg tempera*, he is now preparing an illuminated manuscript of the Bible. And he is as abstemious as a medieval monk.

Vita Company paid all the hospital expenses for Corbie, and in order to assure themselves of Corbie's continued high spirits (and to prevent backsliding) I was instructed by Mr. Cormoran to purchase at company expense several of Corbie's paintings. I keep these paintings out at my summer cottage on the Cape; but I regret to say that they are not holding up well against the salt sea air.

If our solution to Corbie's case seems ingenious, it is elementary when contrasted with our handling of "Z" cases.* When we have a "Z" case, we are obliged to use "Gratitude Shock." "Gratitude Shock" is quite simply a form of shock therapy, except that we use no mechanical devices whatsoever. In this type of treat-

---

* A "Z" Case is one that is classified as basically "Hopeless" or "Catatonic."

ment the client is brought out to witness suffering so brutal that, trembling with fear, he returns prostrate with gratitude for his exemption from pain. After such treatments it is usually a long time before we hear from the client again. The client himself, so to speak, fearful that he may again be subjected to this vicarious suffering, assimilates his own complaints, acts as his own Grievance Adjuster. It works quite simply. When a "Z" complaint is registered with Vita Company, usually by a friend or relative, the client is taken on what at first seems to him a kind of school-outing (there is no point in frightening him so that he is incapable of apprehending the full seriousness of what he is about to witness). A Vita Special Service Officer takes him on what is called a HAP-tour: that is, a guided tour of *H*ospitals, *A*sylums, or *P*risons, or sometimes a combination of all three. Because of their remarkable effectiveness (Vita reports a 99.3 therapeutic capability), these tours are privately referred to by our Special Service Officers as HAP-piness Tours. In spite of what would seem a high initial expense for these tours (partly accounted for by the fact that the Special Service Officers themselves are frequently obliged to file disability claims), these tours have been found to be an excellent resource for the Company. In the long run, they are a time-saving device and then, too, for clients who have been exposed to "Gratitude Shock" there is rarely any necessity for persuasion with Gifts and Prizes.

But of course some cases are naturally harder to deal with than others. On one occasion that I recall, the Company, resigning itself to its loss, was about to settle a "Z" claim. The man had been a prosecuting attorney and had got involved in some political intrigue in which he himself was arraigned, tried and sent to prison (I don't recall the exact charge, but it was an unappealable conviction). After he had served his sentence, he informed Vita Company that he no longer wished to practice any sort of law, that he had nothing to say about crime, penalties and executions. Above all, that he had not a word to say about justice. It was one of those cases where, by a single experience, a man loses touch with the practical realities of life.

Now this client, Mr. Todd, had shut himself up in his room, refusing to eat or drink. He had set his record player to play continuously—some very sentimental song from the thirties. A Benny Goodman record, I believe. When I arrived at L—— Building, he was still playing the same record. The apartment was a shambles. His splendid German Shepherd, Bailiff, was chained to the sink. I give this detail because if a man will not take care of his dog, an adjuster knows the case has become "Hopeless" and/or "Catatonic." Because even suicides, as a final, abortive gesture will often free their dogs or open the cages for their canary. This is a very curious fact, because in such cases it seems to me they wish to bestow upon a mere animal what they themselves no longer desire: freedom. What they do want is imprisonment: imprisonment in an endless, unthinking, unfeeling and painless death. If they thought Death was a *continuation* of anything, they wouldn't do it, you see? I know all about these people. I've heard them rant and rave.

Anyway, this particular client, Mr. Todd, had not even freed his dog. The man himself was lying in bed—or rather, he was laid out in his own shroud since he clearly had no intention of ever rising again. When I pulled him to his feet, he simply stared at me in an exhausted, mindless way, as if he had forgotten how to speak. I hustled him into my car and took him down to the wards for shock.

I poked some adrenalin into him to keep him walking. And we walked up and down the aisles. It was a Solzhenitsyn-type ward: everyone groaning, rotting, vomiting, expectorating, calling for blood transfusions, bedpans, awaiting clotting, searing, cutting, swathing. In spite of my training, it is sometimes more than I can stand. My client collapsed in hysteria. They led him screaming and sobbing back into real life. In my own opinion the man was a perfect case of Self-pity. No other treatment would have been adequate to jar him from his self-preoccupation. We taught him something and I think such moments are the high point of our Company. The man went home sobbing with relief that his mouth was not swelling with a monstrous growth. The idea was: he could *speak*, couldn't he? What matter then that he no longer had anything to say?

At least this is the way Vita Company looks at it. If we seem not to be entirely disinterested, if it profits the Company to have a man live by his terrors and delusions, well—what is a business for? Vita Company has never represented itself as a non-profit organization, although it is true that personally I attempt to harmonize what at first sight seem to be incompatibles.

But these are two severe cases, long become a part of Vita history. I can see now by my appointment calendar that one of the clients whom I am obliged to visit today, for a strictly routine check-up, is Mr. Sardis.

Perhaps you noticed a visible reluctance on my part to do so? But it is absolutely essential to return to High Indemnity Cases such as Mr. Sardis' for a regular inspirational talk in order to avoid backsliding. If the client has had a major relapse during the period and for some reason or other has failed to report his condition, such relapses can turn out to be very expensive for the Company. We are a company, incidentally, which prides itself on satisfaction rendered in even disputed claims. And even if the client himself has gone too far to make a claim, as sometimes happens, we are prepared to reimburse the heirs with a certain number of shares of Vita Company (preferred), now worth three times their original value compared to the going rate at the time the Company first started.

So I tried to approach Mr. Sardis' apartment with optimism, but I confess now, I had a certain foreboding. When he came to the door at my knock, he stared over my head with an odd, blinking expression, his gaze glancing just off my forehead in the direction of a light filtering through a porthole window at the landing: actually, one could see little or nothing out of it. In the silence which followed, while I stood smiling agreeably at Mr. Sardis, I could hear the buzz of a fly which had flown this far toward the porthole window. I began chatting amiably for a few moments but Mr. Sardis gave no sign of listening. I put my hand on his arm to draw his attention, meaning also by this unusual intimacy to show my willingness to hear any complaint he might like to make. After a moment's pause, I entered the apartment and we sat down together at the small table provided in all the apartments. Mr. Sardis continued blinking at me, an indescribable look on his face: neither joy nor grief. Yet I received the impression of a clever client who has somehow outwitted the Company. When Mr. Sardis picked up a bottle of wine and poured me a glass I thought we had finally broken through this ridiculous situation. *"Drink, drink,"* he said at last. "Everybody drink." He had not poured any for himself, however. Although I am not much of a winebibber, especially during working hours, I raised the glass to my lips, nodding it in his direction in a slight but unmistakable gesture of a toast. I drank the liquid down so we could come to the heart of the matter. I began speaking in my softest tones, very sympathetically, asking him questions about his present life. But he remained silent, insisting instead in his strange pantomine on pouring me more wine. Why, this client means to get me drunk, I thought with annoyance. But why? Suddenly Mr. Sardis slapped his palm on the table with a hearty gesture and without excusing himself went to the bathroom. I must confess that at this point sweat broke out on my forehead. If Mr. Sardis should do away with himself while I was actually present in the apartment, it would be a serious reflection on Vita Company's ability to deal with recidivism. So I rose apprehensively when I heard water; it sounded as if the taps had been opened full force and water was pouring into the bathtub. I hurried to the door, listening. No, it was not the bathtub at all, it was the shower, the sound of rushing water on the shower curtain.

Then suddenly I hear Mr. Sardis, and he is *singing* in a loud, joyous baritone. He sings irrepressibly, leaping disconnectedly from one song to another, plainly without any repertoire in mind —an aimless flood of tunes picked up from the radio and television commercials, all running senselessly together like the flotsam of water streaming from his body.

Mr. Sardis is obviously stark mad, and it is a relief to me to be so certain of it, and certain also that it is not one of your murderous types: I prefer a singing madness to almost any other kind.

While Mr. Sardis is busy in the bathroom, I look around for items to be included in the indemnification report. I am also, I must confess it, not a little curious as to what could have pushed Mr. Sardis into this madness of perpetual song. Nearly everything in the apartment seemed ordinary and commonplace, except for a couple of letters which had been pasted onto the kitchen pantry and circled round and round with gold crayon: a memo not to be overlooked. I decided Vita Company would certainly want exact copies of these letters so I quickly transcribed what I read (we are taught a variant of Pittman shorthand during In-service training, precisely for these sorts of occasions):

ALCON ALCOHOLIC REHABILITATION CENTER

July 16, 197–

Mr. Alexander Sardis
2200 Laird Building
Apt. C-2
City

Dear Mr. Sardis,

We regret to inform you that we see as yet no improvement in the condition of your daughter, Mrs. Constantia Adrianopolou. We are presently feeding her intravenously and hope that in time she can be induced to eat normal foods.

However we cannot give you any false encouragement. During her last hospitalization, which as you know lasted nine days, she incurred considerable damage to the kidneys–a not unusual side-effect of dehydration.

In reply to your inquiry, therefore, we strongly advise that some arrangement be provided for the children, as any home visitations at this time would be counterproductive both for Mrs. Adrianopolou as well as for her family.

Cordially yours,

(Mrs.) H. M. Verrechio
T. Berring-Smith
Lydia Mattieu

The other letter was from the shipping company at which Mr. Adrianopolou was employed:

XERXES FREIGHTERS INC.

August 21, 197—

Mr. Alexander Sardis
2200 Laird Building
Apt. C—2
City

Dear Sir:

In reply to your letter of August 10, your son-in-law, Mr. Patroclus Adrianopolou was discharged from our service on March 15 of this year following an incident which took place on board ship. Mr. Adrianopolou was accused of stabbing a shipmate on board the Herakles during a quarrel over a passenger whom they had smuggled aboard at Tangiers. (The passenger, a minor, was released into the custody of his parents.) Although charges were eventually dropped against Mr. Adrianopolou, it was by the unanimous consent of all persons on board that Mr. Adrianopolou was discharged from service with six months severance pay.

We regret that we cannot help you any further in the search for your son-in-law. We would advise you to contact the Greek embassy at Tangiers.

Yours truly,

Malcolm G. Thibiades

This was obviously a very complicated case, one that I felt I ought not to write up for indemnification until all details were made available for Company consideration. In the meantime, it seemed an excellent idea to leave matters just where they stood, at least until I could consult with Mr. Cormoran. As for Mr. Sardis, he would not even remember that I had been there. So I rinsed out the wine glasses, placing them upside down on the drainboard, and without further ado exited Mr. Sardis' apartment. I made certain, however, that I locked the door to the apartment as it was obvious Mr. Sardis himself was very careless of these matters.

I found myself rather nervous after this visit, weighed down as though with the sense of an uncompleted task. Ironically I felt I could have used another little glass of the wine Mr. Sardis had mysteriously pressed upon me, so I decided to finish off the morning's work with a friendly chat with Mrs. Kovic. She frequently offered me some sweet wine which she kept for the holidays. I therefore knocked on her door with a sigh of relief: a few minutes more and I would be on my way home. I imagined Moira smiling. . . . The image disappeared as I realized that Mrs. Kovic was not coming to the door. She rarely went farther than to the corner grocery—even on those days when she felt well enough to go out—so I waited a few moments and knocked again. I thought I heard a rustling of papers inside. She is definitely in the apartment, I thought. I knocked more loudly. Sometimes with these old people you have a gradual hearing loss. At first it's hardly noticeable to them, then suddenly you realize they no longer hear a word you are saying. Sometimes, of course, when it is convenient, they are only pretending not to hear: perhaps this was the case. I waited with a combination of impatience and deference (Mrs. Kovic had been a client with us nearly fifty years); then at last I decided to use my passkey. It is part of my work to account for any mysterious circumstances. Nothing is to go unchecked. So I noisily let myself in with the passkey, hoping that if Mrs. Kovic were asleep, the sound would waken her.

She was sitting at the small table in the living room. Her back was to the door. I stood for a moment, key in hand, uncertain what to do next. She was dressed to go out. Then I noticed that although it had not been raining outdoors, Mrs. Kovic's big black umbrella, widened as if its spring had broken, now lay like an opened parachute at her feet. Her hand lay on the telephone directory. The movement of inanimate objects—the swaying of the curtains at the open window, the tremble of a potted flower—made a strange impression upon me as if I had entered a theater in which the play was about to begin. Mrs. Kovic herself seemed about to rise and play her part.

I approached the body carefully. I am not very good at ascertaining how long a person has been dead, but there was an unpleasantness in the air, obviated only by the open window. I saw now that it had been the wind coming up from the courtyard which had rustled the papers I had heard as I waited in the hallway. On the table beside Mrs. Kovic were several cans of cat food, still in a brown paper bag: but the hungry cat, for whom Mrs. Kovic had apparently made her grocery trip in the rain, had gone out the window probably never to return. The phone directory was open at the Vita Company page. I deduced that Mrs. Kovic was about to call us for help when her heart failed. An error, of course: she should have phoned for an ambulance: Vita does not provide ambulances.

I decided there was no point in removing any of her clothing —she was still bundled up in raincoat and boots, with a scarf wound round her head. I managed to free her stiffened finger from the dial, however; then I put in a call for an ambulance. I decided it would be best to shut up the place in order to protect the property from vandals. Pressing the full weight of my arms down on the window sash, I managed to shut the window; but the lock was rusty and would not lock (I made a note of it).

While waiting for the ambulance I walked around the apartment, filling out my report. I had little doubt that Mrs. Kovic had reported her income with complete honesty. There was nothing to indicate that her situation had not been exactly what my record book indicated. "Pensioned. Disability 100%." Sometimes after a client dies the Company will refuse settlement if it discovers that while claiming 100% Disability the client has been gainfully employed or has been attending classes for educational advancement or has engaged in other activities which indicate that his or her health has not, after all, been 100% impaired. In Mrs. Kovic's case I felt certain she had not falsified any of her reports. I checked to see if she had any living children to whom I should send a copy of my report: Yes: one child, a daughter in Ohio. Accustomed to utilizing my waiting period I made out my report in triplicate (one copy for the Company, one for my personal records and one for the surviving daughter) while I listened for the arrival of the ambulance.

The ambulance came in about twenty minutes. I could hear the drivers calling up the stairwell, trying to locate the apartment we were in. But I decided not to walk all the way down those stairs just to direct them to a dead body: a few minutes more would not matter. I did go out into the hallway and call down the staircase to indicate that I was on the top floor.

They were very angry about the elevator. "What the hell kind of a building is this, anyway?" one of them demanded, glowering angrily until I explained it was owned by Vita Company. He lowered his eyes respectfully after that: no doubt a Vita client himself.

They made no effort to straighten Mrs. Kovic out but heaved her awkward shape onto the litter (with her bulky clothes and dark, wrinkled skin she made me think of some prehistoric mammoth found in the frozen depths of Siberia). The ambulance men did have a great deal of difficulty winding the litter around the narrow staircase, but I must say they maneuvered skillfully. At no time was Mrs. Kovic's body in danger of toppling down the stairs. Once in the street they slid the litter onto a rack in the van with that kind of expertise only experience can bring. However, in backing away from the curb they knocked over a garbage can. I exchanged glances with the driver through the rear view mirror, expecting him to stop and upright the barrel, but he did not. The litter lay in the street in quite a disgusting manner. I noticed a wig had fallen from out of the barrel and lay on the sidewalk, its strands of hair splayed in such a realistic way that if I had picked it up I would not have been surprised to find it covered a shrunken skull. Of course I had no intention of touching any of that sordid-looking trash: orange-peelings, coffee grounds, and that kind of slimy debris from which one averts one's eyes. I turned my head instead to where Mrs. Kovic lay on the rack slightly above me. Her body seemed to take up most of the space in the van, obliging me to squat down while I wrote up the details of this case in my report book. I thought the abandonment of the debris on the sidewalk deserved a complaint against the ambulance drivers, and I made a note of it.

A Brief Biography
of Ellie Brume

To Gladys Schmitt

"Each of us is the other to the others."
R. D. Laing's *The Politics of Experience.*

The idea of being born, Ellie confided to friends, was obsolete. David Copperfield had it all backward: she herself had apprehended nothing during the first seventeen years of her life; all her experience was learned long after the fact, in retrospect. That was why she set her "date of birth" at the time she realized she was not like the others. She was to say, much later, in an interview: "I grew like a carrot. The savage root of me lay in the ground. It was that experience which plucked me up. Suddenly I knew that the frilly lace of the carrot, you know, the intaglioed outer shadow of the thing, was a fake: a female shawl, a cover-up. I realized that whether I was willing or no, I was all tuber, an underground plant; the spiked, splayed body of me had emerged. But at least I was a root that was edible: useful."

It had been one of those moments, she would explain, when one is lost in a crowd, there in the huge gymnasium; all the new students were waiting to be registered, distributed on a Bell curve, sent to computerized classes on pock-marked cards. She had planned to float inconspicuously into college; there, surrounded by waves of people like herself she would be free, at last, from heterogeneity. As a child she had dimly suspected that the strange blooming roundness of her grey eyes, the broad chin, cleft as though cracked by a sudden blow, above all the intensity of her games, her speech, her very silences were an anomaly to those around her, an environmental disaster. When she drew attention, it had not been for her dazzle, but for her motley. . . . But the university was to have changed all that. There, displaced persons like herself were to have been gathered up in a kind of universal freedom. But now on her first day in the gym, Ellie knew nothing had changed. There again she realized that not only was she watching the others, but the others were watching her. Fiercely she asked, what was different about her? Ellie tried to observe more closely. She had come from the same public schools, failed to observe the same religious holidays, played sanguinely in the same city streets and taken the same college boards. Even her I.Q., so they had told her, was in good standing. She stared. She was once more forced to realize that she was less charming, less joyful and altogether less impressive than her companions. In fact, her pale, stoical gaze, looming as it were in public punishment from the pole of her body, made her seem so unexceptional as to be in itself unique: she was somthing irremediable. She steeled herself against the flood of shame, refusing to accept it as significant: it was a mere event in time and not her epiphany, Ellie had assured herself.

But as the day wore on, there had been other things. One of the instructors had read an excerpt about an idiot who was (unbelievably) in love with a cow: and she had cried. Two hours later she had cried again: somebody's sonata. Clearly something separated her from the others, some thong of pain like a rope of fire. By the end of her first day she was exhausted, humiliated; something new was siphoning through like mercury in a thermometer: dangerous, registering temperatures she felt but could not explain.

First year, second year, third and fourth. All through college Ellie had surprised the same look in the eyes of men: a sudden involuntary shock which they tried at once to conceal—not a mere raising of eyebrows but a hasty retrenching of forces, as if there were in her something with urgency in it, like a cry of pain in one's yard which one couldn't shut the window on. Yet they did. She saw them. They shut every window and let her go on talking, pulling at her hair, clasping her hands with such fervor they must have thought she achieved some relief by it; but it wasn't relief she wanted, it was communication. Why wouldn't they talk?

Finally she discovered, after a visit to Europe, that people would listen to anything if she spoke in a foreign tongue, so they wouldn't have to understand it; so she threw herself into literature for a while, spoke only to foreigners to whom English was still a subtle secret so they could evade her nuances. She could be fervent with aplomb. Another thing she did upon her return from abroad: she began to paint. She had lived briefly with an Hungarian artist. It was a platitude she knew for a girl to live with an Hungarian artist: everyone did it, she did not for a moment imagine she was any different from any other American girl in so doing; it was only much later that she realized the others thought themselves an exception.

Painting, however, brooked no argument. It loved her and she it. She grew into it, herself the palette and the canvas; the paint streaming on the canvases issued from her veins. *See, see where Christ's Blood Streams in the Firmament!* was her first exhibited picture. Everyone admired it, it was religious and simple. It was blood on the sky, blood pouring into the universe in an endless radioactive rain. After that she got a reputation for doing religious paintings which she found lucky, though odd, for she believed in nothing at all except the immediate clutch of joy in the laying on of brushes. They were her tools, she said, her *local anesthetic*, borrowing a phrase from her favorite writer. Churches began to call her in and ask her to do altar pieces; some asked her to do murals; she had never done a mural in her life and she botched it badly. Ashamed, she withdrew temporarily from society, only to emerge three years later with a strange new style people called crewelwork, because the paint lay in thick laminated layers as though one could see the stitch of it. But they asked, why did she bother, it had already been done, somebody had already done it, they couldn't remember who, but anyway they said it was using the limitations of another art form, a *"necessary* fiction" therefore unnecessary—neither compelled nor compelling, they said. For a while Ellie was in despair, she tried going back to the streaming firmaments, but people no longer liked them, they seemed immature anyway, they were too imitative, they said, derivative: besides, religion as a subject was dead. Even the churches rarely had a real Christ around anymore, though they did, occasionally, use stained glass windows. Had she ever tried doing stained glass windows?

For a while Ellie was in despair, she tried going back to the streaming firmaments, but they came out looking like crewel work. This new thing was the only thing she could do: she felt like a failure. She took down her *Christ's Blood Streams in the Firmament!* and tried to imitate it; but it was no use. She thought it was a lousy painting anyway and gave it away to an overseas mission.

She drifted aimlessly for several months, then luckily fell in love and married Emmanuel. He was black and he taught her how to paint black. She had never known there were so many shades of black. She painted him in every light, at every season, as a primitive, a noble savage, as an anguished Afro-American, as a Black Liberator. For a while she enjoyed a certain popularity, then one day Emmanuel told her she ought not to paint blacks, it was not her thing: how could she, a white woman, understand *black?* —he italicized it in the air, showing her his beautiful hands, which, when later she painted them, she called *Lazarus's Hands,* because they were so white at the palms, as of a man who has risen from the dead. At the moment, however, Ellie admitted she couldn't; not possibly. Yet in secret she went on painting black anyway; it was as if her brush would take no other color. At last, one day during the war, in the lower left hand corner where Emmanuel's black hands were enshrined as a Liberator's, there emerged a small yellow flame, like the light of Africa. She called it the *Light of Africa* and after that never painted Emmanuel again. Six months later they were divorced. But by this time a strange yellow light like the sands of Egypt had begun to sweep across her canvas. *La Jaune* was all she could call it, it was like a drug, a fix. Wherever yellow went, there went she. She followed its golden lure to the deserts of New Mexico, to the ochered hills of San Francisco, the topaz of New Orleans, the bright blinding sunrise of the Eastern cape. Then suddenly she gave up; it was impossible to paint yellow; yellow was a growth, an effusion, it grew like skin. It changed before one's eyes.

But her yellows had had a mild *succès d'estime*. A few were bandied about in conversation, like ballons: everybody wanted to catch one. If you'd paint one of those lovely cornflowers, those wheats-in-the-field, those piano keys slowly becoming ivory, those pretty oriental children: ah! we'd love to have one of those, her friends said (she had a few friends now, though she knew herself to be even less charming, less joyful than ever); they even knew art galleries, agents, who were crying for yellow. After such an ordeal Ellie would go home and weep a very little. Then she would work, perhaps she'd try listlessly to paint a Van Gogh sunflower. But her work was no longer her own. Useless even to think about yellow. The paintbrush flew from her hand like a witch on a broomstick. She decided she was sick, very sick, she needed a psychiatrist.

What had happened was, she had begun dreaming of things with scales: fish, armadillos, dragons, birds (she'd read somewhere that feathers were modified scales). One morning after one of these powerful dreams in which all night she had quietly plucked one scale after another from the gliding presence of a glorious red carp, she went down to the fish market and pondered Fish as though they were a phalanx of medieval knights clad in armor. After that she became even less charming: she smelled eternally of carp. She moved down near the markets so she could be closer to Fish. She painted herrings, mullets, sticklebacks, bluegills, puffers, the marlin, the tarpon, the dorado, the barracuda, and the pompano.

Her favorite was to be the rainbow trout (*Salmo gairdneri*). She painted precisely one hundred small portraits of Monsieur Trout. Then, overcome by love for Fish, she realized that what she wanted, really was, like God to build one. . . . So she began gathering up their scales like jewels, treated them with a special chemical (three burns and permanent laceration of the inner thumb resulted from these experiments) so they'd "last" ("But nothing lasts," she consoled Monsieur Fish as she constructed him). She lay the crystals one by one, with infinite care, on black velvet. The fish was so beautiful she wept, she was almost terrified of him. She displayed him in a gallery once, and on that day she became Eleanor Brume, Our Lady of Fishes. Her fish was adored.

24

They said that Eleanor Brume had returned to her mystic level; the fish, obviously, was Christ Streaming in the Firmament, only no longer streaming, but swimming. He'd been transferred to more sluicy media. It made Eleanor very happy to realize this. She herself adored the fish; she thought it the best thing she had ever done and she had no objection to the others feeling the same way about it. It seemed, even, a justification of her own foolish joy in the Fish that so many people took him for something else.

But Monsieur Trout died. Scale by scale, he peeled and perished. With horror Ellie realized that her treatment of the scales was a failure, that the gloss and shimmer, the lucent pearl on the black velvet was an all too transitory form. She began to dream of waves of corruption, dissolution. Scales melted like wax in a flame; all was mortal, even art.

But there were arts that were purported to be less fragile: she began to study metal sculpture, stood in the August heat learning about torch welding. But her heart was not in it: the smell of the burning acetylene torch gave her a headache; she looked on her own work as hideous. Yet, she had been mildly successful. Several of her metals works sold; they said Eleanor Brume was versatile, could do anything, but it was not true. Her metalwork bored her; she longed for the smell and rush of oils on canvas. At the end of a day's work she felt as weary as a blacksmith mending wheels. She was nothing but an ironmonger, she thought sadly, and began to contemplate getting married again. Perhaps it would give her some ideas.

Her third marriage (or her fourth, the *Biography of American Women* is taciturn and puritanical on this subject), was a success from every point of view. Having a child or two did in fact give her ideas. For a while she painted endless portraits of children: beautiful smiling children with cheeks of tan, children eating apples, children posing like Goya's royalty in handsome laces; children swinging birches, golden lads and girls playing in the dust. Later she hid them all away in the attic; she said they were sentimental. Altogether narcissistic and counterrevolutionary, she added thoughtfully.

After the failure of her last marriage Ellie discovered Revolution, or it discovered her, she was never sure which. She only knew, in retrospect, that one day she observed that the symbol of the Age of the Aquarius was *the box:* and she began to paint boxes. Huge boxes with people standing upright, gasping for room, long narrow boxes with bodies in them, wrapped in flags, swastikas, rising suns, tricolors, red, black and white shrouds; boxes that were very small, with heads of babies lying in an indiscriminate heap; comfortable boxes with fireplaces; triangular ones with thorns, round ones like universes, and erect, rectangular boxes, boxes made into people walking, each one in his box, like Diogenes in a square barrel. And then she lately had begun doing the same box over and over: it was only a plain bonewhite box with a black border. It's *my* box, was her only explanation, only I can never get out of it.

To her surprise the Youth Movement took over her boxes. They said they understood what she meant; she was glad. She had hated to paint things nobody understood, it had made her feel lonely. Reprints of her work began to appear in the *New Left News* and she appeared before wonderful, beautiful people with flowing robes and golden tongues who explained her work to her. She loved it, she basked in her new role. "I'm so happy to hear that," she said. "You make me so proud . . . I didn't realize." And she kissed everyone of them, with tears in her eyes, she was full of love. Yet somehow she felt dispirited, it was as if she had missed something, some mark of esteem or acknowledgment which (her psychiatrist darkly hinted) she had always longed for.

So she laid a trap for herself to fall into. She accepted, for the first time since that fateful day in the gymnasium, an invitation to the Class Reunion. Her psychiatrist probed deeply, asked her why she was going. She said she didn't know, that *that* was why she was going. So she went. She travelled thousands of miles (she'd happened to be in Tokyo at the time) and to her surprise she discovered upon her arrival that she had already won a Prize even before her arrival, for being willing to come, as she had, From The Farthest Distance.

Then these people who had known each other a quarter of a century ago lined up on the two sides of the stage. Amazing statistics were read from the podium by a man who vaguely resembled her high school principal, only he had got old and his voice had a tremor, as if all his youthful flagellations had turned inward. The school nurse had died. In fact, with shock Ellie realized that nearly nine per cent of them had died: who would be next, who would make it ten? It was a veritable auction of lives. The principal now reverently cited their names, intoning a passage from *Ecclesiastes*. He murmured how the people had died, two per cent in World War Two, two per cent of Natural Causes, etc. Ellie began trembling with something, she didn't know what. It was like that damned moment of realization back in the gym, only this was different because she didn't know what she was realizing. There were endless lists, salutations, greetings, warmhearted reunions of shockingly grey-haired mothers. Women were weeping together, asking questions as though somehow they knew each other, their lives had nevertheless been shared in spite of the separations of space. Then the prizes were awarded. Prizes were awarded with tremendous applause for the One-with-the-most-children, the One-who-looked-most-like-she-used-to-look, etc. Then, conferring among themselves and consulting their Lists, they discovered that it was Doris Smith's birthday. A short, stout woman with legs which seemed to pull down rather than carry her up, climbed to the stage. Tears streamed from her cheeks. From somewhere a birthday cake ("homemade," somebody said) with a fleet of candles emerged and the woman stood at the proscenium balancing the cake, staring, not with gratitude (Ellie thought) but with a kind of fear at the burning candles. "Blow them out! Blow them out!" the crowd shouted from the auditorium floor, and clapped their hands. Dutifully the woman blew at the candles; scarcely three or four snuffed out. She blew again, a few more were quenched. There seemed an infinity of candles blinking more or less merrily. Each time she blew the crowd moaned as though she were stepping closer to a ledge; then with a great wrench of breath the last candles darkened.

After the birthday song, for some reason their activities became feverish; they began ritualizing their questions, each one going up to the proscenium to identify, recall, assimilate their twenty-five years. Someone suggested they ought to make a Guessing Game of it: Who Can Remember What Sophie Wore on the Last Day? What was the score of the High School Football

Team at the Last Game? Ellie began to feel dizzy; something like fear gripped her, a fear of the box, she said afterward, without explaining. She began picking up her notebooks, her sketching pads, mumbled excuses about catching her plane (she couldn't wait to get back to Tokyo). For a moment as she said goodbye, she stood transfixed, her heart contracted with shame. It seemed to her that they were impaling her with the same look she had always known, a look which separated her from them by flames. But suddenly her vision changed, a sweep of insight focused them, and she could see that the light in their eyes had become prismatic; small radii of counter-lights now tinctured the filmy surface. In that flash of vision Ellie grasped that, having fretted their lives away in decency, stability and charm, they now lusted after her private madness; that they believed it had shielded her from Reality, a reality hideous but True. Ellie stared at the vision till it faded in a whorl of noisy farewells.

But at the airport it returned; she sat down in the waiting room and began sketching the people she had seen, people who were to haunt her till her death seven years later. Brume's Gallery, they were to be called. She hastily sketched the faces she had seen, faces full of starvation amid plenty; faces that had meant to grow and affirm, but which had dissolved in an acid of pain and irresolution. They were different from anything she had done before. They were like mere burned out knotholes of despair holding their boxes together.

Although the critics admitted that Eleanor Brume had probably loved her people, ugly and terrifying though they were, they still did not like them: that kind of thing was neither beautiful nor new, they said. They'd seen all that before, and they refused to take her last work seriously. Wait and see what Eleanor Brume does next, they said. Even her new young friends suggested that in the years before her death she had backslid: "Sweeping with a New Brume?" was considered a very cogent, perceptive piece of art criticism, showing how Eleanor Brume had failed to develop into and along with the new technologies, but instead had chosen to revert to Representationalism: she, a painter, they said sorrowfully, who had seemed slated for the invariably various had become a mere imitator of Kaethe Kollwitz and of those who had preceded Kollwitz: of whom, they said, there were a large number.

My Crystal

They say it will help to write it down. Help *whom?* Them or me? But in response to a mechanism built into me before I left, I obediently take up their dull ballpoint. To prove that I'm perfectly aware of where they're at, I write neatly: *Christmas Day*. It helps them keep their records. They cling to these rituals which measure time.

But of course I understand that the social fabric is based on such paradoxes: when at last your consciousness has evolved, when you have emptied your mind of debilitating expectations, when at last you can live in a serene and perfect stasis, they give you a pen and say, *"Write. Remember."* Physician, heal thyself!

And their pen, of course, is blunt and knobby: they live in their mechanized world, they operate with perfectly calibrated instruments, they wind themselves up like clocks to chime precisely the same message at exactly the same hour, and they can't supply you with a pen that writes. The ink leaks out for a drop or two, dries up. A short wait. At last, another clot emerges.

They keep us moving through their time structure the entire day: breakfast, lunch, dinner, exercise, tv, counseling, laundry, letters. Finally, free time. Even this free time is imposed on you. Because, of course, they don't know anything about freedom. They're always talking about being free to go, as if there were anything to go to. I created my own freedom anyway, before they put me in this room (a clean, sunny room, I admit, no bars on the windows: a civilized place). They may say I walked in here of my own accord; but at the time I could clearly hear their minds ticking like time bombs: *if she doesn't go in easy, try injections.* I am against mind-altering drugs. And, of course, the possibility of violence makes one retch. It didn't matter to me anyway. Wherever I go I am in my crystal. I can go in or out, as I want.

Today, for example, I am with Aurelio. We are standing (as always) on the Ponte Vecchio. The sun is coming down like mercy. As always Aurelio is holding me, I feel his tears. Of course he does not believe that I cannot take him with me, that I do not have a millionaire father growing oil in the fields of Texas. He is convinced that back in the States I would be ashamed of him. He is quite dark, a Syrian, his hair shining like wet grape-leaves in the summer rain. He thinks, even, that my children are an excuse to abandon him. Divorce is easy there, he says. He continues pleading, explaining: "There is no use here to anything," he says. "There is no future. Only the *fascisti* getting into power again. Tourism, pederasty, prostitution." I am not certain what he means by this: for me, prostitution is still something women get trapped in, not men. I am silent. Whatever I say is to him all heresy, lies—excuses to return to a life of ease without him. Meanwhile, I cannot, in spite of my best arrangements within the crystal, *cannot* keep the sun from going down. The water becomes black. Aurelio begins to fall. I try to pull him from his knees. Then I realize that it is my hand which in his agony he has seized upon. I try to tear my hand away: but his teeth have set into it. I realize he is dying. Ah, what a revenge this is, and he knows it. He wraps his arms around his own waist as though in an embrace. He sinks, I scream. Screaming breaks the time-aura and I am safe again in my crystal.

The crystal is shaped like a giant sea shell. Barefooted, I stand in it like Venus Rising from the Sea. It is just wide enough so that I can rest either hand on its outer rim as upon the sides of a small sailing craft. The entire inner surface of the crystal is flawless, planed smooth by centuries of effort. I do not know whether it is a "pure" crystal or not. Does that matter? To me? To them? To me it is perfect. Only its color, a translucency as of rose petals shining at once with sunlight and rain, reveals that this perfect vessel does not breathe, has no corruptible tissue to decompose and will be here forever. And I will be here with it. Its iridescent conch echoes with my own breathing, vibrates with my own pulse: and I blend with its whispering surge as I would once have swum upon a sea stretched by moonlight into the horizon. To me the crystal is perfect because it has evolved to the highest principle—perpetual and changeless Beauty. Also, in it one may travel at otherwise impossible speeds, wherever one wishes. Yet it is not the speed of arrival which matters, but the fact that I can go wherever, whenever I wish. Backward or forward.

I admit I don't go forward much. The future brings almost no pleasure and much pain. I tend to avoid it except when they plague me too much. Going into the future is like Balzac's *peau de chagrin*: it is a form of willed extinction. Also (and this is more important), my crystal does not remain perfectly motionless in that aura: there is a trembling, a surge as of waves, then silence. I have trouble coming back; I can feel my physical body fading, becoming astral. There is a slight loss of power, of communication: though visually all is clearer than ever.

The crystal is not an allegory. It is real. Standing firmly in its center, my bare feet balanced on its iridescent floor, the sunlight streaming down as if filtered through some far-off rose window, I can—in it—see, hear, understand all without pain. Now, for instance, I can see Janine (that's me) where she is engaged in her eternal tournament—childhood. She is crying. Nobody comes. That's the way it always is in that *Set*. (In order to facilitate my coming and going in the crystal, I have made my own *Sets*.) What I am speeding into now is *Set Two*. I always go into *Set Two* after Aurelio's Set, because . . . well, I'm not required to explain *that*. That's my affair, not theirs. I see now the deviousness of their handing me a pen. They give you something to write with and, like Heine, you write, you write, you describe the very moment of death. Everybody wants to be Heine.

Set Two Janine is lying in her bed crying. Janine and Mother have been to the shopping center (Bread, Beauty, Bank). Mother has a new coat. It smells like a warm puppy. Mother will wear it to the wedding. Mother is happy because Janine's sister, Mary, will be married to the Navy Ensign who is coming home for Christmas. It is a Sin to have babies before Christmas and Mother is pleased because Mary can now have her baby for Christmas. The In-Sin's baby.

Mother does not lock the car; she will be in the bank only a moment; Janine is a big girl and will not go away. At first Janine burrows in the puppy-warm coat. But she now sits up, waves the red, white and blue flag given her by the beauty operator. Mother's car keys are shining in the sunlight on the dashboard. At the curb, outside the supermarket, Janine sees a dark-haired girl about her own age, crying. She is standing beside a sign which says the USO is [blur] War. Janine has time to think it is a mistake. That it should read USA [blur] WAR. Then she climbs down from the car seat, curious to know why this girl her own age is crying. The girl is very pretty but her face is contorted by fear. She has lost someone or something in the supermarket. The girl is frightened as Janine approaches her; Janine mumbles something inarticulate, a mere indication that she understands why a girl might be crying. The child begins to howl with fear. Her eyes become slits of terror, an oriental caricature. Now Mother is back from the bank. She yanks Janine's wrist, whispering furious words into Janine's ears: "I told you to stay in the car. . . . Out here with dirtyjaps!" They turn toward the car and Janine feels faint; she understands that someone has stolen the car even before Mother turns and shakes her, Janine, like a dirty mop, a dirtyjapmop. She is lying on the bed crying. She is crying with remorse because the dark man with hair shining like wet grape-leaves has stolen their car. But she is crying also in a confusion of terror and longing because she knows that it is not the car he wanted, it was her, Janine.

I can sympathize with Janine in that *Set*. But I realize that she is deluding herself. However, I allow her (in that *Set*, at least) the freedom of childhood. I allow her to feel that she was loved, if however briefly, by the handsome thief. Who was subsequently caught. In my crystal I know, of course, that love is not real, that success is not real, that money is not real, that one's children become strangers, that senility, cancer, starvation, alcoholism, rape, murder, holocaust, skyjackings, bombings are not real. There is nothing to fear from them. On the other hand, I know that there is no joy either: but it is a small loss to suffer to be free from the others—from love, ambition, wealth, family. All eidolons.

Set Three In this *Set* there are FACTS. There is the FACT that although Mother's car is recovered, so that the insurance company does not have to pay, the boy—a Mexican-American from Albuquerque—is sent to prison. He is in prison a long time (he has insisted upon doing things in there that prolong his sentence). Janine is, in FACT, getting ready to graduate from high school when Mother announces that this same man, Juan Cabrera, came into Father's office and asked for a job. Calmly. Deliberately. He said they owed him this job. He said he had paid his debt to society; that now he wanted to get married and he wanted a job. He said that he knew for a FACT that Mr. Snelling was using prison labor while the prisoners were *in*, so why not use them when they got out? Then there was a quarrel, Mother says. They arrested the man (at this point Janine feels a strange twist in her chest, the beginning of a chronic pain like angina, but it is only functional, not organic, her doctor says). They arrested the man, Mother continues. They arrested the man. There is a picture of him in the company paper, his arms held back on either side by two plain-clothes men who are always in Father's office. His chin is resting on his chest, it looks broken; his eyes are squinting into the bright light of the tv camera. His face is gleaming with sweat, making a line like a healed scar down his brown skin and along the edges of his hair which is shining like grapeleaves.

Set Four On the stage Janine is graduating. At the very moment of receiving her diploma, which is embossed in gold and tied with satin ribbon an inch wide, she is certain she sees Juan Cabrera at the rear of the auditorium, this same Juan Cabrera who had stolen their car, but who had failed, at least that time, to steal herself, Janine. Janine's legs begin to tremble and she is falling, fainting. Heat prostration, Mother says, chafing Janine's cold hands, pulling Janine back from oblivion. Janine opens her eyes to a room full of people, a crystalline light is pouring from the window of the auditorium, her head is resting on a rose-colored satin pillow.

Set Five There is no use resisting. The hallway is lit with the kind of bulb that shows dirt but brings no light to the stairs beyond. Janine has resisted long enough. Perhaps he will kill her, she thinks. Perhaps, even, this is what she wishes, that he will kill her. There are two small children, one a dark-haired boy like Juan himself, and a girl who resembles their mother. Janine takes in at a glance the Anglo mother's features. It is hard to understand the wave of jealousy that crushes her, Janine. Perhaps it renders meaningless her act of expiation. Janine is offering up her race: *but he is married to an Anglo, he has no need of me.* She wants to know: she pleads with him. Can he forgive her? She sees at once that he believes her, Janine, to be mad. Does she not understand that he has an Anglo wife who is now at work, that his wife may be home at any moment, that the children? . . . Yet his body understands perfectly. He brushes her breast lightly with his arm as he hurries the children out: "Go find your mother at the job," he says. *"Tell her, stop at the supermarket."* Quickly he scrawls out a list, an interminable list of things for Janine's rival to buy. He looks up bitterly. "And what else? And what else do we need?" The children run off, frightened. Janine's hands are committed to the idea of removing her clothes, but she does not feel her own hands. Contemptuously—but she has seen the tremor of his eyelids—Juan watches as Janine removes her blouse. Then in a stamp of revulsion and fear (perhaps he believes it to be a trap, a final trap to keep him in prison forever) he flings her half-dressed, against the door, throws her clothes at her: "Out, out! *Puta.* Crazy woman. Fascist!"

Set Six It doesn't matter. She pursues him, pursues him, in every man she meets. For three months she spends all her money in Mexican bars. It is not difficult to find Mexican men, they think she is crazy anyway. She does not even enjoy it, they say, laughing at her. But something inside of her is satisfied, nevertheless. It begins not to be necessary to wait in the bars, there are men everywhere—on the highways, in the fields, standing at stop signals, hitchhikers. When she is beaten and robbed by a hitch-hiker, Mother says at the hospital that this must stop. This must stop because *the worst of it,* Mother says, is that Janine now will have a baby. Whose baby is it, Mother demands. Janine smiles, shakes her head. You will have this baby before Christmas, Mother warns, and did Janine not learn from her sister Mary that it is a Sin to have babies at Christmas if one is not married. Mary-ed. It is a FACT that it is a sin to have babies if one is not married, Mother says. Janine will not have this baby. Mother will arrange everything.

Set Seven It seems Janine is scarcely recovering consciousness at the graduation exercises (after Juan's appearance . . . disappear-ance) at the back of the hall, when it is time to go into another *Set.* That is the speed of the crystal when it is working well. Yet it does seem impossible that Juan is now no longer, as Father says, "that Mexican kid who stole our car, y'remember?" but instead is that grown man Janine sees walking down Guadaloupe Street, the father of a son who is already a veteran home from the wars. Juan's hair now has bolts of grey streaking the black. Like star-light, Janine is thinking as she watches him cross Guadaloupe. Like starlight on the blackest, hottest night in Texas. But what is Juan doing? He is not crossing the street, he is leaping, his legs like ramrods, he is bounding with rage, he is crossing Guadaloupe to where his son sits in the sunlight. Janine now turns quickly into a shop, adjusts her sun glasses, tries not to see or hear as Juan seizes his son by the shoulder and is slapping him again and again . . . . ". . . That *shit,*" he is saying, "that *shit.* You goin' be a junkie all your life now, see? All your goddam life. . . ."

And truly that is the *Set* that cannot go too quickly for me. I speed it up so that I cannot hear Juan sobbing. It is the sobbing that I do not hear. I am, rather, just recovering consciousness on the rose-colored pillow. Yes, it is better to turn slightly backward, into that other *Set* because I am, as always at this time, losing control over the crystal and must inevitably, stupidly arrive at

Set Eight. At least, though duller, it is calmer there.

Set Eight I am marrying Ephraim Rothman. I have known him two nights. He is perhaps the thirty-sixth boy(man?) I have slept with since recovering consciousness after Juan's appearance at my graduation. Ephraim has never slept with anyone before, he is barely sixteen (I discover, later, that I am older than he). I am marrying him because he is the only Jew in this small oil town in Texas where we live. He does not know anything about the others, the hitchhikers, etc. He has velvet-eyes, his black hair glistens though not with sweat. During the one hundred and four days of our marriage, before everybody annulled it, including ourselves, I washed his hair seventeen times. I did not let him cut it and by the end of the time that we were happy in, I could plait it for him in a single braid dark as grapeleaves at the back of his neck. When that time is over, our time to be happy in, we each drive away in our parents' cars, guilty at our own relief. I promptly marry "Corky" Stewart whose family raises goats that they sell to the San Martino Sausage Company to make salami with. Most people do not know that the meat referred to by the San Martino Sausage Company is goat meat. (For some reason people do not like to know they are killing and eating goats rather than sheep or cattle—there is no understanding why.) Corky and I promptly have two children. Somebody has told us to do it that way, that it's easier in the long run. We obediently do it that way. That is why, when I finally return from Italy, Junior is old enough to volunteer for Vietnam. I have been in Italy a year recovering, Corky says, from a nervous breakdown. But I know that I have been recovering from Aurelio, whom I sought all over Italy as I sought Juan on the highways of Texas, but whom I did not ever find, and from whom I do not ever recover, not even after Junior has gone to Vietnam.

Not that I ever call him Junior. It is always as if Corky and I are not talking about the same boy. I always call him by the name he used as a child when he played Cowboys and Indians, when he pretended he was the black-headed chief, Manuelito, and wore his hair down his back like an Indian. Like Ephraim. We receive very few letters from Manny while he is in Vietnam but we become resigned to it. Manny reenlists.

Set Nine This *Set* is one I try to avoid but it is no use. It is grooved into my life on the crystal, I can't speed it up or silence it or ignore it or rise above the echo of my own pulse which surrounds me.

It is Christmas Day. They are keeping their promise. For once they are keeping their promise. They are sending the boys home. Manny is arriving any moment. The table is arranged for him with Christmas settings he will perhaps remember: holly at each place, the turkey platter he gave me on another Christmas occasion, all his childhood gifts to or from me conspicuously arranged to remind him of the boyhood he has had and may return to. Kendra, Corky, and I are taking special care with the tree, tenderly hanging all the ornaments the family has collected over the years. Every light in the house is on to welcome him. The Christmas tree blazes with gifts. My hands are cold with anticipation. Kendra and Corky now go to the airport to receive him (I am on my feet for only the second day since the pneumonia and it is presently 4 below zero). So I am waiting in a cold fever at the window.

At last: they arrive. Kendra and Corky and I are all crying, we are ecstatic. But a shiver passes over me. Manny is different. At first I assure myself it is only the army regulation haircut, the hard push of the shoulder. But it is also the voice which has coarsened, the eyes which have become wide, neither shy nor defensive, but very, very hard. He does not ask questions, but during dinner he overrides Kendra's opinions, drowns out her voice before she can speak. Finally, she remains mute, exhausted, staring at her brother with a look of dread. I suggest we open the presents. The word *presents* reminds Manny that he has brought us all exotic gifts from overseas. He leaps proudly to his duffel-bag. He hands Corky some kind of weaponry, it is metal anyway, that is all I see, and then suddenly, with a brusque and cynical movement pours out of a leather pouch, like tobacco, three tiny "Viet Cong ears," cleaned of their blood and preserved by some process, which he explains. A few strands of hair still cling to the trophies, hair still strangely black and gleaming as bird feathers, to which the Christmas lights add an iridescence as of shining grapeleaves in an August rain. I am screaming. I think that I am screaming. I shake the Christmas tree, shatter its lights, stamp on its presents. With a howl of rage I hurl myself on Manny, beating him, tearing his flesh, his black shining hair . . . . When I open my eyes Kendra is chafing my cold hands, pulling me back from oblivion. Through our living room window is pouring down a crystalline light from our neighbors' trees. Under my head is a rose-colored pillow.

Thank God that *Set* is over. It will not come around again for a while. The sound of my own heartbeat, my pulse, echo throughout the crystal. Like Venus Rising from the Sea, I lift my arms like a tiller on either side of the conch, directing the crystal, changing its velocity. Breaking the time-aura, I return the crystal to safety.

Set One I am with Aurelio. We are standing (as always) on the Ponte Vecchio. The sun is coming down like mercy. Aurelio is holding me, I feel his tears. He does not believe that I cannot take him with me, that I do not have a millionaire father growing oil in the fields of Texas. He is convinced that back in the States I would be ashamed of him. He is quite dark, a Syrian, his hair shining like wet grapeleaves in the summer rain. He thinks, even, that my children are an excuse to abandon him. Divorce is easy there, he says. He continues pleading, explaining: "There is no use here to anything," he says. "There is no future. Only the *fascisti* getting into power again. Tourism, pederasty, prostitution." I am not certain what he means by this: for me prostitution is still something women get trapped in, not men. I am silent. Whatever I say is to him all heresy, lies—excuses to return to a life of ease without him. Meanwhile, I cannot, in spite of my best arrangements within the crystal, *cannot* keep the sun from going down. The water becomes black. Aurelio begins to fall. I try to pull him from his knees. Then I realize that it is my hand which in his agony he has seized upon. I try to tear my hand away: but his teeth have set into it. I realize he is dying. Ah, what a revenge this is, and he knows it. He wraps his arms around his own waist as though in an embrace. He sinks. I scream. Screaming breaks the time-aura and I am safe again in my crystal.

John Stuart Mill Goes Home

H e had been determined to Achieve, not only because it was necessary, in order not to surrender to anxiety, but also because he could (naturally) not live without love. If he did not Achieve, they would deny him love, deny him the viaticum of approbation which clung, reluctant, conditional, to their fingertips as they caressed him, or refrained from caressing him. He was their Connie, sanctified and mesmerized by the promise of a future identity. *Prove yourself, then APprove yourself* his foster father had summed it all up in a solemn handshake: underachievers would be sent back to the Home.

As the Home Manager and Connie's prospective father, Dr. Bean, shook hands to cement their new relationship, Dr. Bean asked Connie whether he thought he was good at learning things. Delighted to have this chance to laud the dead merely for the good work of having loved him, Connie had allowed himself the accolade: "My Daddy said I was real smart." It was the last time Connie was to be guilty of boasting (*proveyourselfthenAPprove-yourself*). He was never again to be sure of his standards, he was to become Learning's rate-buster, laboring at all hours for lowest wages. "Well, anyone," Dr. Bean had at once challenged the Home Manager who was pushing Connie toward him, "could—like Conrad O'Connor here—learn to read at four: but if he really *was* another John Stuart Mill, he could go farther, much farther. . . ."

Connie did not know who John Stuart Mill was, and by the time he had discovered the significance of the awesome metaphor, he had already been bargained for and was long out of the Home. *Although*, Dr. Bean had at that time warned (as if Connie, with the Home Manager's prodding fist at his back, might be moved to protest), *although* the tests all tested out, the Beans wanted their proof *on the premises*. They did not want an adopted child they would ever have to apologize for, that was only natural: offspring of one's own, they would have had to accept with all his genetic faults, X and Y chromosomes revealing frailties as if by divine intuition. But a Conrad O'Connor contracted for should have a warranty: it was the wave of the future wasn't it? Chloning before chloning had become a reliable fountainhead of perfectibility. CONNIE CHLONED would be woven into a household sampler, they quipped. Dr. Bean therefore carefully examined the variously-colored charts handed him by the Home Manager. The Manager was consumer-oriented, he had studied packaging, and, moreover, he had known Dr. Bean at college when during their days at dental school the Home Manager, having failed his tests, had opted for "public relations work." Only Bob Bean's name then had been *Bien* and he had logically changed it in order to achieve a name without emotional affect. Bean, he said, was *neutral*; *Bien* was connotative.

So they had listened respectfully as Dr. Bean read aloud: Conrad O'Connor: 8 years old, height, 49 inches ("sure to sprout quickly," added the Home Manager). 52 pounds ("a bit thin, but a skinny kid was always more appealing"). Stanford-Benet 172. Wechsler-Bellevue 165. ("Pretty high correlation between tests.") However, Dr. Bean had pointed out, the Rorschach showed complexities, unpromising shadows: too many deaths in the family, a bit morbid perhaps, but one could count on acculturation to contract morbid influences. Twice the boy had seen a rhinoceros in the inkblots. Was that serious? Dr. Bean wanted to know, or could they rely on it to be merely evolution, an anticipated response to be outgrown like an ugly swollen pupa.

"Well, Dr. Bien——"

"Bean. Bean. 'Make-my-own-affect,' " sang Dr. Bean.

"Yesss . . . ," said the Home Manager. "The fact is, there's nothing to worry about with the kid's Rorschach. It's natural."

"There's nothing natural," Dr. Bean had retorted. "We can make sickness and we can make health, provided the regenerative processes are not deteriorated. At eight, with regenerative cells as good as a starfish's, a boy should be able to overcome a few kinks in his engine."

"Well, if he turns out to be a lemon, turn him back in," observed the Home Manager.

"That's a bargain," Dr. Bean said and signed the contract. "Two years' probation."

The only thing was, as Connie soon saw, the two Beans were not at all identical. Mrs. Bean had her own notion of the ideal son she would have had if she had had sons instead of cats (all dead now, killed off on the highways during successive moves across the country each time there was a war and Dr. Bean was called upon to drill teeth for the Army). Well-mannered, polite, speak-when-spoken-to, seen-but-not-heard, very grateful for all-that-they-had-done-for-him, Honoring His Father and His Mother; and above all *clean*. Thank God he was old enough not to need housebreaking. WHEREAS: Dr. Bean had other views—one might almost say, "naturally" except that the dentist himself insisted that all his views were cultivated. He himself had been a *tabula rasa*, now pretty well reaching the end of his slate: but he hadn't done badly, not badly at all. Best oral surgeon in the state, he *knew* that. When he called Connie to his side their first evening at home (Mrs. Bean had slipped away to bathe: her axioms, theoretically less demanding, were to be laid down later), the boy descended the staircase in his shorts. Instead of approaching Dr. Bean he wandered shyly toward the window where on the lawn a pair of grackles marched to and fro in their glossy black-leather jackets, their delicate ears attuned to the stirring of the grass.

At last Connie had turned toward his benefactor. It was hot in the house, the air-conditioning had been turned off during their long drive from the Home. The sweat lay on Connie's brow. Dr. Bean regarded his new acquisition attentively. Altogether, Connie knew, he looked like a boy of eight after a hard ball game in the sun—but intelligent. Surely he was that, they had guaranteed it.

"You understand the terms, don't you?"

"Yes, sir." Connie was not sure he did, but he had already learned that his learning processes must be speeded up. Saying *yes* (he understood at once) promoted understanding, it was the Coué effect.

"Two years. A boy can prove himself in two years. Even in two *weeks* we could tell *some*thing. Twenty-four months 'll give us real evidence. We didn't buy a pig in the poke, you know. The House Manager showed us you had the numbers: one seventy-two. One sixty-five. Very promising." Dr. Bean smiled. He was sure Connie would do well. "Well, tomorrow you can get out and show us. We'll get you into the best school."

The best of schools, Connie immediately learned, was also the worst of schools (but, of course, that was only from *his* point of view: he understood that he was too young for wisdom, however much learning he ingested). The savage, hour-to-hour combat for success was so fierce that sometimes he was involuntarily ("naturally"?) moved to compassion when he saw on the faces of his vanquished schoolmates a look of fear, self-destruction and irreconcilable hatred. Connie could not explain to them that he was only doing his job.

He continued to do his job, he excelled. His hand pointing rigid as a bayonet in the air signified daily the-knowledge-there-fore-power he was gaining: the power of superior intelligence over mediocrity. During his recitations in language classes, the other boys bowed down like a field of wheat before the windy onslaught of his brilliance.

He felt sorry for them, but really, he couldn't help it: *they* didn't have to go back to the Home if they faltered. Connie forced himself to fling the translations, perfect rings of steel at the throats of his listeners, he watched as they were throttled into silent awe. The sweat broke out on his brow, he gave the synopses of all the verbs, *there* and *there,* he threw out the words, he won the kewpie doll of approval. On the way home, he re-hearsed his victories, anxious to tell Dr. Bean. He scarcely noticed the hunger in his stomach: it had to be hunger—even he knew he was too young for ulcers. *Thank God,* Mrs. Bean echoed him, he was too young for ulcers. Nevertheless the doctors recom-mended the Sippy Diet for ulcer patients and the "hunger" went away.

42

Mrs. Bean's reference to God was part of a secret split between the Beans, a deep and dizzying fault which separated faith (which merely moved mountains) from science which had its eye on the universe. Privately each one acted as if whoever had arranged these things had set the world in eternal conflict. It was Dr. Bean's variation on a familiar theological argument: only works achieved, not faith. Nevertheless, when from time to time neither works nor faith brought Connie the coveted first prizes (occasions which served to remind Mrs. Bean that the Devil was still at his officious Deviltry), Dr. Bean would remind Connie that a lad with his I.Q. should *not* be having problems. He had this Special Gift, which he had inherited, so to speak. When Mrs. Bean ventured to ask if that meant that Connie would have been just as intelligent without the Beans, Dr. Bean replied that he, Connie, might have been just as intelligent, perhaps, but he wouldn't have *achieved* anything, he'd still be in the *Home*.

Since Connie had this Special Gift, it had to be developed: not one language, nor merely two—any vulgar public school kid could be a polyglot. Dr. Bean checked out the numbers of languages. In spite of what he considered in himself a considerable education, he was mildly surprised at the number of languages, and if one considered the dialects—well! He hadn't started Connie too soon. When Connie got to prep school he could extend himself and by the time he got to college he would not only be a linguistic genius but a *recognized* one: what was the point of all Those High Points if you kept them under a bushel?

Connie didn't mind this kind of entrepreneurism. He could swing it when he and the dentist were alone or even at the dinners which Dr. Bean began by asking: "Something good? Something bad?" Good or bad in their moral universe meant only one thing: had he mastered an impressive quota of learning, whatever it was, or had he "slackened his will?" During these tournaments Connie assaulted a huge bean bag of words stuffed with an imaginary enemy—after which his foster parents would assure him, each according to his or her need, that he had done well.

But when the three were on long trips together, it was a Manichean hell. To Dr. Bean the signal of Achievement was pyrotechnics, for his mother, the sign of knowledge was thoughtful silences; she wanted Connie not only to be brilliant but to be modest about it. So Connie couldn't swing it when they were all together, he got his signals crossed. So one afternoon to avoid the problems of firing his brain to catherine wheels of glory while keeping his soul from the Devil, he had stolen away from the camp. He had left a note for his mother. *Dear Mom. Don't worry about me. I'll be home before dark.*

But he had got thoroughly lost, unable to find his way home or to the campsite, and had ended up in the arms of a forest ranger. How that had happened he hadn't the slightest idea. First he was following a creek thinking it would lead him back to where the Beans had parked their shiny aluminum *Airstreamer* and found instead, that—nature or nuture—he had walked around the wood in circles, as in the tales of other fallible persons who had got lost before his time. But the Ranger who picked him up was lonely, warmhearted, fatherly. He helped Connie to undress, helped himself to Connie. It had not seemed unpleasant and besides, it was Experience: as the First Sage of his Century, it was Connie's obligation to learn everything, wasn't it? He was also wise enough not to mention it.

It kept happening. In a baffling inexplicable way, in the midst of an intramural dance, a beautiful girl in his arms, with University Honors, a rosy garlanded bull's-eye of Achievement toward which all he had to do was fling a few paper darts and he'd have all the kewpie dolls, he suddenly left the dance, took a stroll and found himself lost in the surrounding woods. He waited in vain for the forest ranger to rescue him. It was then he realized he would have to go out and find the Ranger himself. That complicated his life immensely. Because "naturally," Dr. Bean expected him to take the most-brilliant-beautiful-promising-girl from one of the neighboring colleges to wife: a wife was an asset on all levels of achievement. A lot of government forms asked about the applicant's family: and what did that mean but your wife? queried Dr. Bean rhetorically.

Connie did finally find the most brilliant-beautiful-promising girl from one of the neighborhood colleges—she was actually a member of one of those I.Q. FRIENDSHIP CLUBS, which astonished him. Connie himself had never thought of his Special Gift as something clubby, but as something negotiable. He married her quickly, because he had an idea Mimi was innocent and that would be a help: what she didn't know she wouldn't miss. His choice was fortuitous. When, seized by loneliness and anxiety, he went out to search for his forest ranger, his wife accepted his absence as a logical extension of his need to Achieve: Her father had achieved, had taught at the best universities. When, while they were on their honeymoon, Mimi's father died of a heart attack at forty-three, she was inconsolable. For weeks she mourned, leaving Connie free to wander through Rome, admiring the statuary, thinking of his forest ranger. When they returned to the States, Connie went on a long back-packing trip through the Bluehill Mountains and there, within commuting distance, he found the forest ranger.

There was nothing trite or sordid about it, it was a permanent relationship. With the tall, lanky ranger, Connie felt healed: he did not need to verbalize his achievements; his silences were not efforts to appease or approve, they were long stases of mutual understanding. He believed he had found a spiritual home, and he spent a great deal of time, while studying for his upcoming Oral Comprehensives, making trips that he said he needed to empty his mind so that he could fill it up again. Mimi understood that too: it was something her father had done, taking them on long boring trips to improbable places as an antidote to (his) laziness, he said: it would never have occurred to any of them to suggest they go some place it might have been a hardship to come home from.

Dr. Bean was delighted that Connie was about to pass his Comprehensives and (almost simultaneously) become a father. For Mimi had become surprisingly very pregnant and Connie said to himself that he was now truly in love with her: indeed after a trip to the Bluehill Mountains he would return with a deeper understanding, it seemed, of human needs and he believed his compassion for her ignorance was unalterable love. He read Proust and Gide and Wilde and Genêt and Burroughs and became, simultaneously, one of the world's leading authorities on Uzbek: it was an easy split, once one got the hang of it. Dr. and Mrs. Bean were preparing to reward his years of achievement with, Dr. Bean recited, (A) an inheritance for the future, (B) a trip around the world, and (C) an architect's dream of a house in Pied Piper Valley, a house surrounded by piney woods and loping rabbits and a nursery big enough for six, added Dr. Bean proudly.

"Six?" echoed Connie in astonishment. "Haven't you heard about Zero Population Growth? We're half-way through our quota already." It was one of the few times he ever allowed himself to joke with his foster father. Mrs. Bean sat slowly peeling a large freckled banana, which for some reason upset Connie so that he was barely able to swallow. The room seemed very hot, the sweat lay on his brow, he remembered the first interview he had had with Dr. Bean on the night of his rescue from the Home: had he not achieved enough? Was he still to be sent back because he hadn't achieved, produced enough . . . Beans. The terror this childish thought stirred in him astonished him. He felt his chest constrict, he was unable to breathe, in a moment he'd faint, he felt, and his whole fine track record would go *splot*. . . . He managed to stay on his feet while his foster father explained the virtues of a large family, preferably three girls and three boys— *gender was still a powerful factor for success in the world,* you couldn't get away from that, Dr. Bean added ominously. Mrs. Bean laid aside the empty banana skin with a fastidious twitch of her finger-tips, then delicately touched a handkerchief somewhere in the invisible depths of her purse, as though performing some holy ritual. She had eaten the whole fruit, Connie noticed.

It was after that that Connie began to have inexplicable seizures, headaches, moments of terror. Did Dr. Bean know about the ranger? Did the whole world know? He pondered and sweated; it made him alternately hungry and nauseous. He ate fruit till he swelled and bloated and sat in the bathroom for hours, memorizing whole cassettes as he sat, his intestines griping like a summer storm. He begged the ranger to wait it out, when the comprehensive exams were over, he'd be his own man—he'd be *his* own man. But he had to have that union card of Achievement.

On the day of the exams he arrived early. His mind was sharp as a laser-beam, he was a "smart bomb" ready to annihilate the Five Wise Old Men at the examination with a single explosion. But they were surprisingly friendly, they put him at the head of the table as if to subordinate themselves to his superior position: but Connie's first irrelevant reaction was that it was the first time in his life he had ever sat at the head of the table. It was somehow an unsettling thought, he was wondering why, when Professor Sterne boomed the first question. Or rather, Professor

Sterne merely posed the question but it roared like a cannon round his ears. The five amiable old men with whom he had worked for nearly a third of his life suddenly took on the aspect of a Manet firing squad. He saw his own head exploding from the simultaneous barrage, his own body falling, the dignity of his dark suit springing an absurd rubbery red leak as he lay in the center of the room. This was not real.

The opening question, designed to set him at his ease, was so simpleminded that he suspected he had not heard it right. Or was it a trap? *How many daughters did Milton have?* Dr. Sterne asked. He pondered. He sweated. Why was it significant? Of all the irrelevancies he had mastered, why this one? Of course Milton was an Hebraist, a Greek and Latin scholar as well. But was the *number* significant? And if so, why? His heart thumped like a rabbit's tail, sweat ran from his eyelids, he could see, suddenly, the grackles on the grass, pecking the silent worm to bits. A wave of nausea, barely controlled, filled his mouth, fortunately he had not eaten. His bowels were . . . . There were smiles of understanding, complicity, around him, the grackles were bowing, they were taking his silence as some sort of a joke on themselves. But they repeated their question: *they are serious!* thought Connie, and tried to think of some quip, some flippancy which would deflect the asininity (as it seemed to him) of such a question. But he was not accustomed to purging high seriousness by persiflage, he was accustomed to performing with hair-trigger response. He opened his mouth to protest the injustice of such a question, but justice was irrelevant here, only audacity mattered. He brought his moist hands together, his eyes bulged, riveted on Professor Sterne's lapel where a key glittered like a gnashing fang. "Well . . . ," said Professor Sterne, licking away the dryness of his own tongue (from his bulging eyes Connie could clearly see with what difficulty Professor Sterne was now swallowing—Connie was Sterne's Best-Student, a showcase of his own erudition). Connie's throat felt as if layers of steel had been welded by the intense burning heat of his own brain into a solid, implacable, strangling band. "If Milton's too big a bite, let's start with someone *more to your taste*. Could you tell us something about Gide or Genêt: or both?"

More to your taste. The threat of it sank like a hook into the steel band; they were rescuing him, but they had to pull him up in such a way that he could not breathe for fear of their knowledge. . . . *Did they know? What did they know? Was this their way of? . . . Was it charity or challenge? Kindness or exposé?* Connie thought he managed to turn his head inquiringly from one to the other, but he was not turning, he was falling, had fallen . . . and they stood over him now, solicitously, reassuringly. His head lay peacefully cradled in Father's—no, not Father's but Professor Sterne's arms. He was to have another chance, they said. This sometimes happened to the best of them. He was not to take it to heart. They chafed his hands, each one went out of his way to clap him on the back encouragingly, as if he had surpassed himself on the exams instead of failing them. And each one repeated that he was to have his second chance.

But Connie knew better. He knew that for orphans of the soul there was no second chance, only a trial period, make it or bust, perform or go back to the Home. Silent, beaded with cold sweat, like a corpse not yet embalmed against the adversities of time, he stared with cunning at each one of his interrogators. He knew what he knew. He expected Dr. Bean to be waiting for him outside the examination room, but Dr. Bean had not had the least premonition of disaster and had gone off to a dentists' convention in Denver. Connie's wife, swollen to her ninth month of pregnancy, awaited him at home with a Victory Party, which she had promised to climax by the delivery of a son in the morning hours. But suppose it turned out to be a daughter, one of the dreaded daughters of Milton?

How many daughters Milton had was to remain an eternal enigma, he never looked it up. Instead, that very evening he boarded the first bus to the old campsite in the Bluehills. He took no clothes, no money, above all, no books. When he saw his tall lanky lover riding up like some illustration of a life they had all altogether lost except in the parks, canyons and bayous, he sank down, silent and exhausted among the leaves and stones and fritillary pinecones and waited patiently for his ranger to rescue him. John Stuart Mill had come home.

Ramón El Conejo

awn, Ramón felt, was perhaps not the best time to get a hitch, since in the unfolding darkness, curled and echoing as a conch, a figure as small as he was, with what must appear to be a rucksack on his back could scarcely impress the speeding tourists from Laredo. Yet he was glad he had worked all night as usual, and had finished out the week at La Hoja Verde—collecting the three dollars pay which would, if necessary, buy him a bus ticket to San Antonio. By the time his mother and his stepfather had realized that he was missing, he would be nearly to Miami. He only hoped that his disappearance would cause his stepfather much trouble with the law on the American side of the bridge—though whatever they did to that *cabrón* would not be enough: it could never erase those weeks and months of humiliation, the foul names boiling like lava in Ramón's memory—nor the brutal mark of the boot heel in his back. When he had got rich as a waiter in Miami, Ramón resolved, he would return to Mexico, kill his stepfather, and rescue his little brother Mauricio.

Except for the thought of his mother's grief, he could relax and enjoy in detail his triumphant departure from Nuevo Laredo: how for the last time he had thrown the crudely starched waiter's uniform of La Hoja Verde into the laundry bin, then had taken a thick crayon and had scribbled into illegibility those words in the men's room which had mocked him for two years:

Puercos y perros
Mean por los suelos

Then he had carefully rolled his own father's cape, the *muleta* of the bullfight, with its leathery congealment of his father's blood still mingled with that of the bull which had killed him, so that the black shroud of satin with its sanctifying stain lay rolled inward, while the brave crimson which had challenged the bull now lay shining on Ramón's back: a signal of courage in the mist of morning darkness fleeing before the first light of the sun.

As he bent toward the highway, he twisted his body into a scythe and raised his thumb into an imploring signal. A couple of returning tourists whipped by, their yellow SANBORN'S IN-SURANCE stickers flashing victoriously, like pennants. . . . Soon, he indulged himself in the reflection, his mother would be knock-ing at the door of every cousin in Laredo. "Have you see my Ramón, my little rabbit?" she would say. "He slept not to his home last night. Last pay night Aguijón took away from him again the three dollars. 'He eats here, let him pay: is he a pimp to live on his mother's work?' Aguijón said. So my *conejo* jumped and kicked him right here—*los hombres temen mucho sus cojones, tu sabes*—an' I thought sure Aguijón was goin' beat him to deat' for that, *el pobrecito.*" . . . Ramón allowed the illusion of his mother's voice to lull him, echoing in his consciousness like a brook followed by the quick chirrup of a bird bathing. . . . But he knew his thoughts were not true ones: *la madre* never pitied him; rather, she had always seemed to fear pity as though it were a form of spiritual bankruptcy, like drunkenness or gambling: the more a man used it, the more he needed it. Nevertheless, he enjoyed the image he had created more than reality, as one en-joyed the marvels of mescal; and he would have gone on weaving *la madre's* odyssey into endless epics of love-rewarded, except that he was reminded by the slashing of gears as a van crested the hill that here was a chance for the long hitch.

The crunch of the truck spewing gravel as it came to a halt before him made him feel like a hero; he stood transfixed by a sense of his own power, marveling at what he had wrought: the truck's thickly groined tires, raised like relief maps, had stopped level with Ramón's eyes; its fog lights still burned watchfully in the waning light; on either side glared restive warning lights, red and lethal as the eye of a bull; and within the cowl of the truck sat the hunched figure of the driver, staring sightlessly down at him from behind a green spread of sunglasses, wide as a mask across his temples.

Ramón said a hurried, breathless prayer as he stood by the opened door.

"Climb up. I'm goin' straight to San Antone with this here load. Been ridin' all night. Think you might could keep us awake till we get there?"

That was all there was to it. Ramón was to fire the consciousness of the machine with a wakeful din while the driver sat immobile, a robot rooted to his leather seat cushion, his arms on the steering wheel like mountain cacti—club-shaped, thick, spiny and bursting with strong juice: the sun-bleached hairs stood up in porcine hackles. . . . The truck now roared through unresisting lateral space. . . . "No Riders Allowed," Ramón read on the door, and at once pitched his voice to a rising strophe of gratitude.

For more than two hours he blew his lungs out, his mouth dry and unbreakfasted; it was a strange kind of torture based on prestige and a sense of honor: without his voice flailing the wind, the over-sized toy at his side would tremble, and with a final click-click, counterclockwise, spin into a silent sleep. Suddenly the machine stopped.

"They got a river here. The Frió. Great for bustin' you in the eyes with a cold bath. I'm gonna have me a swim in 'er."

To Ramón's astonishment the mammoth-haired robot began to strew his clothes around like a madman, wrenching himself loose from the wet undershirt gummed to his skin like tar. For stunned seconds he watched as a bolt of flesh torpedoed the sun-lit water, then surfaced, snorting and blowing a spume of water. Then again the barrelled curve of the back sluiced through the waters, turned suddenly with piscean ease and rested its arms oarlike on the surface; motionless the body floated in the sunlight, the eyes closed in stilled absorption: a buddha.

Gaining courage by the fact that the floating body really ignored him, Ramón hid behind a tapestried willow branch dipping in the riverbank, then plunged into the cool, gently-crescented waves. The water charged at his skin, flayed him with its ice, stripped him of identity: while at the same time his warm blood rushed to the surface to meet and merge with its primordial element. It filled him with a sense of having already accomplished great things to think that this water, perhaps, would go all the way to the sea—starting here with this river, dipping into an estuary at the Nueces River, and so on into a surging flood outside Corpus Christi and the Gulf. El Frió: the Cold One.

He dried himself with his T-shirt, which he noted had begun to thresh small holes under the arms. Then he lay on the river bank and waited for the driver to dress. . . . His brain rang with the cicadas teasing and burring in the sage around him; with his senses he absorbed the world: the pure white yucca blossoms and the womby splash of red gilias, the lissome swoop of the willow branch, all fretted and whirred by an ecstasy of birds. Across the river a lonely gnarled manzanita reared its scuffy black head to the sky.

The intensity of the morning blurred his vision—it was like an eclipse of pain; and he was sure that in all his life he had never been so happy.

Nevertheless, he tried to be greedy about it, to point out to himself that if this patch of earth brought such wonder, what must Miami be? . . .

He was somber and silent as the now wakeful driver revved the motor to a steady roar, as if on an endless elevator climb: they proceeded the short distance to San Antonio in silence.

When they hit the outskirts of San Antonio, the driver asked him where he wanted to get off. Ramón looked around desperately. He wanted to appear as if he knew the city at least well enough to know where to get off. But he could think of only one or two places. . . .

"Just by the Alamo, it'd be a'right. I gotta lot of places to go first."

"Don't want to drive this big load through the middle of town. Look, whyn't you just get out right along here—hop one of them buses into town, they go along Espada Road."

The driver stopped in front of a local cemetery, very neglected and rambling. Ramón would have protested; he had a superstitious fear of burial grounds, but with a conscious rise of valor, he leaped from the truck onto the cracked earth. Evidently it had not rained here in a long while. . . . A network of puffy-headed red ants, looking like a form of future life which was to survive man's extinction, rushed around sending furious messages of invasion. Ramón stamped his feet, shaking them from his sneakers; he could remember how in *la madre's* chicken house, they could pick a piece of chicken clean in a few hours, then perforate and atomize the bones.

With a startling belch, the truck jerked forward; the green-glassed driver nodded from the rear view mirror and was gone.

Ramón's situation depressed him; he saw no indication that this was a bus stop. The scraggly cemetery, scattered with sage and an occasional mesquite tree might have been in the middle of a Mexican prairie for all he knew; but a black American car glittering with chrome in the summer sunlight cheered him by its spectacle of efficiency and its apparent geographical sense. He began walking in the same direction. The cemetery seemed endless; however, it abutted suddenly on the stone stilts of a dun-colored house in front of which a clothesline flurried signs of inescapable life: a cotton shirt, diapers with round holes through which scraps of sunlight oddly capered, a pair of bright red woman's panties —strangely unrecked and shameless in the early light. There was no other sign of life in the morning silence: the clothesline with its crude effigies fluttered across the earth filled in turn with its dead; it waved, it fluttered; it struggled to move, and subsided.

Ramón knocked at the door, hoping to get directions and perhaps breakfast: his stomach felt like cracked glass. A Mexican woman, incredibly uncombed, came out, looking at him with eyes still puffy with white scars of sleep; but her voice was charged with a strangely garish and cheerful energy. She pointed in the direction the black car had taken.

"You goin' fishin'? Need worms?" She showed Ramón their sign, making a cannon of her fist from out of which she shot her index finger. WORMS: FOR BAIT. The sign was meaningless to him. "Here, I'll give you some *free*, give me good luck—start the day with a blessin'. 'Give somethin' away: have *good*-luck today!' " she chimed. She thrust a small can, Hunt's Tomatoes, into his hands, and quickly shut him out.

Ramón hurried away from the woman whom he thought of as a madwoman, a *loca;* he was consoling himself, however, with the thought that at least she had offered him food, when he raised the jagged lid of the can and saw the squirming, writhing clot of worms.

"Dios mío!" he breathed, his heart stopping with horror. There was something diabolical, sacrilegious about it—was the woman a *bruja,* a witch, living on the nearby human flesh? He could imagine her suddenly, with that wild clutch of hair, late at night, digging, digging . . . for the worms which toiled at the bottom of her necrophilis.

He threw the can with all his strength; he heard it hit the side of a tombstone, then roll in the sandy earth. He stood by the side of the road; the glass in his stomach heaved and cracked, but fortunately he had had no breakfast. . . . It would have been an unlucky way to begin his first day of freedom, he thought. With the patience of certainty, a cleansing ritual to rid himself of the ill effects of this brief encounter with doom, he began to tell his rosary beads, feeling a sweet swell of gratitude toward his God for having furnished in His foresight, such an infallible restorative. For good measure he lightly tapped the St. Christopher medal inside his T-shirt, and felt himself again in complete control of his fate.

The bus did come, finally, and he sat down in its fantastical coolness; he found that his experience had swathed him in perspiration; he shivered, but the air-conditioning which wafted around his feet felt good, and he removed his sneakers, allowing the jets of air to tingle his toes. He was just becoming accustomed to this miraculous inversion of temperatures—winter in July— when the bus had stopped, everyone got off, and Ramón stood barefoot in the streets of downtown San Antonio.

Dazzled by the sunlight and the traffic he stood in the street a moment, uncertain where to go, when to his immense delight he saw a familiar sign: Mexican Tourism; he crossed the street and looked into the window as if it were an outpost from Home. Inside, he could see an elderly lady with carefully screwed curls dilating her forehead, sitting at a large desk; another American woman sat in a chair beside the desk, a baby on one arm, a small blue and white canvas bag in the other, labeled PAN AM. The floor was what magnetized Ramón: polished as the human eye it lay in tessellated squares, a dark pool of reflected light, surely as cool to the bare feet as the river Frío. In the very center of the polished redwood wall had been laid a mosaic of the Holy Family, a gleaming rondure of semi-precious stones: the blue eyes of the baby Jesus were made of sharp slices of sapphire; His eyes, one realized, were meant to pierce the Darkness, nothing was to remain hidden to Him. . . . The ascendancy of the Christ child, and the mystic glow emanating from the floor made the place a paradise. For was it not as Father Sebastian had told him was described in the *Book of Revelations:* "In Heaven the floor is laid with diamonds, real diamonds; their brightness is blinding; it is all light, but still cool, very cool, and you walk your way along this path of diamonds till you see Jesus. . . ."

The sight of the Infant Jesus reminded him that he wished to offer up a long prayer before he caught the train to Miami. Opposite the tourist office was the place the bus driver had called out, St. Anthony's: was not St. Anthony one of the earliest of Catholic saints? Its proximity was surely a good omen. . . . He started for the corner, so as to cross, this time, with the traffic light.

He paused at Travis and St. Mary's, feeling mildly edified by this posting of holy names by the wayside, like the Stations of the Cross. A city saturated with holy relics: he knew people who had brought home splinters from the San José mission, and had performed miracles with them. . . . His problem now was so simple that he flushed with shame. He could not find the doors to what he had thought was a church—and stood with amazement as there passed in front of him on the *sidewalk*, a huge black car, as long, it seemed, as a mule team and wagon, driving straight into the hallowed vault of this building. Ramón could see, just ahead of it, dozens of other cars, honking, idling, pushing slowly but aggressively forward, shouldering their way through the crowd. The rear of the car was in the street; he wished he could touch its shiny flank, graceful and silent as a cropping horse, but he dared not. Instead, he walked around it, nearly four feet into the street where the sloping rear panel had stretched itself.

He stood for a moment staring into the faces of the people driving into St. Anthony's; he gazed at them with an almost religious awe, as though they were white Spanish Gods, bringing arms and horses and commerce and misery to his people; but they did not notice him. They were relaxed; blue-haired, black-hatted, as white and clean as boiled rice. They spoke to each other gently; there was no noise within the automobile, one could see that, except for their voices; the blue windows held out the sun, sealed in the cold air. Ramón saw a hand, the color of burnt hay, like his own, adjust the air conditioner to the new cool of the garage, and for a split-second Ramón gazed into the eyes of the chauffeur, brown eye to brown eye, eyes of my people—and there was an exchange, an understanding between them, silent and subterranean, like the soundless explosion of rifles in a dream. . . . Ramón, stunned by the intensity of this look, stood alone on St. Mary's.

He saw at once that St. Anthony's was not, after all, a church, and he laughed at himself, though troubled by his sacrilegious error as he hopped through the door, a door sliced like a giant grapefruit into four equal parts, spinning on its axis.

He stood uncertainly in the lobby of St. Anthony's, his sneakers around his neck, his bare feet upon the red carpet; his eyes clouded with shame when he saw he had left two sooty footprints, so small they reminded him of his little brother Mauricio's toes. He could scarcely believe that it was he, Ramón, a grown boy, who had thus dirtied the carpet: when the dapper brass-buttoned desk clerk raised his plucked eyebrows at him, it made him feel like a dog. *Puercos y perros.* . . . With an illumination of memory, as of a sign in Braille raised by the heat of shame to living words, he remembered something Father Sebastian had read to him in English: " 'Juárez could not forgive me,' " Santa Anna said, " 'because he had waited on me at table at Oaxaca in 1829 *with his feet bare on the floor.'* " The great Juárez, too, had run away when he was twelve—and like Juárez he, too, stood now shivering with shame, his feet bare on the floor, and expecting the brass-buttoned desk clerk to throw him into the street. . . . As fast as he could

Ramón slipped into his sneakers, tied the rotting laces into a knot; then he felt respectable: he cultivated a slow dignified stroll, trying to look as if he were waiting for someone. He even sat in one of the green leather chairs with its winged bronzed back soaring above his head, its graceful concavity to his back; he put his head back on the brass-nailed trimming: not very comfortable, but *caramba*, it was cool against the skin. As he slid off suddenly, violently, his own wet skin made an inadvertent rasping sound against the leather; so that again Ramón stood frozen with shame, involuntarily shaking his head in denial and going through the comedy of repeating the sound on purpose so that the elevator boy would see how he had accidentally made the noise with his bare skin.

But he became at once indifferent to the judgments of the elevator boy as his eyes fell on a beautiful bronze statue of a woman (the sign said *Roman* and he was glad it had been no Mexican *mala hembra* who had posed for it) with one exquisite breast exposed while with the left hand she held up a lamp as bright as the sun. Her breast was round and high and looked soft to the touch as the inside of a melon; but it would never have occurred to Ramón to touch it: he knew that though she was nearly naked it was nevertheless a thing of beauty—as when *la madre* exposed the spurting curve of her breast to Mauricio— and not to be profaned by inquisitive hands.

Ah, how he wished, though, that he might take one long, gliding run on the red carpet, but he dared not; the faint nervous nausea of his stomach reminded him that the excitement of the beautiful place had not fed him. He had begun to drag his sneakers slowly along the carpet toward the incredibly symmetrical radii of the door when he noticed a pair of vases taller than himself—surely the most beautiful urns in the world. Father Sebastian had once told him that in the days of Rome just such urns were filled with rose petals, or even with one's own tears and preserved: the memory of one's grief distilled to aromatic bliss.

He longed to look deep inside, and raised himself on tiptoe, clinging to the lip of the vase for balance, and peered into the darkness. He whispered into it, his susurrating breath returned to him like a dead voice from out of the past; he tried to make a tear, so that like the ancients, his sorrow would be sanctified forever. But he felt no grief, only ecstasy; so instead, with his tongue he scooped up a small bubble of saliva from the soft of his cheeks and dropped it with a tiny *plick* into the bottom of the vase.

It was for this that the hotel clerk threw him out. That was all right—he had to do that, Ramón realized, and felt neither fear nor humiliation for the rude ejection: he had reached the point where he could feel only hunger. So he quickly adjusted his manly pride by inhaling a robust whack of air and raced at top speed for several blocks, in a wild exuberance of freedom. He stopped short at the river, and leaned most of his small body over one of San Antonio's myriad bridges. There, on the opposite side of the river, was a Chinese restaurant. Calm and commercial, a Mexican boy travestied an Oriental waiter in white jacket and silk flowered Bermudas. On the near side, immediately under him lay stretched along the turbid river, *La Casa Mía* Fine Mexican Food.

La Casa Mía—the name attracted him, made a spasm of violent homesickness in his belly: he could hear his mother calling him and Mauricio *Vengan hijos a la casa, a comer. . . .* Almost hopping with delight Ramón descended the granite stairs of the bridge and sat down at one of the tables inlaid with mosaic. Beside him were round tables rooted to the floor by a single stone base, and on the wide diameters of their surfaces, Aztec gods, birds, Zodiacs, Virgins, had been wrought in mosaic. From where he sat perched in his iron chair, he could see on the table next to him the hundred eyes of a peacock's tail, glinting in the sun; piece by piece it had been created, by tireless hands for whom each dainty piece meant a tenth of a peso.

A young couple sat down opposite Ramón: a blonde-haired girl with bangs like a scythe across her forehead smiled at him tenderly, glancing down at his tongueless shoes. The waiter came, hesitated, looked around helplessly, grinned at the blond girl, who was nodding meaningfully. "So O.K. niño, you want tortillas, we got 'em, plenny of 'em. *Con mantequilla*," he added in the tone of a man describing a Christmas tree; and had vanished before Ramón could protest against the butter; it would cost too much, especially in this place.

The waiter brought tortillas, toasted crackers and several

mounds of butter; from the table next to him where the beautiful blonde-haired angel was still smiling at Ramón, the waiter transferred more crackers and a soft drink which *el angel* pushed into his hand. Ramón devoured this rapidly, and left a five-cent tip.

He was about to leave when blind tears stung his eyes, and he realized with a shock that they had simply sprung like a tincture dilating the surface at the very moment the Mariachi music had struck his ears: they were serenading the couple at the next table. While his stomach ecstatically digested the tortillas, he took in at every pore the elixir of sound: oh sweet Mexico, to find you on this river. . . .

The guitarrón was strumming a hat dance, his fingers working with casual perfection. The singing tenor, flamboyantly decked out as a *vaquero* (*we* had cowboys before they did, Ramón silently boasted), stood beside a beautiful Mexican lady adorned with traditional tiara and mantilla. . . . In fact, they looked more Mexican than any Mexicans Ramón had ever seen—his people, masquerading as themselves. Ramón left the restaurant feeling crushed. There had been something about the Mariachis which had reminded him of his father—the pale, yellow resoluteness of their faces, and the sweating back of the guitarrero, whose silk shirt had clung to him in a wet, arrow-like wound, like Papa's shirt at the *corrida*. . . . He was trying, not rationally, but with a leap of personal apprehension to grasp the relationship between those two orbing wounds of sweat; thus he hardly noticed that he had taken over an hour, as he strolled up St. Mary's Street, to find a church, and even then he did not look at the name—it sufficed for him that he saw two nuns emerging in black robes, their heavy crucifixes hanging at their sides.

As he opened the door and stood in the transept of the church the cool beatified air, exempt from earthly heats, swept around him. He dipped his fingers into the holy water, glad his hands had been cleansed by El Frío; then he advanced to the Communion rail where he knelt and offered up a fervent prayer for courage in the new land.

At last he rose from his knees, satisfied that he had been heard. He sat down in one of the polished pews, lucent as amber, and feasted his eyes on God's earthly Temple: on the blue velvet altar cloth with the chastened glow of the chalice and the softly breathing flames flickering like souls from out the red glasses, and beyond it all, above him, a cross of gold on which Christ hung in agony.

From the pocket of his jeans he pulled out the frayed train schedule he had kept hidden for months, ever since his stepfather had first slept at their house. He had studied the schedule many times, had supplemented his uncertain comprehension with patient inquiry darkly reticulated in the pockets of conversations till the information had returned to him repeated, axiomatic: take the Southern Pacific to New Orleans; switch for the Louisville-Nashville; watch out for railway guards and queers. His head nodded over the long-familiar schedule, and while the filtered light from the mullioned window rained silence, he dozed. . . . When he awoke, he was in terror a moment, not knowing how long he had slept; so he jumped to his feet and began running, running as fast as he could, spurred by the vision of vanishing freight cars. He ran, sweating with fear and speed, the entire two blocks to Commerce Street, where at the railway yard, he stopped.

Fortunately he had not missed his train; that would indeed have been a bad omen. What remained now was merely to find a place to wait, so that when the train approached and the railway guards flew their lanterns of consent, he too would fly, silent as the hawk, and descending upon the box car with a swift swoop of arm and limb, would lift himself into the car and be—free.

When the train came at last, it proved to be interminably long—freight after freight of cotton, lumber, oil products, and Texas beef—freshly slaughtered, flash-frozen, to be made into steaks worthy of a nation of conquerors. The thought of steak made his stomach rage suddenly with hunger; but he had not time to think of his stomach now; for he must be watching, watching, for the moment when the flares descended and the cars bumping together in their blind haste would begin to move forward. Now the train jerked, spattered, steamed like the ejaculation of a bull, and began to move—one car following another like some thundering herd hard behind its leader.

The noise was terrifying, but even more terrifying was the

possibility that this controlled acceleration of a miracle might vanish without him. . . . So he leaped . . . and the roar and motion of the cars was like an earthquake, in the midst of which he clung, clung to the opened door, till a momentary stalled jerk of the car allowed him to pull his legs up; and he let go. He was flung with a lurch into deep sawdust, for which his brain flashed a marveling wink of admiration as the shavings cushioned his fall. The train roared on, and he found himself alone, triumphant, looking outward from where he lay on the floor.

Keeping his head out of sight, he gazed on the city from his vantage point. The usual railroad outskirts pricked his vision, kaleidoscopic and searingly familiar as they sped by, ugly shack upon ugly shack, like his very own street, spotted here and there with geranium pots: a huge scab covering the wound of the City, healed now and then with a concentric beauty and health only to break open from time to time in suppurating disease as they sped away from the festering little homes and ruts of streets out into the infinity of Texasland, a land as wide as the Salt Sea. . . .

When they were out on the open road, Ramón felt at last protected against vagrant eyes that might wish to take over his squatters' rights. . . . Stacked on one side of the car were a single bushel basket, and several empty pinewood boxes with various labels: Texas Peaches, Buford's Huisache Honey, 100% Pure, and Sam Slaughter's Packing House: Fresh Frozen Produce. He was kneeling in the sawdust, looking for any stray bits of food that might have been set adrift in the boxes when he heard the cars come to a screeching stop. Without a second's hesitation, Ramón rolled himself like a pill bug under the empty peach basket and lay there without breathing while he listened to grunts, groans, heaves and what seemed to be the rolling wheels of a dolly. After about twenty minutes (which felt infinitely longer) the marching and dragging subsided and darkness shrouded the staves of his basket. He was safe; for the first time in his life his small unfleshed body had been an asset; he squatted for a moment on his haunches, then stood up, chilled with relief, his hands cold from the prolonged fear. . . .

On their way out they had slammed the doors to, all the

way, and locked them, and in the gloom he could not at first make out what food his benefactors had left him; but as he raised his head he collided with the flayed and dangling limbs of a cow, evidently so recently killed that it had not yet begun to smell dead; as he stood beneath it a drop of blood, like a raindrop, fell to the sawdust. Such was the inert company they had brought to share his vault: he saw them clearly now, hanging from hooks in the ceiling on which were skewered the delicacies of edible flesh: hams and shoulders and legs of mutton and carcasses of beef: there were even two or three blue-eyed, rosy-cheeked heads of porkers spiked to the side walls like condemned victims beside a medieval drawbridge. A whole hennery of fowl lined the wall, and a rabbit, which for some reason had not yet been skinned. It hung head down, slender-footed paws nailed to an iron tree, its delicate nostrils and fine whiskers still alert with fear. The other animals, stripped of their deep cow-eyes and bleating tones, were mere anonymous flesh meant to renew and construct the body and mind of man; but the rabbit's fur was still dappled grey, stippled with the colors of the prairie, dogwood blossom and cenizo-colored leaf. . . . Ramón felt suddenly a great desolation and wished they had left the door open for him so that he could stare out at the rolling escarpments of color—at the orange clay and blue gentians and purple paint brushes and yellow star grass and white shreds of thistle, so that he might close his mind to what seemed to him the still echoing shriek of the slain animals, their not even memorable grief—the mere pitiless pain of the charnel house.

He had found a softly rotting peach, but in spite of his hunger, he could not eat it. The grizzly spectacle had chilled him to the bone; he realized suddenly, that his teeth were clenched and chattering, though he could feel drops of nervous perspiration congeal under his thinly woven T-shirt. He shivered and tried the door, eager for the now-fading sunlight, but as he had suspected, it was immovable. If only there were a window through which he could watch the moonlight and stars during his all-night vigil across the Louisiana delta: twelve hours before their arrival in New Orleans, and he would not once see the glory of the heavens.

More practically, he murmured to himself, if there were a

window he could dry his perspiration, hold back this progressive chill: was he getting a fever, hot and cold as his body seemed to be? He unrolled his father's cape and enveloped himself in it, with the black side, the side with Papa's blood close to his heart; but still his teeth did not cease to chatter; his hands remained stiff and cold. It was odd, too, that the *muleta* had no smell: almost always, and especially on hot, humid days, the smell of the dust and blood of doomed bull and father would pervade his nostrils; but now he could smell nothing. He breathed only the icy fumes of his own nostril; his breath made a cotton-like burr which eased away from him, refusing to cohere.

As he sat on the sawdust floor, shivering and peering longingly at the sharp blade of light slitting the throaty darkness of the door, he became aware of a humming in his ears, a bedtime murmuring as if *la madre* rocked him, cunningly, to sleep. Was it the sound of the wind—or the sound of a motor? He rose, gasping painfully at the cold which now burned at his chest like dry ice— he felt he would not be able to endure it, and he began whimpering softly to himself, clutching his rosary in rigid hands: *oh hace frio, o god, oh Jesús, hace frio.*

He remembered suddenly that moving about might keep him warm, and he began, not walking but hopping—his left leg had scraped against the side of the boxcar and now was numb with pain—hopping to and fro beneath the contorted limbs of the friable bodies. He was still stubbornly hobbling back and forth in the car when with a loud shriek the train began to cross a trestle and threw him against the wall. His hands clutched the wall in amazement: it was lined with coils and covered with a light, damp frost, like rail tracks in mid-winter; and his fingers pulled away with an icy burn.

In despair he threw himself down on the sawdust-covered floor, sobbing. *Oh Jesús help me,* he prayed with blue lips that made no sound as he moved them; but as the unarticulated prayer sounded in his heart, he clutched the sawdust which oozed through his fingers like sand: like sand that one could burrow in and be warm. With a sudden rush of energy, he moved all the hanging bodies to one side of the car, and with his arms and shoulders began shoving the sawdust into a corner of the car.

The floor had been liberally covered with sawdust, and he murmured little orisons of gratitude as he swept. And *oh Jesús mío*, how good it felt to crawl into it, submerged almost to the chest. Covered by the black and red cape and buried in the sawdust, he felt as content, almost, as when swimming in El Frío—when beneath him, sustaining his body, had reposed the infinite shales of immovable time, and above him, skittering across his naked chest like dragonflies, had darted the sunlight. . . . And as he had trusted then to the maternal, caressing rills of sunlight, he trusted now to the ooze and ebb of the blood of his body, the very treachery of whose congealment seemed to warm him as he slept, lifeless, his rosary in his rigid hand.

L'il Britches

Sam here is goin' to write it all down so's he can take it up from Texas to *Nooyawk* with him. He write down just about everythin' anybody say 'round here; he a real writer for sure: he an all right guy, and he *straight* too. Sam's just about the only white boy I ever knew to call a friend, I mean a *friend,* if you know what I mean. But I knowed he was from up yonder the first day I seen him at that Akarena *Motel,* and he step on my bare foot tryin' to walk both ways at once 'round the wet whiles I was waterin' the grass, and he say "oh *par*don me," just like that, "oh pardon *me,*" like some kind of church hymn.

(Now don't be lookin' at me like that, Sam; just you write it all down. That's *yo'* job, ain't it?)

Now in San Marcos colored folks like me and L'il Britches here can fish right there by the dam—you know where you turn off the expressway comin' down from Austin to the college—yes siree, LBJ's college. It's integrated now so's colored folks can go. You know Mr. Jefferson Davis?—he our preacher down by the Colored Baptist; he a plumber by the week, only on Sunday he say he plumb for the Lord, ain't that a good one?—well, Mr. Jefferson Davis' daughter, *she* goes there now; and if I ever *do* get through that there junior high school, I'm goin' there too, 'cause I sure enough want to be a doctor. Boy, like you got *five dollars* for maybe three minutes seein' is Miz Liza got a fever in her chest, or *no?*

But you don't go as far as the college if you want to fish. You just get you some bait and you go down by the dam. Ain't nobody goin' stop you. I mean, I always tell L'il Britches, if that there woman who owns the motel there, she tells you to go away, don't pay her no mind, just you go 'round to t'*other* side of the bridge, 'cause she don't pay no taxes on the *whole* river, does she? But like I say to L'il Britches, if one of those cedarchoppers, one of those skinny, hungry-lookin' ones with eyes what don't never open all the way to the sun (it *hurts* them 'cause they ain't got no piga-mentation), if one of those with their knife-hand in a pocket, and with those Elvis Prezley sideburns cut away like sawed off shot guns, come by—why you just shut up and *get*, I'm tellin' *you*.

That's what I done told L'il Britches, but he ain't exactly like we-all. It ain't that he dumb, no siree, he real smart that boy, *real* smart, but he awful scared. Seems like it was born in him. If he hear a car zoom by our dirt road, kickin' up a storm of dust and stones, why L.B. he would just wake up from his nap like a dog done bit him. Or say an airplane was comin' through this way from S'Antone—why, he run to Mama and climb up all *over* her, to get away from that thing! And one time, Mama took him to Miz Cook's house 'cause she have to vacuum those white carpets, 'cause they were havin' a supper party to get money for the San Marcos library (you oughtn't to laugh at that library, Sam, maybe it ain't *Nooyawk* but they got over a *thousand* real nice-lookin' books now) and Brother was so scared of that machine, he wet his britches on their white carpet. "I wet my l'il britches," he said to Mama, they're the first words he ever said, and she sure whipped him hard at Miz Cook's, but then she kiss him all up again when they got home. . . . Next time Mama went to Miz Cook's house Miz Cook said, "Miz Johnson, you know you the best maid I *ever* had, but I have to ask you to leave yo' pets at home till they are *house*broke." It was a joke, Sam.

One thing he scared of, anything dead. How it happen we know that even before he can talk is, I'm goin' be a doctor like I told you, so I got to know what's inside things. Well, about two years ago I was just cuttin' up a frog like Mister Benson, he showed us to, when in comes L.B. He just took one look at that frog and started squallerin' like a hound dog—and *sick?* I never did see a boy puke so much. He just that way. After that Mama wouldn't never mention no meat we ate by its name—we never ate catfish nor pigs' feet nor hog chitterlings—and though we used to have the *best* fricassee out of chicken legs and giblets, now we couldn't even have that 'cause he knowed those legs, so all we ate was just "meat." Mama would fry us up some *real* good pork brains and fried corn bread and she'd say, "Now see here boys, what-all good meat I got here."

Mama said it was just the smell of that old form . . . forma-*hal*dehyde what made L.B. sick, but one evenin' I left my best Monarch butterfly under the space heater so's to dry, and I guess there must of been a little too much carbon *die*-oxhide *com*bined with the oxygen, 'cause that little old heater just blew the roof off and ruined my Monarch. I tried to patch it up some, 'cause they're a tourist butterfly, what spends only the winter in the South and go back North in the summertime—they're hard to get this time of year—but it was ruined, so I just threw that butter-fly away in the trash not thinkin' about L'il Britches, y'see? And when he seen me throw that insect away, he had it out of the trash before I could think to stop him.

"Put that there back," I said to him, mad-like, 'cause I knew Mama sure would get after me, if she knew I done a dumb trick like that. "That butterfly ain't no good no more, he *dead*."

He just stood there holdin' this dead thing in his hand, very gentle-like, by one wing, like he waitin' for it to flutter (he seen me do that plenty-a-times, I reckon).

"I say he dead." I'm goin' to be a doctor, I figures to myself, and I ain't goin' to start now by tellin' no lies to no little brother.

Well, you should of seen my baby brother's face, those big black eyes watchin' me like I was God or somethin' (those butter-flies always fluttered in my hand, y'see, Sam?).

"Make him fly," say L'il Britches. Can you beat that? Make him fly, he says. And I sure as hell had to make him fly. . . . I picked up that old dead butterfly and shot him so high up in the trees, he just stayed there. . . .

Next thing you know, a couple days later we were sittin' right there by the dam catchin' catfish, I mean *live*, Sam. We always carried a big two-handle washtub of water on our wagon, and when we got home, Mama would take care of everythin'. Whissh! We never see those catfish again. L'il Britches, he think fishin' is just a *sport*; he naturally don't know we *eat* them. Well, we were sittin' right there after that big rain, boy that was the biggest rain I ever see in Texas this time of year, six inches right here in San Marcos, and the fish were just crawlin' out the river, like those *amphibians*, you know those animals that lived in the Messozoic, the Age of Reptiles?—just happy to be caught. It sure was pretty out too, like that walnut tree out there, it was all fretty and frilly and clean like a woman glad when she all prettied up. (*That* one by the *magnolia*—don't tell me you don't know a *walnut* tree, Sam?)

It was just one of those days for fishin'. Say, you know what day it was? Now I'll tell you what day it was. It was the thirtieth of May that's what; it was the same day that the President of the United States was givin' a Commencement *Address* at the University in Austin. That's why this town was just empty. All the white folks with cars were gone off to Austin, hopin' maybe to see LBJ on campus—no, not *my* LBJ, the President who I mean. L'il Britches, he ain't President *yet*.

Now, come to mind, it may have been just that shirt L.B. was wearin' with the initials on it what made those cedarchoppers mad. I mean, they were teed off the minute they seen us. Boy I knowed they were lookin' for trouble when the two of them scrambled down from that bridge up there and the short, snakey-fingered one put his hand in his pocket, and the Big Slim he say: "Whatcha catchin' in that river—*niggers?*"

I started pullin' in my line right away then. I mean there ain't no use of you fightin' that kind—leastaways when I had L'il Britches worrin' me. He small, and he delicate; he born that way; he ain't cut out for no roughhouse stuff. But L'il Britches he surprised me that time. He wasn't scared a bit—shows you can't never tell what to expect from a little old baby. Me, I was scared. We don't have hardly no policemen walkin' 'round this here small town, and if we *had* of had, he'd been over to Austin watchin' out for the President. So it was *quiet*. My, I could hear myself breathin'.

L'il Britches, he pointed to the tub. "We-all catchin' catfish

—see we got two of them already. Calvin, he goin' fill the tub up to here." L.B. stuck his little finger out and pointed to the top of the tub.

Slim, he put out *his* finger, pointin' to L.B.'s shirt.

"Whatcha got there, boy?"

"My shirt." L'il Britches looked down to see did a scorpion drop on him . . . or what?

"I mean *there*. Them letters."

"That's my name. L. B. Johnson."

That sure broke them up. I heard them say somethin' about LBJ was sure enough a dog lover and a nigger lover *both*, but I couldn't rightly hear them, I was so busy gettin' myself ready for to *de*part. I noticed the wagon's done got sunk down in the mud for sure, but I wasn't fixin' to ask *them* for a push. Fact is, I had a pretty good idea which way they'd be pushin' me, and I didn't aim to get drowned. Anyway, I was tryin' to be inconspicuous, tryin' to look real calm, like I was mainly interested in gettin' my line out of the river and my wagon out of the mud—not lettin' on that I was scared.

But Slim wasn't goin' let me alone neither. "Say, boy," he said sudden-like, "how came you usin' minnows 'stead of worms? I thought even a nigger knew better 'n that. Don't you know *nothin'* about fishin'? This river's full of bream, and you can catch 'em too, but you gotta know whatcha doin'. Get you some worms, boy. Bream just love them juicy worms. . . ."

I wasn't fixin' to tell him I didn't care nothin' about bream; that if L'il Britches ever see me spike a worm on that hook it would make him sick. Now a minnow, Sam, it stays clean, it don't come apart, and I can keep it live in the can till just before I drop my sinker. . . . Meanwhile I was pullin' up my line fast. In spite of all my troubles I done caught me a whoppin' big cat, which I took off the hook fast and *careful* and I splashed him in the tub with the rest of the catch.

L'il Britches sure do love to see them plop in the tub. "Nother one! Nother one!" He was just laughin' like a baby, jumpin' up and down. "Plop!" he said, jumpin' up and down like the fish. "Plop! Plop! Look at that big one swimmin'!" And that catfish sure was swimmin' 'round in the tub, big as a seal, man, I tell you.

"That sure is a big one," said Slim. "Say, you goin' eat all that catfish, boy?" he said to L.B.

L'il Britches was lookin' down in the tub, he was just laughin' like he been at the circus—which he ain't, never. He don't even *hear* Slim at first. He was too busy laughin' and chasin' the big catfish with his both hands. Looked like the big fish was enjoyin' it too, like some kind of game between L'il Britches and the fish.

Slim tried his joke again: "I say, boy, you goin' eat all that big catfish *yo'self?*"

L'il Britches, he stopped laughin' and he just stood there shakin' his head and kind of grinnin' like he knew white folks was always makin' jokes he don't understand.

"You ain't big enough to eat all that by yo'self. Why that fish's bigger 'n you are, boy. You sure must have a big gut for fried cat!"

L'il Britches, he shake his head—negative.

"Well, whatcha catchin' so many of 'em for if you don't *like* 'em, if you ain't goin' *eat* 'em? Boy, when it get to be about suppertime, there ain't *nothin'* I like better 'n fried catfish. You just fix me up a platter of fresh cat fried in bacon grease with cole slaw 'n french fries with plenty of ketchup—mmh! . . ."

Slim, he looked like he was salivatin' but L'il Britches looked like he was sick. How was I goin' to make that fool hush?

"Say, nigger, you cain't tell me no story. You ain't never goin' to be able to eat all that fish. So just you hand me out that there dead one for Mac and me here. Might as well let me take him on home and put him in the fry pan—he ain't goin' be no good to you time you get him home—he goin' get spoilt in all that sun."

L'il Britches put his head down by the tub, like he lookin' for somethin'; the fish Slim was talkin' about, it was floatin' side-ways on the *top*, but L.B. don't notice that—he was lookin' for somethin' to be "dead."

"Ain't no fish dead," said L'il Britches.

"Whatcha mean, *there's* one dead—he's deader 'n a pistol."

"Ain't dead. He just swimmin'."

"If that fish ain't dead, I never seen a dead fish."

"I say he ain't dead!" L.B. was shoutin' then. "He *ain't* dead."

"Well, he damned well is dead, and ain't nothin' you can do about that, nigger!"

"Ain't dead! Ain't dead!" L.B. threw himself on the ground screamin' he want his Mama, he want to go home—and I sure did wish I *was* home.

Big Slim grabbed that old catfish from out the tub. He threw it on the ground right by L.B.'s face where he was lyin' there kickin' and screamin'. "There now, boy. You see that fish move? No, he don't move at all. Do he flap? Do he *swim? This* son of a bitch is dead, that all there is to it." And he stomped on the fish for fair, till the head scrunch off. "There now," he said to L.B. "Is he dead or is he?"

Well, L'il Britches commenced hollerin' like the dogs was after him. He was yellin' and kickin' and so mad he forgot to be scared; and he picked himself up and he bucked into that big cedarchopper like he was goin' to buck the livin' daylights out of him. And before I could catch my breath to pull L'il Britches back, that Snakey-fingers grabbed him from behind ("You little black bastard," he said) and picked him up and pitched him head first in the tub of water. His head banged down to the bottom of that tub like a rock, I tell *you. . . .* Then they run away, scared and laughin' both.

They didn't do L'il Britches no harm. L'il Britches, he's all right now, though he sure was powerful sick to his stomach that time. I mean he's all right, exceptin' it seems like he don't hear so good sometimes—one of these days I'm goin' to take him on the bus to see one of those ear specialist doctors in Houston— they got the best doctors in the world in Houston; they got doctors what don't do nothin' but look at yo' bones or yo' stomach or yo' eyes and ears, why, they got doctors for almost everythin' —but, Sam, you done read a whole lot of books about what happens to yo' mind when you been scared, scared real bad? Do you think, just you tell me the truth, I'm goin' to be a doctor ain't I, ain't no need to be lyin' to *me*—is L'il Britches goin' to be scared from now on?

Nails

She would try to believe them, really believe them, not just pretend. She had never been very good at pretending anyway; the pretending wearied her more than the rest of it. Why couldn't they just sit and be still; her daughters had talked to each other more in the past six weeks than in the past six years. Living across town from each other, they had nevertheless acted as if they were on opposite Coasts. Now they came to the hospital every day to see their mother, arriving separately—carrying their knitting or bringing a book which they read themselves, casually leafing through the pages as though curious to see what might interest the dying. Above all it wearied Cornelia when, flushing guiltily and looking around as if for visible proof, they talked about her looking better and about miracle drugs. Such lies were a waste of energy, *her* energy: she felt she had just time left for her memories, none at all for delusion.

What she liked best was to lie quietly, her gaze fixed on her folded hands, that relieved the pain or seemed to. It was as if her hands were all that remained to her—comfortable companions that she could be sure of now that all else was corrupted. It was as if time might wash over her in a wide surf stretching farther than she could see, but her hands, at least, were near, a map of her lifetime. The webbed puckering of her thumb was familiar to her, like a wrinkle of pain on the brow; the ridges of the nails held secrets she had kept or lost, even from herself. Above all, her nails gave her pleasure, they were perfectly clean for the first time in her life. Never before had she been able to get those final, eternal specks embedded in the flesh just below the quick. Her days at the tv factory, her evenings in the vegetable garden pulling leafy things till their heads trembled with the fresh earth—these had always left some darkness at the root of the nail. Now at last they were clean, white as a priest's collar. Only they were broken and rough at the edges, she didn't like that. When, churned by a spasm of pain, her body roiled beneath the sheets as if by its own will, not hers, her nails would scrape across the white surface, making a coarse sound of accompaniment to her moan. What she childishly longed for was a file with which to smooth out those sharp edges: an odd desire, perhaps, but one she irrationally clung to. She believed, even, that she had asked Beth (or had it been Henrietta?) to bring her one. But perhaps she had only thought she had asked.

Cornelia sighed patiently: at least she had meant to sound patient, but perhaps it had come out as an angry moan; for Beth, who had been looking in her purse for a birthday card their father had sent, now turned apprehensively toward her pillow.

She was glad Beth could not find the birthday card: she wanted no stupid sentimental mementoes from *him*. She slid her hand across the sheet in dismissal, meaning: "Never mind. Nothing your father does could ever interest me." *No reconciliation possible* as she had told the priest years ago. Because you can only be reconciled with someone you have loved, Cornelia went on explaining to Beth's slowly welling eyes. But some one you never cared for: how can you be reconciled to him? Indifference carries its coldness to the grave. To Rikki Advenuto she could be reconciled, whatever mortal sin he might have committed without her, or even against her, in the years since she had last seen him: but to their father, never.

But Beth was not even listening, Cornelia realized irritably. Or else she had failed to make herself clear. That was the trouble, she had never been able to explain herself to them: other things, useful things, perhaps, she had explained to them: but at some point she had forgotten to make herself clear.

What they had understood was that she had destroyed their freedom by clutching at her own, with a divorce which had rocked their small Pennsylvania town as if the story of her adultery, hers and Rikki's, had been a flash flood wiping out all the surrounding areas. What they never failed to recall were the hardships they had endured as a result: "Pa was always a hard worker," Henrietta would say ruefully, rubbing her chafed hands, red with cold from carrying potatoes up from the unheated cellar.

And Henrietta was right, of course: Solomon Vanetti was a hard worker; they had taught men to be hard in Italy. When he had arrived in their town he had soon earned himself a reputation for being able to mortar more bricks in a single day than any man in Moreland County. He had saved his money and one by one brought all his family "over."

Shortly before Cornelia's first menses—Cornelia's grandmother had not failed to notice a fine fold of pubescent fat rising above a triangle of new hair—Cornelia had been given in marriage to Solomon Vanetti: for he was a hard worker and a laborer (St. Paul had said) was worthy of his hire. Cornelia's wedding night, steeped in archetypical ignorance, had brought, along with other surprises the first flow of womanhood; and for months afterward Cornelia had believed that Solomon in the violence of his conjugal rites, had inflicted upon her a mortal wound: she not knowing it was God's curse. And now God had begun her bleeding again, as though the only way He had discovered to break a woman's will was by striking at her like a stone, till the red flood flowered forth.

Like her daughters, Cornelia's own girlhood had been a paradox of intimate isolation among women—that half-harem, half-convent so peculiar to Mediterranean women; thus she should have known that by her divorce she would be depriving the Vanetti girls of everything: a stable home, a secure income, a father to protect their chastity (seduced and connived at, both girls had married, not the men of their choice but of their necessity). Even now, when Henrietta came to visit her, she brought always—as if free at last to express it—huge bouquets of bitterness. Instead of talking to her mother, Henrietta would glance across the white void of sheets which in her pain Cornelia had twisted into ropes around her feet and ask idly of her sister: "And who's taking care of Charlie?"

Henrietta's hurried marriage had been a deep disappointment to Cornelia—the more so since Henrietta held *her*, Cornelia, responsible, as if her mother should have warned her that a fine bosom and a narrow waist were a marriage trap two could irrevocably fall into. What should have brought mother and daughter together in mutual compassion had been embittered, ironically enough, by Henrietta's stoicism. For Henrietta would never admit that her marriage was a scourge of necessity—a sacrifice not a triumph—but had wrapped up the whole mess in a spotless wedding gown of antique satin, sporting a bouquet of white flowers which she had twisted and shredded all through that unforgettable mockery of a ceremony; then afterwards, she had gone through the travesty of removing herself from the public eye by a long honeymoon in Mexico until after the baby was safely born and baptized.

What had hurt Cornelia most had been what seemed to her the irrevocability of it all: Henrietta sealed into her doom and determined to die of it, if necessary, without a word of complaint. The depth of her daughter's bitterness was measurable by her absolute silence. When Cornelia herself had been a young mother she had clung to the belief that *hers* was to be the last sacrifice, that her daughters, at least, could not be retailed in the market place. Her own life had been settled by *fiat* when The Grandmother—still wearing the perpetual black mourning cloth of Italy—had come to her saying: "Well, and what do you *expect* to do if not marry Vanetti? Go into the streets? Your mother a widow with three small children? How long do you think *I* can support you all?" That had seemed to settle it then, though The Grandmother had always done very well with their yield of tomatoes and yellow squash: an intrepid woman, fit for the dynasties of the Renaissance, with a will like an ironmonger's rod.

"And who's taking care of the baby?" repeated Henrietta, as if to impress upon their mother how exigently *they* took their maternal duties, in spite of the bad example she, Cornelia, had set for them. . . .

They had always, it seemed, wanted more of her than she

was able to give—partly through exhaustion but also, she knew, from temperamental differences. Cornelia simply had not been the way The Grandmother had intended the women of her dynasty to be. . . . After a day at Tee-Vee Tubes, testing, tapping, wiring the tiny filaments together, it was more than she could do to air the squabbles and confusions which had congested in her absence. Even before the divorce she had preferred to work in the vegetable garden till dark, using necessity as her shield. And then, of course, all those vegetables had to be canned for winter: a labor sufficient for the entire staff of girls at Tee-Vee, yet she and the girls had done it alone every summer. During these annual crises of gardening and preserving, Solomon would be out earning as much extra money as he could, laying a new terrace for the people on the Hill, or doing landscape gardening at prices kids charged now to mow your lawn. For the big thing had been, Solomon used to say, to work hard, save money, buy your own land. Book-learning was for the idle rich—a hereditary rank Solomon never dreamed of aspiring to.

Vanetti had been considered a good catch for a girl not yet sixteen, with a widowed mother. For it was understood in a family system such as theirs, that Solomon's obligation to the needy women on his wife's side was implicit in the marriage contract; he could no more evade it than Cornelia could shrink from her conjugal obligation to bear children every year: Henrietta and Beth had been born so close together that they had been as exhausting as twins. It was not till after she had had two miscarriages that Cornelia had discovered one night that she could say *no* to it all: that if Solomon wished to run after other women, it was his soul that was in jeopardy, not hers, whatever St. Paul said about it. It was at that moment that she became a heretic, as later she was to sink (as she thought of it) into agnosticism, and finally into unbelief.

"Of course. I understand that. . . . You can't just leave children *alone*," Henrietta was saying, glancing outside the hospital window. In Henrietta's life questions of this nature had achieved the level of moral discipline. She kept her house like a pin, and refused to admit, after dropping out of high school where she had excelled in math and chemistry, that she ever once lusted after the fleshpots of learning. Henrietta was now looking down at her mother's face; but what she saw there apparently pained her. The pretty face, piled high with curls, seemed to melt for a moment into fear, recognition, prophesy. Then the gaze steadied itself again to the mundane. "Are they bringing you what you like to eat, Mama? I told the doctor what you said, that it was no use pampering you, that your stomach, at least, was made of iron. . . ." Her voice faltered on *at least*; and Cornelia hoped that Henrietta wished she had omitted that phrase. Other things, surely, were not made of iron in her: her womb now rejected sanity and would have nothing to do with moderation, but metastasized madly, as though the body, tired of love and creation had rooted itself, like the Devil's rump, into a massive theology of error.

Funny how she remembered that image. Rikki had used it once during her "lessons." (She still did not use any other word: he had said he would give her *lessons,* and that word had become the symbol of their time together, though he had taught her much besides grammar—love and the special torture and creative inventiveness of lies, and the exaltation and defeat of Art which was supposed to transcend suffering (it didn't, but somehow that was a lie which didn't matter). "The sixth grade?" he had repeated over and over with astonishment. "The *sixth*? I thought no one had to be that ignorant any more. . . ." When she had explained that above all the thought pained her that one day her daughters would be ashamed of her because she spoke English like two rusty nails crossed in a creaking box (Rikki had laughed at her image, showing his white teeth like a scar of joy, an ineffaceable memory in her life), he had at once offered to give her grammar lessons. She was to stay a half hour after the regular night class on Mondays and Wednesdays.

It had been a happy struggle, a paradise of effort. Long after Solomon lay asleep, exhausted from *his* work—she could not deny it, his life was a long prison sentence of heaving and hauling, a life even more bitter and empty than hers because Rikki's vision would never enter it—long after he was asleep, she would sit up with her lessons. At last the girls would have been put to bed (in her frustration and eagerness to get to her studies they were sometimes first slapped in exasperation, then wept over in passionate remorse), and Cornelia would sit at the kitchen table conjugating Latin verbs in their exquisitely expanding forms (like the opening of a peacock's tail, Rikki had said). Then on Monday evenings, she would spread page after page of synopses before Rikki's admiring eyes (she had known instantly that he loved her).

Rikki had thought Latin grammar should come before English because of the 'rules," but in his own hot Latinity there were no rules, only passion and guilt and absolution and again guilt, like the stone of Sisyphus on his soul. Once she had sworn she would kill herself if they did not run away together, that she could not stand the endless lying and meeting in corners. It was after they had made love in the cloakroom, and she had buried her head in their coats, sobbing with a sense of irredeemable sin. That time he had taken a weapon from his pocket, a knife or a file—in the darkness she had been unable to discern its true shape, only its glint of steel, its lethal edges—and offered to open their veins together and both be eternally damned. Finally, after a night's remorse they had agreed upon a childish, romantic pact. Rikki had taken a coin from his pocket and slowly filed it into two ragged pieces: "Here, take this," he said. "And when you want to die, send your part to me; and I'll bring you mine. We'll do it together then, neatly. . . ." As if anyone ever died for love: what one died of was this harrowing pain, like centipedes devouring the flesh.

She had learned not to sob after that, but to be silent. She had learned to turn faceless with indifference when, openly suspicious, Solomon had examined her books, flipping them open so that any fluttering thing trapped in their pages would fall to the floor.

Fortunately a dried maple leaf had been the only token of those evenings when Rikki's last student would stand at the door saying, *goodnight, goodnight,* over and over again, and eyeing her speculatively. But once Solomon's friend, the barber Agrelli, who was studying bookkeeping and English at the night school (because, he said, he didn't trust his son-in-law with his accounts), had observed ironically from the doorway: "Coming *signora?*"

"One minute, in just one minute," she had called out, dropping her books to gain time. "But don't wait. . . . You'll lose your bus. . . ." As if the shrewd old *paisano* cared about his bus. What he had waited to see, had evidently succeeded in seeing (though she had always unflinchingly, and as she thought heroically denied it to Solomon) was Rikki's hand on the light switch plunging all into darkness before—long before—her own dark head had emerged from the school building.

Shortly after that, Solomon had begun trailing her wherever she went; his suspicion was fiery, blatant, he scorned to invent a pretext but simply followed her. . . . No ingenuity on her part could shake him: impossible for her and Rikki to come together again. . . . Nevertheless she had remained fixed in her will to have, if not love, then the "lessons" which Mr. Advenuto had promised her free. "Free? Why free?" Solomon had demanded. "Who gives his brains for nothing? You, what do *you* give?" "I *will* go," she had declared promptly, haughtily. But Solomon had only looked at her, his dark eyes sullen and knowing. In her bravura that evening she had packed her books as usual and taken the long walk to the school.

Arriving as usual at twilight, the church bells in the distance were ringing, she remembered, and the students filed in slowly, as to a monastery. All that evening she had sat with her eyes glued to her book, not daring to look up at Rikki, for fear his already breaking voice would collapse as he read *nunc puella timebat,* and the roomful of tired students would hear his desperate confession to God and the wilderness.

But Rikki had held himself together on that last night. It was she who, after a bitter quarrel with Solomon, had fallen into furious heresy and, in spite of everything the priest could say, had begun the divorce. I must, at least be *alone* in my suffering, she had said to him. Suffering with Solomon, I feel only hate, hate, hate. If you want me to love God, she had begged the chancery priest, help me to be free. So she had won, at least, from *that* the Church's sanction for their legal separation. But from her own women, she had won nothing. The Grandmother had said simply that it was a man's prerogative, that she was lucky Vanetti hadn't killed her, and went on to give examples of expeditious executions in Italy for no less than Cornelia had done. No one even bothered to listen to Cornelia's ritualistic protestation of innocence; she realized, finally, that even if she had been innocent (she shamelessly thanked God she was not), they would not have believed her because they spent nights longing for a lover unlike their husbands—a real lover, such as they felt Rikki to be. Openly they envied her opportunities; their own husbands, they said, would never have allowed them the liberty of night school.

Once during the divorce she had walked by the barber shop where Solomon's friend, Agrelli stood, flanked by three others from the town—a tough, Italian Sanhedrin all ready to cast judgment on the woman taken in adultery. She had thought they would jeer, laugh, nudge each other obscenely; but their faces had been silent and anonymous as masked executioners, the four faces becoming one face in her blurred vision. "Get out of town," she heard one of them threaten her. "Get out of town unless you . . . ." The threat faded indistinctly as she quickened her pace, but she had seen something more than vindictiveness in their eyes—something which was surely fear and which proclaimed to her that she was *guilty, guilty* of having changed their world. If the chastity of women was not guaranteed, on what keystone could the ancient rituals rest? And here was a woman who had defied husband, family, the Church itself, to go seeking after heretical knowledge—deserting her children, committing adultery with that sly hypocrite, Ricardo Advenuto, who for some time, doubtless, had been fathering bastards.

". . . but *why* is he coming?" Cornelia felt certain she had heard Beth say. "Isn't it enough? We've had enough. Oh, Mama will be upset. For years now, he's been quiet, and now . . . to disturb her? For what?"

Beth had always been sweet; and now here was Beth protecting her from something—or someone? A wild hope stirred her breast.

"Well, he has a right," said Henrietta, bowing her head as though reading a prayer. "He has a right to see her . . . this last time—."

Beth scowled, widening her eyes and shifting angrily in her chair.

"—this last time," repeated Henrietta, as if determined to be cruel in order to be kind. "After all, no matter what the civil law says, he's still her husband. . . ."

The hope died. Impossible after all that it should be Rikki summoned from unspeakable distances in the southwestern deserts. And after such a life as his, after so many years, she might not even recognize him. He had entered the seminary the year of her divorce, and what could those three years of abortive priesthood have done for him but to have made him wonder what he ought to have done instead? She had heard that he had, at first, taken to the abstinences and vigils as an idle man might enjoy an inheritance and a life of ease; but then that he had given them all up in disgust, turning first to stoop labor in the vineyards of the Coachella Valley, and then to teaching Navajo Indians in Arizona. Abruptly he had begun drinking, as if, having tried sanctity and failed at it, he had taken on corruption as a surer thing. And steadily the reports had drifted back, of a life of vagrancy without honor, of alcoholism and illness. Now for the past year and a half, his address had been that of an asylum for alcoholics.

". . . arrangements," said Henrietta. "After all, who knows better? And who else has a better right to decide?"

"Better than *Pa?* Almost anybody!" exclaimed Beth with contempt.

"But he's paying for it," hinted Henrietta darkly. "And if that's what he wants, it seems to me he has a right . . . ."

"And what about—?" The ardent whisper stirred Cornelia to open her eyes long enough to rest them on Beth with what she hoped was approval. But things were a bit blurred; sometimes she didn't know whether what she saw was a dreaming sleep or a drugged wakefulness. But her approval wrought no change in Beth. Though they knew she listened, they seemed not to be able to remember that she listened and from time to time the girls would talk as if she were not there. "Oh go ahead," Beth now said with exasperation. "Do it then. Do what Pa wants. You've never really—."

Carefully Henrietta interrupted her. Everyone knew, even Henrietta, that such a sentence must never be finished, not even after their mother was gone. But it was true, true, Cornelia felt it to the scalded marrow: Henrietta had never loved her; she was her father's child.

"Just ask Pa, then," Henrietta now naturally said. "He's talking to the people downstairs. When he comes up, ask him yourself. You'll see."

When her grandmother had died, Cornelia recalled, the children had fought over the inheritance. Standing at the foot of the bed, the children had begun their sacrilege by swapping off a marble-topped table for a porcelain Blind Cupid which The Grandmother had brought over from Italy. Then a quarrel—bitter, repressed, conducted in a high tense whisper—had begun about the old clock which Cornelia remembered had chimed through all the hours of their lives, breaking the silence every hour like a senseless, importunate bird. To Cornelia it had not been worth fighting for, a mere recorder of hours which could never restore to her one single hour of those stolen from her by The Grandmother's primitive barter with Solomon Vanetti. Yet the clock had proved important in their lives; the quarrel, vicious and sterile, had been irreparable: there were members of the family who had never spoken to each other again. Perhaps if she could remember why the clock was so important, the recollection might help her understand what it was Henrietta and Beth now seemed so angry with each other about.

What they were fighting about, she realized after a moment or two . . . or an hour . . . was love. Henrietta's love for her father, Beth's love for her mother. A horrible, necrophiliac division: why bother? Only let me die and be buried: no need to talk about love at all. Yet it was bitter, bitter unto the last that Henrietta should wish her to be buried alongside Solomon.

For that was precisely Solomon's wish, she realized through the buzzing questions—his utmost need, his final extortion. Briefly she opened her eyes, not to Rikki as she had been still childishly praying, but to Solomon.

He was standing near (too near, she thought) to her pillow, holding in his right hand the kind of weathered summer hat which he always wore in the sun. He was so close to the bed that her angle of vision caught irritably, not at his face, but at the sweatband of his hat, stained brown with wear and, inside, a ticket to something: something he looked forward to seeing, some harvest of joy to which he might yet aspire, a day at the Stadium, or a lottery. *He still has hopes of winning something.* This clumsy inadvertent display of life yet to be lived made her seethe; she could feel her insides boiling: she wished she could die now, now, with a burst of blood upon his bumbling head, this man who had fathered her children and who filled her with nausea. She could not, even now, forgive him for filling her last reveries with bitterness. Blackness and drugs were preferable, and she sank back into them, into the pillow.

But he called her back, Cornelia, Cornelia. *No, no,* she refused to come back, refused, above all, to have him lie beside her in death as he had in life. *Consummatum est,* as Rikki had taught her to say.

"Cornelia, can you hear me? I want your permission, Cornelia. You and I together. I want to look for a place. Quiet, beautiful, with marble plaques. A family . . . . After all," he explained with uncompromising plausibility, "I haven't much longer. And it's been a long road together—."

Together? She set her lips; if her eyelids which she willed to blindness, continued to flutter, she couldn't help it. But her eyes, now, were burning, she would have to open them. She rolled her head on the pillow, in a movement of anguish which somehow resembled ecstasy, and a silent howl like a death rattle issued from her. *Rikki!* she cried, *He's beating me, beating me into the dust. . . .*

Stones

harles Mandell was a lonely man at the midpoint in his life, whose chief source of relaxation was taking walks and collecting things—not in any scientific, organized way, but mere trifles: a stone, a leaf, a shell. He was relieved to think he had given up fleshpots, the things you saw on television that they wanted you to buy, and had made instead a kind of hobby of retrieving colorful fallen objects which he carried back to his small apartment. His little habit gave him, he felt, that touch of reality which he needed to balance out his daily life, which was dull (he worked in a credit office), and his fantasies, which were rich and riotous.

His nature, like that of migratory birds, followed the seasons. In the spring he picked up speckled birds' eggs fallen from their nests; in the fall he brought back to his apartment bright-red leaves still crackling with their mysterious fire. Summers were less predictable; it might be a shining agate, a piece of marble, or even a crab apple, burnished red as mahogany. When the snow melted, exposing cracked sidewalks, peeled buildings, molting bricks, that was the best time of all; it was then that from the winter's devastation he collected multi-colored stones, their veins enigmatic as lifelines in the palms of strangers. Mandell would burrow them happily in his pockets, warming them with his hands as though they were still alive.

That was how he had happened to go into the bombed-out house—one of those Victorian frames with stained glass windows crimsoned with sunlight, and cupolas raised heavenward from the rooftops. The house had coexisted for decades along the razor's edge of a slum, and now one side of it lay gutted by fire, in ruins. As he had passed the house, Mandell had drawn himself up short at the sight of a shard of burnt glass, like a live coal on the sunlit sidewalk. At first he had failed to understand why the house was such a wreck and had turned to an old woman who stood on the doorstep to ask her if there had been a fire. "A fire?" she repeated, laughing harshly. "No, a revolution they called it." He had understood then that he was standing outside the house where the two revolutionaries (sisters), had been making explosives and had themselves been blown to bits. Mandell experienced that flicker of curiosity felt by those to whom the world of crime is remote, entertaining, unbelievable. It was beyond belief to him that pretty young girls anywhere in the world could hate banks, for instance, enough to blow them up, as though they believed that capitalism was a kind of heresy which could be purged by fire.

The old woman seemed at once to grasp both his curiosity and his reluctance about the house. "Go in, go in," she said. "The police were here a long time ago. Everything's done and over with. Their bedroom was blown to pieces, it was like an airplane exploding in mid-air . . . ." There was a vindictiveness in her voice which repelled him. At whom was it directed? At the dead girls? Or at him, one of those who merely Let Things Happen. "Used to be a good neighborhood!" she added. "*Now* look!"

Mandell looked. The destruction of one part of the house was nearly total; the other stood looking dark and defiled by the scarification of its neighbor. He wanted to ask her: "And you? Why are you here?" But something in her manner prevented him. It was as if he feared some false accusation, something meant to distract him from her own role in this devastation. Instinctive self-preservation made him avoid old women, anyway. Drained dry with the past, they were always needing new lives with which to revive themselves: his own perhaps.

"But isn't there any? . . . I mean—," stammered Mandell, not wishing to say the word 'trespass,' as if avoiding it might prove him innocent at least in intention. Yet of course there were signs: ABSOLUTELY NO TRESPASSING: VIOLATERS WILL BE PROSECUTED.

"Who's to stop you? Go ahead." It was almost an order. Clearly she knew the house and had defied the signs. She waved him inside and Mandell noticed on her left hand a bright stone, either a garnet, or even a ruby, perhaps, he wasn't certain; but it was a stone mellow as burgundy, with a warm breathing core of light.

He would ordinarily have commented on the beauty of the ring or even on its value; but he wanted to break off this conversation, which seemed to him morbid at best.

"Who's to stop you?" she repeated. Her tone implied that *she* had been in the house and that he must be something of a coward to take such warnings to heart.

As though to prove her wrong, he quickly crossed over the pile of rubble in front of the house. The old woman followed him; glancing down Mandell noticed that she wore thick black shoes, wide at the base as though to support her crippled feet. They gave her a look of having been built right out of the shoes, as though she herself had been poured in after, to fit. "My name's G.E.," she said, which struck Mandell as very odd. "I let people call me G.E. because Geraldine Ellenboren is so . . . hard. . . . You'll admit that?" she added, as though they had argued about it.

She was obviously in some way crippled, Mandell decided, and clearly as old as sin: so he ought to try, at least, to be polite. He nodded, and tried to look absent-minded as he pocketed the shard of glass.

"What's that? What did you take there?" she demanded. "Did you find something? Sometimes you find . . . you don't know what. I came right after the police left. They're so stupid, they don't know where to look." Her voice dropped to a conspiratorial whisper: "See this ring?" She held out her hand: over the deformed knuckle of the index finger the stone shone vivid as an eye. The tone of her voice made him feel ashamed and alone, as if something contagious, venereal in her could break out all over him.

"It's a real ruby. I had it evaluated." She pointed toward a burnt-out mound of grass where, evidently, a fire had briefly flashed through the damp leaves, extinguishing itself. "Found it right there. Laying in the grass. Who cares? *I* say. They were ready to kill us all, weren't they? Why should they even own stuff like this? All *I* get is ten apiece for foster-mother . . . ."

The idea that the woman was entrusted with the care and mothering of somebody's children made Mandell wince, but what, after all, could he do about it? He decided to say nothing; he feared any personal remark would bring the woman right into his life; she'd follow him, she'd want to share his thoughts, read his mind, talk to him world-without-end. He shrugged and concentrated on avoiding her eyes, eyes like a pair of gray headstones, the color of a void.

She continued as if she had read his mind. "Oh, I may be old, but I know how to live. I don't starve. . . ." She stood now in the doorway, like some dark debris flung against the house by the force of the explosion.

Quickly Mandell tried to sidestep her, but she put her hand on his arm, her head canted upward in warning: "Watch out for the ceiling." Black rings of sweat were visible around her neck: sickened, Mandell rushed past her into the house.

For some reason the lights were on and he was taken aback by this strangeness; it was as though there were still some sort of celebration going on to which he had come uninvited. He stared around him; everywhere there was a mood of Victorian comfort, an air of decorum and ease, a slowly fading splendor. The chandeliers were of facetted glass, the hallways were still carpeted; it would have been easy to imagine red velvet ottomans, lounge chairs with antimacassars, silk screens before the fireplaces. Above the mantelpieces cherubim stood, poised on one foot, looking as though they were about to return to their heavenly abode: the very perfection of their gilt and naked bodies in view of the devastation around them seemed somehow ghoulish: why had the revolutionaries lived here, of all places? Mandell had always thought people like that (starved, bearded creatures—he had always imagined them), hid in freezing basements or rotting garrets. Obviously these girls had been brought up with all those amenities known vaguely as: Civilization. Why, then, when they were so clearly already masters of all that he surveyed, had they chosen the risk of imprisonment and death?

As if he had spoken aloud the old woman echoed him, her eyes lightless as portholes on a grey sea. "You'd think they'd know better, brought up in a house like this," she said enviously. "Good family, plenty of money. What business did they have to get mixed up in a mess like this?" She clucked her tongue as an ordinary person would have done in shared sorrow; but in her it sounded like some parody of grief.

Mandell confessed himself baffled. He regarded such antics by those who were lucky enough to have money as sheer madness. He allowed his imagination to wander a moment to what he might have done with such wealth: the trips he could have taken, the collections he might have made, not of stones and trifles but of works of art . . . masterpieces. The upkeep alone on such a house must have cost more every year than he had put aside out of his life's earnings. The realization that he would live and die, not destitute, but wretchedly poor, lay like the taste of dried blood in his mouth. Contemplating bitterly what seemed to him his unlucky fate, his missed chances, his abortive 'promise' he wandered, scarcely realizing it, into the girls' bombed-out room.

The fireplace had survived the blast, although pieces of the marble mantel were flung like feathers everywhere. He felt at once that he would have liked to gather up a few pieces which were of a particularly attractive green serpentine marble. But he did not wish to demean himself by scrabbling around while the woman stood staring at him (she was watching him, he thought irritably, as though he were some giant fowl about to pounce on her barnyard corn). Her gaze infected him with a kind of shame as though her very presence there made his natural desire for a few pieces of stone seem, like herself, cold and larcenous. He decided first to look around the house, appearing always as casual as possible, then he would return to pick over the lot, taking only the most attractive pieces.

So he let the old woman show him about while, patiently, he bided his time. Together they examined the parqueted floors, the inlaid wood panels in the library, the artificial pilasters of the dining room, the window seats built right into the curved bow of the cupola. When he thought he had given over enough time to these things (showing a polite and proper degree of interest), he turned and, with a just barely accelerated pace, made his way back to the girls' bedroom.

Here he strolled about, his hands stuffed into his pockets—wishing still to appear casual, but aware that his pose was stripped away from him at once when he could not refrain from eagerly bending over to something he saw glitter amid the rubbish on the floor. Certainly nothing of any value, he told himself quickly: only a bit of broken mirror or a piece of gilt from one of those naked angels. Nothing could have survived the destruction of the bomb, the pillaging of the police and the systematic depredations of that old woman who followed him around as if she had discovered in him her *alter ego*.

But to his surprise, nearly buried in a muck of ash lay a wallet, nearly consumed by fire now, but which had once been tooled with an edge of gold. It was, of course, empty. All identification tags, money, pictures, had been removed. As the pieces of leather crumbled in his hand, only a flake of ash remained, leaving black traces like stigmata. Within the black dust lay a ring; a simple wedding band, it seemed to Mandell without value. Such plain white-gold bands could be had for a few dollars at any pawnshop. He ought simply to leave it, it was hardly worth the bother—or the risk. But the idea that the ring might eventually turn out to have special value which he could not guess at the moment made him quickly shut his hand.

The empalming of the ring, as though it were a secret signal, brought the woman at once to his side. "Let's see it. Let's see it," she said with excitement. "What did you get? Oh . . . ." Her voice strung out to an obscene note of shared pleasure. "*You* lucky! I missed that, I did. And there it was all the time. Those stupid police. There, what did I tell you? Didn't I say they left things laying here right before your eyes. Let's look around. . . . Maybe we'll find more. . . ."

The "I" and the "we" jingled strangely in his ears. A faint flush of disdain mottled his brow. Yet, why not? Overcoming his physical revulsion he let her now, for a second time, show him around the house. At the realization that he had joined her forces her voice shrilled with excitement, piercing his ears; but Mandell was determined to tolerate her now: she knew the house much better than he. For a few moments she babbled about how they would help each other, how two heads were better than one, how they could move the furniture in the attic, how they could in all things assist one another; but as he turned upon her a look of wrathful impatience she fell silent.

The silence became intense as they began this time methodically examining the house. They gave microscopic care to corners, cupboards and cabinets of every kind. They pulled down a moldering mattress, plunged their arms like midwives into the rotting womb of cotton and rooted out objects which they had not time to examine for value. They parted shredding blankets, they left the kitchen stove a skeleton of grates and grids; they pulled down a few scorched paintings and, with the scrupulous attention of loyal servants, shook out the blackened drapes. At the old woman's suggestion that they remove the lids on the commodes and fish among the waters, Mandell gave her an involuntary look of admiration: she was a genius in her way, an artist of depredation. But in spite of this stroke of genius, the commodes turned out to be a disappointment. There they found only a floating tampon, a cracked molar, and a contact lens. Somehow this struck them as funny and although the woman's high nickering laugh repelled him, Mandell discovered that he, too, was laughing and enjoying himself—enjoying himself hugely. In their daring and inventiveness they seemed to him to have transcended that boundary which separated his quiet reveries from his most riotous dreams. . . . Yet on the whole they had been careful, Mandell considered judiciously, they had destroyed nothing irreplaceable, they were not Barbarians.

When they had finished, they sat down on the floor and shared the plunder; a certain expertise guided them; they were momentarily comrades, and to his surprise there was no dispute over the booty: she had a sense of the proprieties, or perhaps of his inherently superior position as the younger, the male. Or perhaps she merely sensed his craving. . . . Whatever was small and sparkled she let him take. If it were heavy and would need conspicuous lugging, as with a wheelbarrow at night (like the picture frames, or the gilt angels which they had discovered were detachable), they pretended to leave them behind, knowing she would return alone in the night. . . .

When the spoils were divided, they sat silent, as in common understanding. The woman stared at him expectantly, pushing back the lank hair from her face. The grime around her face and neck forced him involuntarily to glance at a mirror for his own image. He was amazed at the dust which had accumulated on himself, like a growth. He tried to brush it off but it was powdery as plaster and it clung to him. He realized then that their search through the house had been so exciting that he had forgotten the bits of marble in the girls' bedroom. But he now determined to hurry and take what he could.

"Excuse me," he said firmly, anxious now to get rid of her; he even bowed slightly, or thought he did. Back in the bedroom, he squatted to the floor and filled his pockets rapidly, taking as much as he could carry. When he tried to rise he felt as swollen and encumbered as a deep sea diver in need of a hoist upwards. But he felt, also, strangely exhilarated. "Goodbye," he called to the woman with heavy emphasis as he walked stiffly toward the front door. "Goodbye." God knew he never wanted to see her again; the very thought made him panic. And he hurried toward his apartment as quickly as his burden of stones permitted him.

That evening he showered and went out to an excellent restaurant for the first time in months. He dined lightly, though as he felt, superbly, on a supper of *escargots*, an *omelette aux herbes fines*, and several brandies. Such food, he speculated, made one feel invincibly civilized. Then he returned home and took out, along with the few fine stones he had collected over the years, the new ring he had picked up at the house: he began carefully, with the patience of an artist to clean them all. To his joy, the ring turned out to be, not white gold, but platinum: inlaid chips of diamond around the inner band formed the letters VEN-CEREMOS. Mandell was delighted. He hid the ring away in a drawer and waited several days before taking it to a well-known fence in the neighborhood. The fence paid so much more than Mandell had expected, and with such alacrity, that he regretted not having tried several others first. But on the whole, he was content with the exchange. Then, on the way back to his apartment, he bought copies of all the Sunday papers, which he took home and read with extreme care, listing the disasters: the explosions, the bombings, the fires: you never knew what the police might have overlooked.

Selma

For Viola Liuzzo

March 8, 1965

I asked myself, suppose a brick should enter through my window, as it did the car of my father many years before? Transfixed by love, by pain, I should be unable to speak to my dear ones. For fear of this, I have begun to write these things down, though in a jumble. It is a way of being with them always.

I came after I saw them on television, beating people on the Edmund Pettus Bridge. This was not bearable to me. I said, Why are they striking those innocent people praying to their God? And Nicola said: "Because God has not *answered* their prayers." I thought about this a long time; then I went to pack my bag. Because the way that God answers is mysterious. In me, He answered.

I kissed my children. Hardest of all was it to leave Francesca. She is only four, but suffers already when others are in pain. How does she recognize suffering so as to experience it? I do not know. Perhaps she absorbs it from the wind, from the radioactive air. Perhaps from my eyes. . . . But she is concerned with good and evil. She asks, Why must *you* go? Why not the mother of Carmella? I could not explain this. Why indeed? I put on my green cloth coat. I like its color, though it is old—the color of winter grass. I gathered together a toothbrush, a blanket, several pictures of the children. Should I take a camera? I decided against. If I shall have time to take pictures, what need of me to go?

Nicola drove me to the train station, where Cynthia, Bob, and Charles were already waiting. They had called me earlier, they were going, too. After much discussion it was decided that Charles would drive for me to Alabama our blue car, as Nicola wants me to have "safe transportation" when I arrive. I think that it is because of the Michigan license plate he does not wish me to drive it. But after? He does not expect that I shall remain quiet in Selma? That Charles will be there to drive the car for me? But Nicola tries to think of everything. It is strange that he has not yet thought of a way to make me happy. Perhaps this one thing is impossible. Perhaps it is merely one's fate—whether one has been happy or not.

From the moment we entered the train a strange peace descended on me. I have been for hours in the lounge, leaving Cynthia and Bob to themselves. I am sorry to be alone, yet I feel "purified" that I shall do this thing and others—friends, relatives, children, even loved ones from the past—shall not see me. But this is a corrupt thought: I become proud. What virtue can come of an action which already admires itself?

Therefore is it that I have been sitting alone. I wished to read from my missal, but I am ashamed to be seen reading my prayerbook like a priest. Yet it happens sometimes that the greatest desire for God is in a public place. They should make these books to be inconspicuous, so that we can, without false pride or immodesty, open and read.

Montgomery
March 9
A long tiring trip. Was it necessary to waste so many hours? I should not have listened to Nicola, but should have taken the plane. But Nicola says that a mother of small children should not take risks; then he gives me the statistics concerning air crashes, how many are fatal, etc., etc. But it is because he himself cannot breathe in high altitudes; as he fears for himself, so he fears for me also.

I am staying with a teacher from the Loveless Elementary School—Mrs. Criss. She is a very brave woman. She has been a teacher for many years. She says school teachers have not been active enough. She says she was on the bridge Sunday when they gave the order for the troopers to go forward. Some of Sheriff Clark's men had made holes in their clubs and put metal rods inside. She says it was very bad. I saw it also on television; but it is different when she tells me about it. She tells of the awful silence when, as the marchers kneeled in the dust, the posse-men put on their gas masks. I begin to tremble when she tells me this. I begin to wish myself there, humbling myself with the others, in the dust. I begin to feel a thirst for virtue.

We have many veterans from other struggles here: from SCLC, from SNCC, from The Mississippi Summer (last year). There are those who claim we are already betrayed, that there are "black racists" rising up who hate the white man as bitterly as ever the Klan hated "niggers." I do not believe this. But even if it were true? Every religion has its Betrayer: the belief that all men are brothers is not a philosophy, it is a religion. Can there be a religion without those who pervert it?—the Christ without anti-Christ?

There were four ambulances from the Medical Committee for Human Rights. The doctors and nurses were not, at first, allowed to pick up the eighty-four people who were lying on the highway, on the bridge, among the bushes—wounded. At last, leaving a trail of blood on the highway 80, they rushed the injured persons to the Good Samaritan Hospital. This is a hospital for the black people of Selma, established last year by the Edmundite Fathers. Those hurt very bad were the children and old people. They could not move quickly enough away from the clubs. The tear gas sickened them. They were torn by barbed wire. In the crash of horses and whips Mrs. Criss lost her blanket roll. She regretted this very much, she says, because a blanket can save your life. One young man (from Arkansas), she says, was being beaten with a bully club; but he shielded his head with his blanket. That saved his life.

It forces me to think: by what threads we are saved. A bullet flies, a boat overturns, a clot of blood forms. Our doctor once said that he became a physician in order to overcome death, that he felt himself to be a failure. Of course. It is as if a man were to become an astronomer to overcome space.

This young man, Mrs. Criss said, was nearly blinded by tear gas shot into his face. She said she saw the face of the man who did it, that it was done deliberately.

Afterwards, they threw tear gas into the First Baptist Church. They went inside and threw one of our people through a church window. . . . They stood in the streets, fighting with the children, throwing big bricks at them. They tried to run down our people with horses.

Martin Luther has scheduled a second march for Tuesday. That is today. I have debated whether I should carry a blanket. I will wear a long skirt. It is good to have cloth on the ground where one kneels; otherwise the skin may break on the sharp stones. I have seen them with the blood streaming from the broken skin. And I do not wish my blood to be seen.

March 9

It is so beautiful here, it hurts me to look at it. I sometimes think: at this moment someone is dying. It is not believable.

The earth here is constantly alive; the tiny insects like jewels fly everywhere around you. And trees like ships. If we could have such trees to look at now and then, the winters would not seem so hard. Even poverty would not be so ugly. For instance: outside Mrs. Criss' house there is a tree in blossom (I do not know its name). The house itself is all flaking shingles but the fernlike leaves flutter with hundreds of blossoms like pink and yellow butterflies. It makes me feel as if I have begun another life, in Naples perhaps.

But I am so ignorant I do not know whether such trees grow in Naples. When I think of my ignorance, I become ashamed, speechless. When I am in the cafeteria with the students, the *other*(!) students, they talk and talk. I listen attentively. I do not interrupt. Though they are young, they are wise, much wiser than myself at their age. Only after I have left them, I run to the book: *lapidary, existentialist, dominion.* I look them all up. Hypocrite that I am, I am ashamed to reveal my ignorance. I said to a student once as we stood near the Art Museum, and the summer sun sank, making lights on the ground: "Look at these beautiful polished stones," and he asked, smiling: "Since when have you become a lapidary?" I was frightened. I thought I had done something wrong. I threw away the stones. He picked them up and taught me: *quartz, obsidian, tourmaline, gneiss.* How is it some people, though young enough to be my children, already know everything? After all, it is I who am the lapidary one.

I have wasted my life. Ignorance was my crime. . . .

Because of the court order, there is much confusion about whether we will march. People say that because so many have come Martin Luther will be forced to march. I do not like this way of deciding. We must march, some say because of an "absolute principle." However, I do not know, really, what that principle is. So if the others march, I also will march.

Mrs. Paul Douglas is very dedicated; she says we must march. She looks very beautiful in her white gloves and pearls and small lavender-colored hat. She has the face of a saint. I would not mind one day to look like her.

About a thousand people have been waiting by Brown's Chapel. At last Martin Luther has made up his mind. . . . He made a beautiful speech: "I have made my choice," he said. "I would rather die on the highways of Alabama than make a butchery of my conscience." We are relieved to get started. The waiting brings out our fear. . . .

This was very strange. As soon as we reached to the other side of the bridge Martin Luther stopped. Major Cloud ordered us to stand where we were. Had we quickened ourselves to this great action only to stand submissively before the Blue Helmets? The sun was blinding. I looked upward, beyond the phalanx of troopers to where rows of telephones were standing like crucifixes on a hillside. We knelt on the stones: I was glad I had thought to wear my heavy skirt. I saw many priests and nuns. (The people of Selma say they are not real priests and nuns, but Communists in diguise.) Rev. Abernathy prayed over us all. He said: "We come to present our bodies as a living sacrifice."

There was one priest who did not uncover his head as we prayed. I wondered why. I thought St. Paul had made some rule about this. Then it occurred to me that he was not a priest but a rabbi. Here are all churches made one church. At such times we have a Vision of what the world may one day be. We are ready to die for each other. As Rev. Abnernathy said: "We don't have much to offer, but we do have our bodies and we lay them on the altar today."

I wonder how my children are. Sylvia will take care of them. She is old enough. But it is a responsibility. And Nicola is not well enough. There are many things I should have told Sylvia. Though it is true she knows many things better than I. Mother and daughter in the same school!

Between radio news and writing letters home I have been trying to do my schoolwork. It is difficult to study at my age. Most of the students in this sociology class, for instance, are young enough to be my children. Yet it is only in the mirror that I am thirty-nine; I blush like a child when Teacher smiles at me: "Angelina has the right answer!"

Reading the *Negro Revolt* when you are in the middle of the revolution seems, as my fellow-students say, "academic." I like better to be reading my *Walden*. If we are ready to live as Thoreau . . . but we are not: we must, always, carry our blanket. Lord, give me courage to carry, not a blanket but a cross.

King said at the church: "When Negroes and whites can stand on Highway 80 and have a mass meeting, things aren't that bad."

Mrs. Criss came in from chuch. I did not have the radio on. I was lying in the darkness, my rosary round my neck. It helps me when I worry about my children, what accident may befall them in my absence. I press the crucifix to my bosom. Sometimes it seems I can feel a heart, a pulse, beating against my palm.

She told me about Reverend Reeb's murder. (She called it murder, although there is a chance that he will live.) As I listened the cross in my hand seemed to burn; I cried out in pain.

We knelt and prayed together, though she is a Baptist. I remembered how Mrs. Chaney who is also a Baptist said: "I don't quite know how my boy wound up joining the Catholic Church, but we all worship the same God. . . ." Thus Mary was a Jew, and Christ? A Christ–ian.

Mrs. Criss recited the Lord's Prayer. I leaned on her shoulder. We mingled our tears.

He had left his church in Washington, D.C., so that he could give himself up to the meek and the poor. He had been working with the American Friends Committee in Roxbury.

Four or five men outside the Silver Moon attacked them (the ministers), calling, "Hey nigger!" Mrs. Criss says that his friends escaped, but that James Reeb's skull was split open. No one helped him. People from behind the window of the Silver Moon gathered to watch. There was no help anywhere. There was no Samaritan to succor him.

Reverend Reeb has four children. Who will care for them?

We do not ask ourselves these questions before we come. If we did, our hand would shake, our mouth would go dry, our foot would slip.

March 10

He is still in a coma. His wife has flown to the hospital at Birmingham.

We have been standing in a vigil, waiting and praying. The rain never ceases. Hundreds of priests and nuns, with umbrellas and newspapers, black and white, we cling together so as to shield one another from the downpour. The rain falls like bullets on our tired bodies.

A clothesline keeps us walled off into a kind of compound here in Sylvan Street. In defiance, with ecstasy in their voices, the children are singing: "A Clothesline is a Berlin Wall." We also sing, We Shall Overcome, but at times it seems to me we lack spirit.

Some are covering themselves with canvas. I must admit it is a blessing to be sheltered from the rain. We need blankets, for the nights are harrowing, and the ground is cold.

March 11

Mrs. Criss and I were standing together, leaning against the rope staring into the headlights of the police cars when suddenly, like a low thunder, the people all around us began to moan with grief. We knew at once that he had died.

March 15

Some say a senseless death. Four children orphaned. If his death is senseless, then no life is meaningful. For we all die, and who of us could say as the priest enters to anoint us, feet and head: It was well done. I hold fast to the belief that when the blow descended and he felt the agony of it throughout his soul, he prayed: "Now Lord, let thy faithful servant depart."

But perhaps he experienced only a longing to see his children.

Other people have died. But his death obsesses me. I yearn to ask him: Why—? Others have died, but they left mourning parents; his death leaves mourning children.

They held a memorial service at A.M.E. this afternoon. I asked permission to attend. As there were to be hundreds of nuns and clergymen from all over the United States, I felt my presence "unnecessary." But I asked a priest here who said: "We are all *necessary.*" So I went.

Martin Luther King spoke last. I have never seen so many different priests, ministers, rabbis. It was as if they had been gathered up from all lands, speaking all tongues. Greek Orthodox and Fundamentalist and Hebrew and Baptist and Catholic and Methodist, white and black, we sang *We Shall Overcome* together. A rabbi sang the "Kaddish." I had never heard it before. I think I would have liked such singing at my grave.

But I am in awe of his widow. Would I have had the courage, to say as she did that the cause of equality was so important that if her husband had to die for it, she accepted his death. . . .

There is to be a memorial march to the courthouse around sundown.

We started out from Brown's Chapel, arms locked. The Alabama sun was beginning to fade into twilight. With the darkness came the nightbirds, the whirring of insects, the singing of katydids, the chanting of tree frogs. They are there in the daytime too, but it is as if when the night comes, we hear these things.

Three abreast, we walked. When the front line had reached the green courthouse, we stopped. Then Martin Luther spoke to us, standing on the steps as on a hillside.

Afterwards Mrs. Criss and I walked home together. It was very hot. I took off my shoes and carried them. I had cut myself on Sylvan Street, which is unpaved. In her home Mrs. Criss set me down by the kitchen table; she knelt and washed my foot; a stone had pierced it. She crossed it twice over with white tape and bound it carefully. I did not protest. It was good to be comforted. I felt very weary. I wished it were over.

Awoke in terror during the night, and wish to write this down before the image fades.

I dreamed that I lay on a table, like Gorki's father. Around my feet my children played. They did not know I was dead. Nor did I. I rose from the table. I beckoned to them. My face was white. Though I wept, no tears ran down my cheeks. I lifted my hand to my mouth. I was toothless and could not speak. My children, seeing me, my moving mouth, speechless, my tearless eyes, my white face, shrieked in terror. Nicola appeared and touched his fingertips to the wound which Mrs. Criss had bound: the blood spurted out. Then I lay quietly, accepting what had been wrought. My children picked up their toys and left. I was alone. Though I loved them, it hurt me that they would not stay by my body, but preferred their toys.

As I write this, the first birds of morning are beginning to come from the trees like a gradual increase of light. First chirping, then with a clear call.

March 16
Voter registration keeps me too busy to write. There are 29,500 people in Selma, about equally divided, black and white. Only one per cent of the people on the voting polls are Negro.

In Detroit ten thousand people, led by Mayor Cavanagh and Governor Romney marched in protest against brutalities here.

March 20
Busy as we can be, preparing for the Long March. I am to be in charge of the oatmeal "detail" at breakfasts and (once we are at St. Jude's) will be part of the transportation committee, shuttling the footsore and heavy-laden from Montgomery to Selma.

March 21
There were about three thousand of us. It was a clear morning. The air smelled like freshly baked bread. Dry, crisp, as though

to feed our hunger. We were not noisy. Perhaps we were a little afraid. The women just outside the Chapel, as we turned on Alabama Street frightened me most. Why do they hate me so much? Their faces as they yelled at us were ugly with rage. They insult the nuns. Do they believe their own stories of birth control pills and black and white "orgies?" Or is it that, like children at vindictive play, they do not understand what they are saying? A Jewish boy once told me that as a small boy at the Bishop School he played a game in which one child was set in the center of a circle while the others chanted:

> Here comes a Jew
> All dressed in blue
> At the door he bends his knee
> But no matter what you say
> No matter what you do
> A Jew, Jew, Jew are *you!*

He said that they would scream the last line, pointing their fingers at the child kneeling in the school yard. Did they understand that their game was filled with their father's hate? I cannot believe it. Only children, chanting hateful tunes whose story was lost long ago.

Toward the noon hour the sun became very hot. We were very thirsty. The line was led by Martin Luther, with Rabbi Heschel and Dr. Ralph Bunche. But my favorite among the clergy is this Reverend Dom Orsini. He reminds me of Papa; he has the same eyebrows, though of course Papa did not have this black patch over the eye, about which there is something at once noble and pathetic. It is that a man with a dark eye-patch becomes more vulnerable: we know a single grain of dust from the highway could cripple his greatest work.

There is in fact a blind man among us. He is from Atlanta. I do not know his name.

When we walked past the Selma Arms Company, the women screamed "White niggers!" They were well-dressed, grey-haired ladies with hats and white gloves. I think they had just come from church.

We had no trouble at the Edmund Pettus Bridge this time.

Only that a woman with a little boy no bigger than my little Francesca hurled filthy words at the Sisters. I sang as loudly as I could to drown out their words. Never before have I sung so— insistently. One of them (the Sisters) turned and smiled at me. It made me ashamed. Who was I to protect her from the foul words? She is protected by her innocence. But I sang in pain and anger, because having lived in sin, I know well the meaning of their words.

We sang Freedom songs, then rested, saving our breath for the march, for the gaps in our ranks that sometimes force us to run to catch up. We camped near Trickem Fork. It is cold, very cold. Temperature below freezing, I think. There are only two tents, with kerosene heaters. We had spaghetti for supper—*not* Italian style. I am still on oatmeal detail. Breakfast will be at 7:00. Am too weary to write more. Feel as if I'd been stomped to death. . . .

Perhaps there will be a letter in Montgomery when we arrive Thursday. A note from my children would help me remember, perhaps, why I am here—cooking oatmeal in new garbage cans.

Someone pointed out Reverend Jarvis to me. He is from Detroit. Perhaps I will speak to him tomorrow. But tonight—.

March 22
Three hundred people to feed this morning—most of them cold and humbled with fatigue. Few of us slept well, in spite of the protection of the National Guard. The kerosene heaters did not work well, or perhaps they let them go out, perhaps it was safer in the tents without them. But everyone agrees it was cold. They find my oatmeal delicious. I say to them I wish I could fix some *lasagna* which my husband well likes. They laugh. There are teachers, ex-soldiers, psychologists. One of these analyzes aloud our "reasons" for being here. He does not say why *he* has chosen this place to be.

This morning, our numbers seem diminished. I try to remember who it is that has gone. Doubtless they left because according to the court order our number must be kept to three hundred (there is only a two-lane highway from Trickem Fork.) But why did they permit themselves to be sent away? I do not know. Perhaps a weakening of their will, of their physical force. One priest has been sent to the hospital. They say he became terrified during the night, that he was weeping like a child. What torment for men. . . . We too are afraid. We see it in each other's eyes, but we pretend it is not there. Or we joke. On the longer marches it is always hard to sing. It is better to have some silent symbol, a voluntary burden to carry—a flag, or a child on one's back.

We passed a dirty, peeling, splintering shack, set up from the raw earth on stumps of bricks. Five rickety steps. Windows like a warehouse. Somebody said: "There's Rolen School. My grandson go to school there." I looked at the shack. What could my Sylvia, in spite of her natural gifts, have learned at such a school? At the sight of this shameful poverty I made the sign of the Cross as though I had passed a wreck on the highway. Father Sherrill Smith (he is from Texas) saw me do so, and gave me such a look. But I meant no irreverence.

Martin Luther told us: "You will be the people that will light a new chapter in the history of our nation."

But we were not thinking of history, only of the heat, which was like an inferno. From the blacktop highway the flames were licking our feet. They were burned, blistered, swollen so as to be impossible to put our shoes on again. We wanted only to bathe them in cool water.

During the last few miles (we made sixteen today) the wound of my foot reopened. There was blood in the shoe. I took off both shoes and carried them. A young black man walking by my side offered to carry them for me, but I only shook my head, too tired to thank him. I was ashamed to show the blood.

March 23

The rain was a blessing. I felt I could not have walked else. But I wished very much to keep off the burning highway. I tried whenever I could to sink my feet in the wet clay-like earth. The damp smell everywhere was like a *benedicite*. In the rain we were united. We lifted our faces to the heavens. Again we sang songs. We were cleansed by the water, which came upon us in great pounding rushes of rain, like the pounding with leaves at the ancient baths. Just as we passed the Big Swamp, the skies opened upon us their heaviest downpour. Birds which in the slanted rain-light resembled doves or peewits flew up from the swamps to the trees. On the trees the Spanish moss hung like the wet tangled hair of a woman. It was beautiful. There is something mysterious about the way that the host and the parasite together make a beautiful tree. The National Guardsmen would not look at us as we passed. They were angry, perhaps, to be out in the rain.

We are a strange-looking procession. We must look like fools to the people watching us. A blind man, a one-footed man (he too is from Michigan), a one-eyed priest, and nuns in plastic coats, like sailors. I have a strange habit: to look down at people's feet. There I see worn sneakers, always with the small toe boring through on either foot, and heavy boots, Wellingtons, and those they call "roughouts" and sandals, and leather oxfords, and some few like myself, wearing bare feet.

There is a saying I heard once: I complained that I had no shoes till I saw a man who had no feet.

Not far ahead of me I see the left leg and crutches of one of our marchers. His name is James Letherer. The tough teen-agers never tire of taunting him. Perhaps they are shamed by him: having both shoes and feet, they do not walk. They mock him as he marches: "Left . . . Left . . . Left. . . ." But he ignores them. He has endured worse things.

Above us, suddenly, a plane. In spite of myself I feel a flutter of fear, for it would be easy for some psychopath to destroy us from off the face of the earth. But it is only leaflets, a message from the United Klans. They say Martin Luther is a Communist.

We did eleven miles today. Everything is wet, and it is difficult to cook anything. Still, I prefer it. My foot swells desperately. Impossible to write. The pencil smears on the paper. Also, I had nothing on which to write except my knee. A curly-headed boy with a beard (I do not know his name but he is one of those carrying a child like an amulet about his neck) said to me laughing: "You can use my back." So I made pretense of writing on his back. Somebody said: "She is a gentle yoke. . . ." But I thought the clergymen did not like this levity concerning the yoke of Our Lord, so I stopped writing.

March 24

I am weary unto death. Sixteen miles to go today.

More people are coming every hour, it seems. We left our

camp this morning at seven, after oatmeal and coffee. (Mrs. Criss had some peanut butter sandwiches which she shared with those around her.) Now leading us is the one-legged man (who, they tell me, is from Saginaw, Michigan), the Reverend Young from Atlanta, and someone from SNCC. There are many American flags. It rains a little from time to time and our clothes are never really dry. A strange odor pervades the air, as of ripening melons, or love. My face has become nearly black from the sun. When I touch it, it is so dry from the heat that it wrinkles as if I had lived a whole lifetime on this march, and had become old in four days. If Nicola were to see me he would say, you must cover your head —protect yourself. But I cannot protect myself against anything anymore. I feel only a deep need to sleep.

Fourteen more miles to go tomorrow. As we crossed into Montgomery, suddenly there were many hundreds to join us. The clouds parted and as from a fountainhead, water descended. Then almost at once the sun came. We sang *We Shall Overcome.*

The new people who have joined us seem very fresh, very rested, very white. All of us from the first day are as burned as if we had been walking in the desert.

Many famous people, including Harry Belafonte, singing on coffin crates built into a temporary stage.

March 25
We waited around St. Jude's this a.m. for what seemed hours. Something detained Martin Luther. We sat quietly waiting in the mud. The more energetic ones, the younger people, wandered about, looking at the "delegations" from Hawaii, from Denver, New York, Los Angeles. . . . Many are wearing UAW chef-type hats; others—more striking yet—are wearing yarmulkes, as a symbol of the solidarity between Negro and Jew.

Finally we started. Martin Luther's wife was with him this time. I had never seen her before. The people in front wore orange vests. Somebody played Yankee Doodle Dandy.

It was strange and wonderful to see so many barefooted priests. Because they were barefooted, I put on my shoes. It was not seemly for me to appear to imitate these saintly ones. It was well that I did so. The crush of thousands as we walked down Oak Street to Dexter was a kind of ecstasy. We tried to hold onto each other—six abreast (women and children on the inside) but the momentum was often too great. Our lines broke, reformed. We panted, we ran to fill the gap in our ranks. People ran to give us things to drink, as we were thirsting. Cold drinks, soda bottles passed from hand to hand, black and white. People cried to us from the porches; "Freedom!" But it was restrained, as though it were a Passion Play. People ran to shake hands with one another. Somebody ran to me and took my hand as though to kiss it. He called my name: "Angelina!" he said; but it sounded like a question. He stood, smiling strangely, like a man filled with love or hate or both at once. Then he bowed, and raising up his camera slowly, like a weapon, took my picture.

One girl spat upon the ground as I passed: "Go to hell, nigger lover," she said.

I had placed a handkerchief at the bottom of my shoe, to ease the wound. At a stop street I paused to fold it; the handkerchief fell from my hand and was kicked away in the crowds. But it was not much farther. So we hobbled on. . . .

3:00 p.m. It is finished. We have made "the Selma-Montgomery March." I am sitting on Dexter Avenue with about twenty thousand people. Speeches are being made, but we barely listen. Most of us are resting. We still have work to do when the speeches are over. King is saying: "They told us we wouldn't get here. And there are those who said we would get here over dead bodies. . . . Segregation is on its death bed in Alabama . . . and Wallace will make the funeral. . . ."

There is much yet to be done. We can't stop here to eat. Nearly all shops and restaurants are closed. Those that are open show their unveiled hostility. Even getting back to St. Jude's where many have parked their cars, will be for some people, a formidable hike. In a few hours it will be dark, and we are, all of us, exhausted. We have arrived at our destination in a fever, an exultation, but also with despair. The despair comes from the feeling of not knowing why, exactly, we have consummated this particular act. It is a momentary terror, our *eli, eli*.

The Playhouse

"I shall gladly look upon hell
as a playhouse."

Gunter Grass, *The Dog Years*

When I heard her footsteps on the porch, I'd just come to the end of one of my usual days spent making Lists, and had at last begun to write these copies of my bequest as I'd been instructed—one to the hospitals that needed donors, one to my lawyer, and one to my ex-wife Delsie. So far I'd listed:

Kennedy	Spock	Corneas to Girard (Baylor U.)	strychnine
Malcolm	Coffin	Heart to DeBakey (St. Luke's)	arsenic
Schwerner	Goodman	Kidneys to Starzl (U. of Colo.)	Prussic acid
Chaney	Mora	Blood Type B-negative	morphine
Goodman	Johnson	(Texas Blood Bank)	atropine
Liuzzo	Samas		mercury
Medgar Evers	Berrigan		potassium cyanide
King	Lewis		hydrofluoric acid
Kennedy	Levy		carbon monoxide

You'll understand at once that I was not keen about this Sweet-youngthing interrupting me. So I walked slowly over to the locked screen door and stood there in my bare feet, waving the pencil at her menacingly—I wanted her to think I was some kind of a madman, so she'd *get:* "Whatever you're selling," I said with heavy sarcasm, "I'm not buying any."

Now it would never have occurred to me that a smart-looking chick like this one would have taken me literally. But she assured me, addressing me interrogatively as "Mr. Meyer Bernstein—is it?" that she wasn't selling anything, and explaining to me in that tone of eager plausibility middle-class kids develop the way the rest of us catch measles, that she was a representative from the Concerned Voters' Action Committee.

"Who's concerned?" I demanded without inviting her in. "*You?*"—and my voice offered that full contempt I reserve for straight chicks from the unpolluted suburbs.

Again she explained to me as patiently as if she were teaching an elementary school class of slow learners that the colored people they were especially trying to reach, in this important election, were the middle-class Negroes.

"Middle-class Negroes? What's that, baby? Being black is a *caste*—."

She stared at me, intimidated in spite of what seemed a natural courage (or innocence?) by my familiarity and rage. Really, I felt so low I just wanted to shove her off the porch—her and all the other brain-proof, bomb-proof, shit-proof chicks like her who sell their guys to the Establishment for a bag of polyethylene toys. But at the same time, staring down into those cinnamon-colored eyes, it seemed to me I'd never seen such innocent orbs, the pupils banded with yellow like some medieval nimbus designating the virginmary. Her ash-colored hair fell caressingly around her ears, and at my bitter glance (did she sense the repressed lust, or did she think my glance was a reproach-to-tidiness?) she tucked the errant strand behind her ears with an impatience which told me plain enough that her hair was not what she'd come to talk to me about. . . . It was that gesture that trapped me.

Because it reminded me of Delsie, of course. I'm one of these conscious cynics, bitch-haters who's still hung up on his ex-wife: wouldn't you know? Her gesture reminded me now of how about ten years ago, or was it only eight, when Delsie and I were picketing Woolworth's in Berkeley, it had suddenly started to rain. I didn't have a raincoat, but Delsie did, a huge tarpaulinlike affair, because she was seven months pregnant with Paul. I'd had a bad cold for a week, and Delsie insisted I come under the tarpaulin with her: so I did, tucking little Betty under one arm (she was only two then and lithe as a fish). And there we'd stood, huddled like the first family driven out of some improbable Eden. . . .

So, as I say, when this kid pushed her hair back like that, I felt that stupid lump in my throat, the way I did back when the world was young. And like any goddammed fool who believes he has fifty years of The Good Life ahead of him, I said: "Come on in." I held the door open for her and she passed right in front of me without a moment's hesitation, though I knew for a fact I must have smelled like a four-day Mississippi corpse after sitting in front of those Lists all week, doing nothing but chewing on my pipe and picking the lint from my beard.

Well the bitch walks into a guy's pad pretty cool, I thought, as without waiting to be asked, she sat down in the very chair I'd been sitting in myself (the only comfortable one, in fact) and began her spiel. She had to raise her voice because I made no move to turn down the record player where Dylan was coming on strong with *The Times They Are A-Changin'*. Just for a moment or two her eye wandered to the posters on my wall—Baez, Gins-berg, Malcolm and King (*confuse* 'em, that was my strategy)—to where I now rested my bare feet on the coffee table alongside a recent copy of *The Wall Street Journal* (she looked a bit surprised, the creep: where else did she think we knew how they were lappin' it up since the war?)

Anyway: the idea was, as she explained to me, to get as many Negroes as possible to vote. ("New idea?" I mused sarcastically as I reached for my pipe, but she hurled herself into the subject like a kid who's just discovered the pill.) The white volunteers, she pursued, like herself . . . like me, she hoped . . . were driving down to the Negro areas ("The ghetto, baby," I interrupted. "Let's face it: every isolated economic group is a cultural ghetto.") She lifted her sun-bleached brows at this, but nodded in quick agree-ment that smacked of humility, and went on to explain that if we would provide transportation, many Negroes who ordinarily would not vote would have a ride to the courthouse and—.

I knocked my pipe impatiently on the ceramic ashtray Delsie had made for me (one of the few things we'd collected that she'd forgotten to take with her): "Yeah. Yeah. I know all that. But *why?* Why should we do it?"

She looked away for a moment at the posters. Then those gold flecks lit up in her eyes and began generating their own brand of electricity. She leaned toward me intently. "Because we have to beat him. You know what'll happen if he becomes mayor, don't you? Every liberal program in this city will go under. Twenty years of progress, down the drain. The kind of guy who builds fallout shelters in his backyard—."

"Ah yes, the bomb," I said. And yawned. "So what about it? Let 'em drop it. Serve us right. . . ."

She sat staring at me, silenced a moment by what she must have believed was my gargantuan joke.

So I added, as if in reasonable explanation. "They've killed off all the best guys, haven't they? Well, let 'em have a taste of it. . . ."

Her eyelids quivered slightly and she raised her eyes when she spoke, as if in invocation: "They? But 'they'—that's everybody. . . ."

"That's right, baby. THEY. US. EVERYBODY. Guilty. All of us guilty as Judas for every damned death of the decade—." I tried to control the emotion in my voice (Don't get *involved*, Meyer, I kept saying to myself), but after all a man who's just signed away his liver and lights is entitled to a bit of passion. "They've killed all the best guys," I repeated, hypnotized by my own phrase, "and now you want me to go out and campaign for some political *symbol?* Symbol of what? Of our stupidity? Our greed? Our nuclear insanity?"

She seemed to sit up even straighter to reply, and as she spoke she pronounced her words with a faint righteousness that made me want to crack her right across her beautifully straightened middle-class teeth. "We have to work with what's left," she said. "As intellectuals, we're responsible for the future as well as for the past."

"I'm not responsible for a damned thing anymore," I said hotly, glaring down at my Lists, as if to prove it. Then suddenly I added another item: *teeth.* I'd have 'em sent to Ted Bettleman in dental school up at U. of M., see if he could use them for anything. "My last will and testament," I observed to her conspiratorially, and the Sweetyoungthing thought I was joking. She began smiling at my sudden change of tone, and it was now my turn to stare, at the exquisite proportion of canines to bicuspids—all those murmuring white monoliths, like a row of perfect headstones, each one inscribed: *Ego blanca sum, ego dea sum....*

"Teeth are a funny thing, though, don't you think?" I remember Lenny Perlman complaining to me in a hoarse whisper after he'd been beaten up in McComb, Miss. "Your teeth, dig, you like to keep 'em. Like they're a status symbol. You lose 'em out of the wrong side of your mouth and you're not Prometheus anymore, you're Sancho Panza. Lotsa guys worry about getting their brains bashed in down here. But not me. I worry about teeth ... Vanity, you'll say. O.K. so it's vanity. But I remember how Ma used to say, "Chew it up well, Lenny. Chew it slow. Es gibt gezundheit." And the guys on our block used to swear by the chew-and-screw criterion. Meaning, dig, that you enjoy your food, you enjoy your screw. Who wants to make love to a guy with his teeth on the nightstand? And then, too, you could always make the scene with a SMILE. Without your upper plate jiggling—you know?—a guy can con his way out of any situation." And Lenny pointed to his gaping mouth: "Man, I almost wish they'd busted my head. My brain never was that good. But my teeth—that's a bummer, man."

Then last summer they'd picked up Lenny in a phone booth, naked as a catfish and high on acid, trying to make a person to person call (collect) to Sirhan Sirhan. ... I saw the best minds of my generation destroyed by madness, starving hysterical naked ... THAT was a summer. ... Three six-month sentences for contempt of court, two nervous breakdowns, one fractured hipbone, and one turncoat for law and order.

I finally became aware that this chick had been digging around for some time, trying to find her cigarettes ("What'd you say your name was?" "I never said: Nancy." "Nancy what?" "Nancy Whitesell." "Well, wouldn't you *know* it!"), and now she was searching through her pocketbook for a match. Evidently my silence while I'd gazed upon her teeth had made her nervous; she looked more scared than she had a moment—or was it ten years?

—ago. Now she stopped rummaging and waited for me to hand her a light. But I didn't move a muscle—those amenities just didn't mean a damn to me anymore.

"We have to work with what's left," she repeated as, at last, with a deprecating shove of my bare heel, I inched the box of kitchen matches toward her. "I know how you feel. Afer they shot Bobby Kennedy, I was in despair, too. . . ."

Oh Christ no. Not that. That's *my* role, baby. And I shoved my pipe between my teeth as though they were a metal vise.

"But we have to stop this man. . . . He's dangerous. He's well —a fascist, you might say. A racist. . . ."

"The whole fucking country is racist. So what's new?" Now that'll drive her away, I thought. If being a wild-eyed barefoot Jew with a three weeks' growth of beard wasn't enough to scare the lily-white pants off her, obscenity should do the trick.

But she was not swayed by smut. She looked at me as sweetly as though we'd once been hot lovers, but were now calmly reasoning together: "We need bodies. . . ." she said. "People to help. If we can register five thousand in this precinct—."

"Five thousand *bodies*? 'Live or dead?" It was no academic distinction to me. I had my Lists, and I'd seen 'em both ways.

"I mean to *help*. To drive them to the courthouse."

I dropped my bare feet at this and looked up at my posters. Malcolm-baby, you're dead, I apostrophized. You're deader than the conscience of the white liberal, deader than Our Saviour, than OurFatherWhoArtinHeaven. Deader than me. . . .

Aloud I said: "Oh yeah. I know that scene. You finally get a few trembling white-headed old blacks who've been living on the burnt-out side of Gehenna for the past fifty years without ever having registered. You get 'em there and what happens? Either they pass out with fear and escape to the bathroom till it's closing time and too late to sign, or Missy Election Commissioner finds out they can't read or write. Can't you see that you're about a hundred years too late? that you got to run to hell like Alice in Wonderland just to stand in the same place? Who the hell cares anymore *what* mayor is going to be elected in what city, when it's all *go-ing, go-ing . . . gone.*"

She gave me a soft, intelligent, yielding look of those cinnamon and yellow butter eyes of hers, but I could see we weren't connecting. Everything in the place, including Dylan's voice, was yelling *Ave frater* to such as she, but the pitch wasn't getting through to her. It was like we were talking to each other through a white parchment paper: we could hear each other, see each other's lips move, even—on a lucky hunch—go to bed together, but neither of us could understand a word the other was saying. We were just a couple of softshell, hardnosed Do-gooders, one of whom—myself—was already the anachronism of the decade; the other, Little Missy still dreaming drowsily of the Goodwhitelady bringing baskets of love and apples to help (Mother of God!) middle-class Negroes. We were on a bummer all right.

The upshot of it was that we arranged to go off the next day to Do-good together. And it was all so bad, it was good, so I've decided to jot it all down and mail it along with my teeth to Ted Bettleman. He'll die laughing. (How you like it, Ted? So far, I mean?)

But listen. The first gig was, we hopped into her shiny new AU-TOE, a small sportscar, all red-wine color and seats as white as a dove's ass, you know the kind I mean (the thing was so new that when I slammed the door shut I couldn't hear for the air pressure), and at my jolly grin, she explained: "A real economy move . . . saves so much on gas, compared to using Daddy's car. . . ."

I said nothing—what was the use? Should I have explained that carting black citizens to the courthouse would have been much more dramatic in one of those slatted trucks strewn with straw that they use for migrant workers? Nothing doing. Would have been like complaining about motherhood and savings bonds— they'd just tell you that if you don't like it here, go back where you came from. . . .

Maybe I could go back to Delsie. Who loved me because, as she said, I couldn't take care of myself. She was there when they cracked my skull—that long, lost time ago during the sit-ins, when white and black sang together against a common enemy. She saw me just standing there with bowed head, the blood gushing from my forehead, my face a fugue of desolation, and facing death—she said—bravely . . . She decided to marry me, she said, because I looked like Jesus Christ. We all looked like Jesus Christ in those days, starved, beaten, spat upon. . . . So they picked me up in a litter and drove me to the nearest hospital. I've owed my life three times to those hospitals, that's why I'm paying them back. . . . Or a reprieve anyway. . . .

The third time? You could guess that one. That was when Delsie left me.

And it all turned out as I expected. We arrived about eleven that morning, at a spanking new Federal Project, already furnished with indoor plumbing (I calmly took in a frockless tot peeing on the kitchen floor as we passed: "Their mothers just aren't around to teach them any better," Nancy apologized. "Gone to play bridge I guess," I observed), and furnished, too, with outdoor mudholes surrounding the project like trenches for the beseiged. ("There's going to be a garden there later," said Nancy. "Yeah," I said. "Later. . . .") But at least it was a beautiful morning; the sun was dying off the shreds of fog; each quartet of apartments stood high in the air on concrete stilts which made them seem to rise from the mud like cubistic waterfowl. From a nearby ditch one could hear the shreeing of frogs.

Nancy approached the apartments as though crossing a medieval drawbridge. Referring to a map which she held in her hand at all times, she knocked on the first door, introduced herself and her Cause before the occupant could say a negative word —and went off on her spiel. I followed her indoors without greeting anyone: I believe they took me for her special, silent, and morose bodyguard. While she talked I let my eye wander idly around the small apartments—at the kitchen, the furniture. They aroused in me no specific reaction. I'd lived with furniture like that all my life—you can get fifty dollars worth of it to fill a room so that it looks crowded. Always the same sectional pieces, the plasticized tables, the deformed, craterous-looking red lamp on a doily with a green-glass dime-store ash tray set beside it. ("Why is poverty so ugly?" Delsie used to groan, and finally left me because, she said, she was through making love on broken springs.)

After she left they had to pump my stomach out to save me. Save me? For what? For this? I should have used strychnine, but hadn't the guts to talk the druggist into letting me have it. It was

115

just one more damned fight with the Establishment, and I hadn't wanted to bother. So I botched it. I'd used what was left of Delsie's phenobarbital, which she'd left behind—along with our photographs, our unpaid electric bill and an eye-of-God thing I'd woven for her when we were first married (I'd had all the talents then, it seemed). And she took the car, my first lousy sellout to the System, you can't live without one. She took it even though it wasn't paid for and she'd never be able to keep up the payments: guess a car is the ultimate rescue when you're running away from being poor-all-your-life. The other way is just to run away from your life: like me.

Meanwhile I continued to follow Nancy around, glowering like a kid who's been turned off from an exciting rumble to serve tea biscuits in straw baskets to little old ladies. What grabbed me were the omnipresent photographs of Kennedy and King, usually in metal frames and ornamented with flowers or candles. Real icons, the two-headed, biracial god always shown with His hands outstretched: Kennedy's giving, promising; King's exhorting, blessing. . . . After coming across three or four of these little altars I began to accept the Worship of the Dead as part of the scene. If god is dead, you make one out of whatever tools you have handy, everybody knows that. I began listening instead, in spite of myself, to Nancy's routine.

You had to hand it to her, she was good. She turned them on like a handful of bennies. Before you knew it, tired, pulpy-looking women with their legs propped up on chairs, nursing their thrombosis, would struggle into their clothes and be dressed and ready for the courthouse in ten minutes. And weary old men who stared at you with a clearly recognizable bitterness, as if this was the Ultimate Betrayal (they'd hoped to die, at least, without seeing Whitey in their homes)—these old men, too, would soon be buttoning up their shirts, cleaning out torn, invalidated tickets from their wallets, and arranging their social security cards for handy identification. She even persuaded a couple of tough-looking kids who looked too young to drive, let alone vote, to absent themselves from felicity awhile and come down to the courthouse to register. They looked, in fact, so young she demanded to see their proof-of-birth, just to be sure they weren't trying to bug her.

So they sing-songed out at her in unison soprano: "We been born, lady, we been born, and we knows how and when. . . ." Nudging each other.

They showed her I.D. cards proving they were exactly old enough to vote.

"Kind of sneaks up on you, doesn't it?" I commented with jealous triumph—nobody's asked to see my I.D. card since I spent a month in an Alabama jail. But I guess she didn't get me, or she just didn't have time for petty warfare. She was into this big thing.

Altogether, within three hours, she'd rounded up about twenty. Impossible, of course, to load them all into her sportscar, so she phoned the Ararat Church, asking them to have a couple of station wagons from the Concerned Voters Etc. Etc. come over to the project at once. While she did this, the prospective registrants, dressed up in their Sunday clothes as for a wedding or a funeral, gathered together out on the gravel parking lot beside the mudholes, where one day the garden would be. They stood there, waiting uneasily in the hot light of the afternoon sun, casting sidelong glances at each other, as if they had all been caught guilty of something.

While we waited for the station wagons, trying to look happy and confident in the sunlight, Nancy glanced at her map to see if she had covered *her* "area." With an annoyed shake of her head she complained to me *sotto voce* that she'd become confused, all the apartments looked alike, and she'd omitted 201A, the corner one up there with the fake balcony: would I like to stay down here with Them while she checked to see if anybody up there was voting age? "Not on your life, baby," I whispered back. "You're not leaving *me* here to explain to these citizens why you've taken them away from the serious work they've got to catch up on on Saturdays because they've been working like hell all week. . . ." For people like you, baby, I might have added, but she interrupted me irritably: "Hush! Then just come along with me, then—you—*baby!*" I remember that at that point she seemed to me a bit nervous. She didn't like to leave all the people alone and unattended, and at the same time she obviously didn't think it would be "fair" to overlook anybody.

"We'll be back in just one minute," she explained to the

crowd. "We're just going to check out that corner apartment there." And she pointed to 201A.

A cautious murmur, a rigorous *refusal* to exchange glances seemed to pass through the group. They would never have presumed to give white-missy the advice she so badly needed, but they were all of one mind about her visiting 201A: I can't explain how I knew that except by their unanimous silence. One teen-aged looking cat who seemed to be standing around waiting for some hard bellylaughs, began grinning: *that* should have warned me. But even after we'd climbed the stairs to Chop Davis' apartment, and Nancy had rung his bell, and I'd heard his muffled exclamation behind the screen door: "Goddammit, what do they want *now?*" I wasn't absolutely certain what territory Nancy had landed us in, till Chop said: "Oh yeah? You been wantin' to talk to *me?* Well, I been wantin' to talk to *you.*" And he glared at us as if *we* were a couple of blacks who'd skipped parole in Alabama and he was the white State Trooper at last. My impulse was to grab Nancy and get her away—we were on the small front balcony, in full view of all the spectators below—because I knew that voice. The rage of it was sweeping across the land, uniting in a single roar of fury; it was a voice that was getting itself locked up in a thousand jails—for profanity, for loitering, for driving without a license, for carrying a gun, for looting, for arson, and finally (it no longer cared, that voice), for murder. . . .

I tried to kid our way back downstairs to where the safety of the crowd lay. "Come on, Nancy, this cat's too young to vote." And for *her* sake, dammit she'd got me into it after all, I *smiled* at him propitiatingly, though I know he loathed me as much as at the moment I loathed him: because we'd lost our big chance at Loving-one-Another, and we were both (who else?) responsible for that failure. So we hated each other like a pair of convicts who've both turned state's evidence against each other, but are doomed to hang anyway. . . .

I thought Nancy would run when the axe fell directly on her: "And what the fuck do you think you're doin' here?" Chop demanded of her almost at once, pushing away the leaflet of identification she offered him. But she was a brave kid, I got to hand it to her, and she stood her ground, murmuring in a breathless voice (she *was* scared, I realized) ". . . we've organized . . . in the hope that . . . it being an important election . . . and thought maybe you'd like to come with us . . . if you haven't yet registered. . . ."

"Well, ain't that just grand?" exclaimed Davis, his hands on his hips. "You want us colored folks to get out there and *vote*, to save us all from that big bad buggering *racist*. And you think that's a real fine liberal you've got running for us there—he's swinging with the Latins and the blacks. Well, let me tell *you*, he ain't nothin' but an asshole, and even *before* the Civil War we didn't need a shithead like him. And as for your pimp here—." Davis, enraged by my silence, turned suddenly to me: "What you doin' with this jive mother, sendin' her around with all those whiteass lies? 'We gonna help you, you gonna help us. God gonna help everybody. . . .' Ain't *nobody* gonna help us now except the sweet black kissin'-curve of a gun. . . . Now you get your white asses off my *property* before I shoot you for trespassin'."

Nancy was frightened, but she'd had special training in Christian Forgiveness and Psychological Understanding; so in spite of her fear I could see she was making allowances, forgiving much, understanding-his-problems. . . . As she drew back from the doorway, her beautiful hair straggled like a last leap of sunlight across her face. She turned toward him sadly, one hand already on the freshly lathed, unpainted bannister of the balcony which was joined by long metal stilts to the mud-bottoms. "I understand how you feel, Mr. Davis," she began sorrowfully.

That was too much for Chop Davis. Before I could come between them he had rushed forward from his perch on the threshold of his apartment, where he'd been guarding the entry, and swirled her around so smoothly and violently that they might have been doing some teen-aged dance together. Nancy's wide skirts fluttered in the breeze.

"*You* understand, you little chippie—."

I laid a firm grip on his arm. "Cut that out," I said. "She's only trying to help."

"Well who *you* shovin', motherfucker?" he demanded of me, but with a certain bitter raillery in his voice, as if his fight were not actually with me and we both knew it, but with Nancy. It was as if her very innocence infuriated him, an innocence which, with all its myths of purity and decency, had brought black men like himself to their knees.

"I ain't shovin'," I retorted in the same tone of voice as his own. "I'm keepin' *you* from shovin'."

"Listen," he said, bringing his face up to my face and speaking in a passionate whisper, his shoulder slightly hunched with eloquence, and punctuating every word with zigs and dashes toward the sunlit corner of the balcony, so that I was caught for a moment by the sight of the slashing shadows his rage made upon the concrete slabs like those of a man shadowboxing. "When I shove, I *shoves*," he threatened. "There won't be any doubt about it, hear? There won't be any Missy-please, and oh-pardon-me. Next time she get in my way, I'm gonna—," he flailed the shadows with a fierce striking motion, like the sweep of a machete. "I'm *tired* of your kind, both of you. . . . So don't come round here no more, y'hear? Less'n you want to get—*get* it? And I'm gonna keep my people away from you too. . . ."

With a sudden brilliant barefoot leap he had passed in front of us and was down the stairs three at a time; I became aware in that moment how surprisingly small he was, not much taller than a well-fed seventh grader. In his bare feet he ploughed through the mud surrounding the stilts, with the furious dedication of a man caught in the swamps with the dogs after him.

As Nancy and I descended the steps, carefully, timidly, one at a time, we could hear him haranguing his people.

"Don't let these crackers eat all your vittles. You grew it for them, you cooked it for them. Now *you* gonna eat it. Let them vote for their own selves—we ain't *got* a candidate yet. But when we do, I'll tell you who's going to be the next mayor of this here city. . . ."

They all knew the answer, and began smiling and whispering to each other in anticipation. Now and then they shot a look of triumph at Nancy and me, as if this was really what they wanted to hear: that it was worth sacrificing the vote to see the real parade. Above all, they wanted to hear it right out loud, so Davis gave it to them.

"Chop Davis!—that's who!" he cried ecstatically, and a flare of joy seemed to light up among the group. The teen-aged cat began banging on the lid of a garbage can with a sharp stick, seized (as it seemed) from out of the air. "Chop Davis! And you-all know how I got that name. By *choppin'*, that's how. 'Cause I been choppin' cotton since the day I was born. And my mama before me. And her mama before *her*. But now we *thew* choppin' cotton—we choppin' heads. . . ." And he slashed his arm out with a gesture of fury as though to block out the sun.

I looked at Nancy; her face looked grey; her mouth was slack with revulsion—and with fear. I felt a little sick myself; a concentrated dose of hate can make you feel like you got a bad hangover. And a phrase kept jamming into my brain, like a log that's stuck and gets hemmed in by flotsam: *It was the best of times, it was the worst of times. . . .*

As though we were of one mind, Nancy and I made our way to her car. Even as we drove off we saw two station wagons approaching from the opposite direction, but we never found out who went to register and who didn't. We didn't even hail the folks from Ararat. Nancy had begun crying and was unable to drive, and kept sobbing harder and harder every time we'd hit a miserable bump in the unpaved roads. There was a minute or two when we got stuck in a ditch near the swamp; our wheels whirred meaninglessly through the half-dried mud and sand. Nancy murmured to herself: "Oh God!" But I wasn't scared. . . . I knew it wasn't the hour yet for head-rolling.

After I'd driven Nancy home—her folks stared at me as if I'd just got her pregnant—I walked about three miles back to my pad (Nancy was so upset, it didn't occur to her that I had no way to get back, and I looked so ratty I couldn't even hitch a ride). When I finally got in, the place looked strange to me as if it were no longer mine; then I realized that the new tenants who were moving in tomorrow had come in my absence and had taken down my posters to make room for a couple of Vermeers and had shoved the rest of my gear into a corner. I rushed over to make sure my Lists hadn't got jimmied up, and felt grateful that they, at least, had been left untouched. Lighting my pipe, I climbed on top of my gear like a sailor on a raft; then, to the Names of the illustrious dead, I carefully added my own.

The Girl Who
Was Afraid of Snow

Intolerable, without mind
The snow drops its piece of darkness

Sylvia Plath, *The Munich Mannequins*

During her childhood Marilyn Perales had been fearless. Send her alone to the store, she never had fantasies: strangers did not pursue her, shadows never became real sculptures. She had lived a free spirit, sauntering pleasantly around the plaza of Nuevo Laredo, delighted with the delights of the poor: cold Cola in the hot summers, a trinket from someone's birthday *piñata*, and plenty of *mariachi* music on holidays. She had scarcely dreamed she was disadvantaged. Perhaps because both her parents could read and write; in a border town that could make all the difference. When her father had intoned from his Spanish text: "Yea, though I walk through the valley of the shadow of death, I will fear no evil," that had seemed to change things. From such trifles a girl imbibed spoonfuls of courage, like garlic and olive oil which were good for the complexion.

Her mother's method of transfiguring the slums of Nuevo Laredo had been Work. Like an insect circling the trunk of a tree whose circumference she could not measure but whose existence she never doubted, her mother had wrestled with thieves, lechers, addicts, and drunks as calmly as though she were a church deacon sweeping out the back room. Mrs. Perales had done her thing, and in the process Marilyn had grown up—scorning such psychic lacerations as a pimply adolescence and learning how not to look like a wallflower. As Mrs. Perales' friends had assured her frightened mother, Marilyn was not like other girls. No feeney-finey airs for her. On Name Days, with an air of ritualistic decorum her strong fingers had deftly parted the heart of the slaughtered goat from its soul, never doubting it was the function of goats to die and of the Perales family to live.

Since she had been reared in a home where courage, like salt, was a staple item—used casually yet from a sense of necessity—it was no surprise, years later, that when her hour of heroic confrontations came upon her, Marilyn was almost conventionally heroic: the civil rights battleground, the anti-draft battleground, the women's liberation struggle—wherever there had been battlegrounds, Marilyn had battled. Courageous, gamesome, chunky but not fat, the folks Downhome had decided that Marilyn was not only brave but existential: she ran to meet danger like her Redeemer.

Then, a few years before the cut-off age of thirty she had suddenly directed all her energies into formal education, had remastered her own native tongue and taken a couple of degrees in Linguistics at the University of Texas. With these trophies she had migrated North to carry English-as-a-Second-Language to Spanish-speaking peoples everywhere. Her new Yankee friends welcomed her into the fold: no race prejudice, they assured her, no malarial insects, no dysentery, no broiling summers, and above all: the joys of winter. Had she ever seen real snow? (reality measured by quantity, that is). Well, not to shake a ski pole at, she admitted. And awaited the advent as though it were the Second Coming.

When the white winter arrived suddenly one morning, she was totally unprepared. As a matter of fact she was on her way to the grocery to buy eggs for breakfast when the mills of the gods began to grind out snow, exceedingly slow and exceedingly fine. She paused in the middle of Fifth and Center as the curious drowsy stuff began first to flicker, then to fall . . . assiduously. As the wind increased, the snow seemed to increase in intensity—opaque, mysterious, terrifying. Marilyn discovered that her Yankee friends had lied to her: that New-fallen Snow was neither beauteous nor lyric nor even (as they had hinted), ethnic; indeed, it aroused in her no esthetic reaction at all, but only symptoms of mortal terror. After years of marching, militancy and *mensch-ing* (her linguist's neologism intended to combat the male chauvinism inherent in *wench*ing), after years of bravery, to wake up one morning and discover that Sister X, Madam Super-spy, and Freedom Fighter of the Seventies was scared shitless: well, it was a bit of a comedown.

What's more, it turned out to be the worst winter in More-land County (they always say that) in thirty years. The snow fell thick as tail feathers in a duck shoot—the difference was that the soundless shooting never stopped; the birds fell and fell, covering the universe with their soft fleshless bodies. Marilyn tried logic. It was a great natural art form, wasn't it? Photographers froze them-selves solid in their dedicated efforts to snap sinuous snowcaps. Whereas, she—Marilyn Perales—stood by the window and trembled like a dog. Was this a punishment for something? Hubris? She would have given a decade of freedom-fighting for the sight of an armadillo in the grass.

She racked her brains for the cause of her terror, since she prided herself on her rationality—she who had probed to the relevance of forgotten objects, of slips of the tongue, of dreams. . . . Could it have been the goose feathers she had plucked for her mother on holidays? Or the night her father's car had broken down in the desert of White Sands, New Mexico? Or what? Or where? The cause, if there was one, eluded her. The white flakes, however, found her—on street corners, in the park, under trees. . . .

Actually, it was not that it was so *very* cold outdoors (she was nothing if not rational). In fact, since bravery was to be her thing, she proved she was not afraid of the cold by hiking her mini-skirt another inch and parading bare-kneed through the elements, literally flirting with Death and Transfiguration.

Which was fine until the third day of their first winter storm. She was standing alone then, in Northside Park, while white flakes surrounded her, whirling their silent dervish. Courage here was not enough, she saw that. The stuff could not be routed, slain, pulverized, assaulted, melted, or ignored. It had the tang of guilt, like venison. It was fear-and-trembling-and-sickness-unto-death made visible. Swelling conscience-like underfoot, slogging one's very heartbeat with envy and lust, it insinuated one's mortal soul, whispering: *destroy*. Destroy what? Not herself, dammit. She hadn't travelled straight to the midpoint of her life (as the poet saith) to be routed by a case of the Snowy Slobbers.

So she folded herself beside the slats of the park bench and glared at the enemy—its fantails and curlicues, its curvetting and waddling—all evidence of an idiot consciousness that had lost its bearings somewhere in outer space. If God was nothing but the Silence, Marilyn snuffed angrily, we were in for a hell of a run for our money. She'd have to stop believing in this travesty of the Absolute: let Him stop this mad fluttering of His will first, this *peeling* of His epidermal universe. . . . Then we can negotiate.

Now, to be fighting psychic battles in the snow is sufficient conflict alone and unto itself. No need for Climax and Catastrophe, she was in the thick of it. The only thing Girard Tippet could mean at this point was more trouble: but there he was, the antihero of the Linguistics office, not made but created—erupted in the image of someone, one forgot who.

Tippet was one of those of whom it was said, seeing is unbelieving. He had bulbous eyes and a vague whine in his throat as though he'd been run through an electric grinder once and was still purring with it. His legs stood akimbo like an overturned hull of a ship. His hair, cinder-colored, was cut in an homogeneous clip, each hair perfect, like one of those packets of free matches offered by your local veterinarian. And on top of his head he wore a long knitted ski cap which came around his shoulder like an arm caught in the wrong place. Otherwise, Marilyn summed it up, just a nice normal guy who had wanted to be a cowboy, but flunked the physical. What he and Marilyn had in common was that they were both from Texas: a demographic error which was to assume tragic proportions.

Marilyn was trying to think of some nice way to say fuck off and leave me alone, I've got enough trouble, when through the swinish white swirl she heard Tippet's motor rev uncertainly, like Orpheus with a bad cold: "Howdy!" he called (he really did) and in spite of herself Marilyn felt herself respond tenderly to this echo of the fatherland. So she over-reacted as the shrinks says. She planted her legs solidly in the center of her snow boots and rasped, as ruthless as AT&T.—

"What the fuck are you doing out here?" One thing freedom-fighting had taught her was that the only way guys could differentiate between a revolutionary woman and a free lay was by not screwing around with the amenities. When speaking with idiots, she'd discovered, one four-letter word was worth a thousand ideograms.

Tippet made an effort to tip his ski cap (migod, in the snow!), but finally settled for flicking the tail of it at her, like a horse flicking flies.

Again he intoned his magic word: "Howdy!" he called and a sweeping tropical breeze rose straight from the palms of Galveston Bay and hit her in the ovaries. Watch out, baby, she told herself, he's not a man, he's just a compass pointing Home.

"What you say to a hot cup of—." Looking into her gelid indifferent eye he amended quickly, without a smile: "A right smart shot of whiskey sure would warm us up now, wouldn't it, m'am?"

The worrisome thought hit her that if he was parodying himself he was not all that dumb, and if he was not all that dumb, in her present low state she might get fond of the idiot. But for the moment she was, in a very Freudian sense, stuck on the Longhorns of a dilemma: this stuffed stud with real button eyes was offering her sanctuary from the snow.

"Where'll we go?" she challenged. "Pizza Parlor? Pub?"

Apparently he sensed it was some kind of Rorshach test, because he crooked his arm like a bandy-legged teapot and seemed to smile (without moving his lips): "The Black Angus'll make us feel more to home, y'reckon?"

Numb with nostalgia, Marilyn nodded her acceptance. The Devil, she had to acknowledge, has been known to invade the bodies of ninnies. As they entered the restaurant Marilyn looked over her shoulder to see if anyone they knew had seen them together. She thought in a moment she was going to cry: one thing she knew—no guy with real balls would ever look at her after being seen with Girard Tippet.

Thus began the most talked-of romance of the year (as such things go in the dullness of Linguistics offices): the squiring of the leader of Women's Liberation (southeast campus only) by Girard Tippet, nobody's incubus. They (Marilyn and Girard) took long walks every day, pausing in the pint-sized piece of park near the Museum, where the wind blew through the barren trees and the path lay solidly strewn with white—with—.

" '—bodies!' " he echoed (for unbeknowst to their randy-minded gossips, they talked not about love but about Her Problem).

She defended her vision. "Of course bodies. Look at them. What do they look like to you? Zillions of them, falling through space. Alighting for their brief moment of joy, then pouf! cough! dissolution: dead bodies."

"Wa—el. (*Weigh-yell*, she transliterated at once). "What Ah would have said is, they look more like a Texas sky at midnight, like upsahdawn starrhs, sort of."

She had difficulty concentrating on his meaning; his drawl lured her like an aphrodisiac. Don't listen to him, you aural slut, she warned herself. He's just a midget Texan. Even Texans can be dwarfs, eunuchs, abortions, wizened old men. To shut out the siren call of his speech, Marilyn tied herself to the mast of dramatic hyperbole:

" 'Stars'! Lousy little motherfucking corpses streaming through the air. Faustian malignancies, spirits, malevolent *los aires* spreading germs, making colds, destroying life limb and the pursuit of happiness. Just look over there. *Look.* Do you see a single solitary leaf on that tree? No!" she answered herself, feeling ready to weep, so she stirred in herself a look of triumph and blew her nose. "Not one leaf! That snow-stuff is deadlier than Operation Ranchhand. The whole raw dealie is one grand defoliation stunt: God, the Grand Defoliator." *How*, she was asking herself, could she be attracted to an epicene dwarf with adenoids, just because his screwed-up vowels reminded her of cottonwood trees and huacamole salad, red beans and rizzo con pollo. The guy didn't have a teaspoonful of the blood of *la raza* in him. . . .

He whistled at her—in admiration, she was supposed to believe. "You sure are a trigger-fingered hot-blooded Messican gal," he sighed. "And that's for sure. Though there's a mite of sense in what you sayin'. But it ain't *defoliation:* it's decomposin'. It's conservation of energy and all that. Baby, God ain't *serious* about destroyin' the world—he just playin' at it, so to speak."

"What the hell's God got to do with it?" she growled.

"Well, Ah didn't bring Him into the conversation—you did," he said reproachfully.

"Oh God!" she exclaimed in despair.

"See what Ah mean? . . ."

"Bah-humbug with that conservation of energy stuff," she said. "Just a bunch of coprolites. Turn everything shit-brown, then they suck it up again."

"They? Who 'they'?"

"Ha! Ha! Betcha think you got me on that one, don'tcha, Girry-boy? Well, that's easy." She scooped her legs up onto the bench and burrowed her hands and wine-dark nose toward the warmth between her knees. She winked her thighs at him a bit, to give him a peek. With what was meant to be a sensual leer, she explained: "The people. The people in the snow. . . ."

He looked a bit frightened then, as though she had gone too far. He glanced up the deserted path: checking escape hatches?

"Now, now Tippy-lad. I shan't hurt you," she assured him. "I am but mad north-north-west." She stuck her finger in her mouth to moisten it, then held it up in the icy wind.

The sight of her index finger seemed to restore him to phallic meditations. "Marilyn," he said suddenly, his natural whine switching to a whirr, as though an egg beater were frothing him up somewhere. "Le's us go to my place."

She thought she detected a note of lechery in his tone and accepted quickly, before it whirred away.

She threw herself on the bed the moment they came to his room (Don't let them get the idea that they're seducing *you.*) "Well, Tippy-boy, what do you say, will you or won't you?"

"Will I or won't I *what?*" whirred Girard from the depths of his tucked-in scarf.

"Will you or won't you surrender your vital bodily fluids

to satiate the mad passion of one whorish, hottish, sluttish fe-male?"

"You are not a slut, Maa-ry," he assured her. (He insisted she had had a nice simple name once and must have changed it when she became involved in Women's Liberation.) "You ought never to say such things. . . ." (*Sich thangs:* it rang like German lieder in her ears so that she scarcely knew what he was saying; the soft syncopations of Dallas Gothic kept hoo-hooing in her mind like a flea in her crotch.) The fuzz could not break in upon nor custom stale the infinite variety of his Texas vowels. When he paused to swallow, she waited as if for a familiar aria. "Lovin' a man don't make a woman a sl-uh-ut. . . ." Syllable held for three beats: beautiful! Repeat. Deep down inside her, he went on to assure her, she was pure, she was virtuous, she subconsciously desired to be dominated by a strong, superior intelligent man. ("When Mr. Raa-t come along. . . .") That like every normal woman, she secretly longed for booties and bassinets and floured hands. Hadn't her great grand-daddy been at the Alamo?

"For Chrissake, that does it!" she said. "My grand-daddy was an Indian from Cuernavaca, and my daddy fathered three kids, most of them black as your Angus, and we rooted around in the slums of a border town for a way to smuggle rum for *los yanquis* —which we traded for United Juicy Fruit. My mother was strung out on United Juicy Fruit. By the time I was twelve I'd slept with both my big brothers and one uncle, and *since* then—."

Tippet held his hands crossed before his face, as if to ward off evil spirits. "You oughtn't not to talk lak that, Maa-ry, I know you and you a *good* woman. . . ."

"And you know what else? You know what I think about you? I think you're a faggot."

"A what?"

"A queer. A queen. A fairy. A gal-boy. I don't believe you can even get it up. Not for a real woman. Like me," she bragged huffily.

"So that you, is it, Maa-ry? A Ree-ull woman. And what about that snow?" he taunted. "You can't stay here screwin' the ranch hands forever. You got to git out and git yewzed to it."

Yewztet, Yewztet, Yewztet sucked at her brain like a new

ewe lamb, while to his pride and to her mollification her Texas transplant with the prepubescent larynx did get it up tolerably well. Then they got down to earth, as it were, and talked about the snow.

"O.K. I getcha," he nodded. "You scairt to death that stuff's goin' cover you all *over*."

Plumb over, she corrected him silently, then helped him out: "Yeah. Like a tomb." She'd been In Therapy and knew the links the shrinks loved to elicit.

"Wa-el. They ain't but one thing to do then, is there?"

She shuddered. When one of her countrymen considered final solutions, anything could happen.

"We got to go out there and *see* 'em."

"See whom?"

"*Them*, I said, *them*."

As a linguist she was ashamed to admit a failure in simple denotative communication. "Of course, *them*. But *who*?"

"The tombstones. In the snow. You said, didn't I hear you plain as daylight, 'like a tomb'. Well, that figures, don't it? We'll hie us on down to the Holy Trinity Church and we'll just *sit* there till we have a yew-know-what: a confrontation."

She should have known a Dallas boy would be daring all right.

"Put on your clothes," he ordered. " 'N put on a lot more *of* 'em. You lak to freeze your butt off, goin' to a Yankee cemetery in a short skirt lak that."

"Wa—el. Look around you," he said grandly about an hour later. "What do you see?"

"A cemetery," she said glumly. "A goddam motherfucking cemetery. What do *you* see? A herd of Brahmer bulls?" The snow continued to fall, swallowing up the air, welding earth and sky in one smothering cud-like mass. She clung to her companion's arm. Tippy as a more-or-less-Human Being was beginning to look better every second.

"Wa—el. What they put you in mind of? That's what you got to be lookin' for."

"Dead people. Funerals," she said, affecting an air of informed intelligence. "Cemeteries always do seem to remind me of dead people and funerals. My association-syndrome is queer that way. . . ."

"Aw, git down off yer high horse. No use yer fightin' me. We got to git to the bottom of this thang. L'es us sit down."

She shuddered. *"What? In—on the snow?"*

"Ain't goin' hurt you none. I kin *promise* you that."

After she had slid down to the icy surface she decided to punish him for making her sit (*sit!*) in the snow. "For Chrissake," she exclaimed, "why do you go on talking like that? I got the point long ago. A regular Ph.D. and all that, you don't have to talk like an idiot."

"Talkin' lak home ain't bein' an idiot. *Runnin'* from home's what's bein' an idiot. I homesick as a dawg, and I don't aim to change none either. I aim to *stay* homesick long's I live."

She shrugged. "Well, if you want to sound like Buffalo Bill in a rodeo show. Every man to his obsession. . . ."

"Wa—el. Don't you want to know why? (*whahh?*)"

She nodded and shrugged her simultaneous compliance and indifference.

" 'Cause Ah don't want to fergit nuthin' I ever been. 'Cause I don't want to wash my whole life unnerground. 'Cause bein' a goddam P. H. & D. don't matter to me as much as *not* bein' ashamed of what I used to be (*terbee*). Hell, when I first come up here, what I wanted to be was an actor."

Marilyn raised a rhetorical eyebrow. "An actor? Well, that's just what you are. The whole damned thing's an act. You *can* talk plain LBJ Amurrican then, can you?"

"Whenever it's expedient," he replied succinctly, and the shapely vowels of "Ideal American Speech" went round and round like a can opener circling an empty can. She stared at him with what she knew to be fear, as though like Humpty Dumpty, he were about to fall and break, irrevocably.

"But shucks," he added quickly, as though he sensed her reaction, "you don' wannoo hear none of that. What I'm fixin' to do, I'm fixin' to explain to you that what's under the snow, what the snow's coverin' *up*, so you cain't see nuthin' left, is your own life. . . ."

Marilyn turned to stare at the miles of tombstones, each one covered with a mound of snow, capped by a white monolith. She began counting, counting, as far as her eye could reach. Then her vision blurred.

"Nothing special about me," she observed. "Plenty of them covered up to their noses out here."

"That ain't what I mean," he said with something like passion. "You been fightin' and fleein' and forgettin' as fast as you was able for as long as you could—tryin' to forget all that border town jazz (oh don't try to make out to *me* you don't remember: I been to plenny of border towns and they the most godawful places God did ever place on this earth). And that's what you been hustlin' 'round here forgettin'—that you lived half your life 'fore you ever sawhr a Yankee. And then you seen the snow. . . ."

"Yes, Dr. Tippett." She made an effort to yawn, but her jaw felt stiff and she was as cold as . . . as cold as Death. (Man the torpedoes: who's afraid of a metaphor?)

" 'N you wuk up one mornin' and your life was clean washed away, nuthin' but a vast empty white plain openin' up before you. . . . Like fallin' into another planet. First thing," (*fust thang*) "you had to ask was, who are you, Marilyn Perales—and that was too much for you."

"Jesus!" exclaimed Marilyn. "With a line like that you ought to have gone to Hollywood."

"I been there," he shrugged. "It ain't much. I done *tole* you, I wanted to be an actor. And everywhere they said, 'You gotta drop that accent, southern boy. You cain't make it from *there*.' In New York, in the dramer, you cain't hardly get a part without their tellin' you: 'Drop that accent, boy.' Then I got me a part as a mime—."

"As a who?"

"You know. Where I wouldn't have to talk. But you know I got tired of *keepin' quiet*. So here Ah am. Take me or leave me, sugarbaby."

She stared at a snowflake melting on his nose (not a bad nose to be stuck between a pair of Sousaphonic ears), and at another which melted on his mouth. He licked at the stuff as though it were circus candy.

"Why don't we get the hell out of here?" she said.

"But why (*whahh*)? This is good for you. This is facin' up to Reality."

"I don't want to face up to reality," she said. "I want to lick that Texas drawl right off your lip, that's what I want to do. . . ."

This time he was much better. She tried to persuade him toward the end of the evening to drop his masquerade. She wanted to hear the Real Man, she challenged grandly.

"This ain't no masquerade," he protested. "This is me. The real me. You know how Jews go around talkin' up their Jewishness, and you'd think an Irishman'd never been out of County Cork? They're professionals. Like me. I'm a professional Texan."

"Well you must admit it sounds pretty kooky: a guy with a string of degrees from Harvard—or is it Yale—walks around sounding like the local yokel."

"Not Harvard," he said with distaste. "Johns Hopkins. Did my dissertation on the Victorian Novel and the Fallen Woman," he ended with a note of pride.

"What the *fuck* is a fallen woman?" she demanded.

"A fallen woman," he defined, "is a woman who commits fornication or adultery. A woman who gratifies her senses with a male partner—out of wedlock that is. A fallen woman is a sinner. Like you," he added blandly, momentarily dropping the lids over those hyperthyroid eyes of his.

"Oh come off it, Dr. Tippet. Do you really believe that crap?"

"Ah sure do," he nodded ponderously. "You know what's goin' to happen when you-all women get 'liberated'? You goin' to destroy the family, that what (*whuut*). . . ."

"You're kidding, Tippy. I mean, you're really putting on an act again, aren't you? There's no one in the nineteen seventies A.D. (*After* Domination) that really believes that it's the hymen that glues families together."

"You sure do put it crudely, m'am," he said and began zipping up his fly with an air of dismissal.

"Well, I have a first-night confession to make, Tippy-boy. I'm no virgin. I swear to you I'm not."

He shrugged. "Trouble with women today is, they want to sleep with a man and they want him to tell her lies. Now you *think* about that. . . . Are you liberated when you can't listen to what's true? I say, I don't believe what you say. I say, I don't believe women can be biologically free. But you want me to say that Ah do believe it. You want me to cozy awn up to you and say, 'Sure, you-all, you're equal to any man alive, now let's screw. . . .' You want me to change the old lies for new lies. Why cain't you just go to bed with me and let me believe what *I* believe, without making up a whole lotta script about when the revolution come, women won't have to have no more babies. . . ." In his excitement he had lost more and more of his accent and began to sound to her like any ordinary graduate student defending his thesis.

Marilyn rose from the bed and began putting on her clothes. It was about ten o'clock and a glance out the window told her the thick evening snowfall had come, the first flurries flinging themselves obliquely across the lamplight. Girard Tippet raised himself on one elbow to watch as she dressed.

"You goin' to run out on me, aren'tchoo? You ain't but a woman after all. Here I was tellin' you the truth 'cause it's the damned truth gonna make you free, no headshrinker nor no liberation committee either."

Marilyn nodded as she thrust her head through the port hole of her sweater. "O.K. So I'm biologically *not-free*, not yet anyway. You win. I got to have the kids, while you can go off and screw every chick in Texas if you want. If I were to be pregnant, I wouldn't be free to get myself thrown in jail in a protest movement, or get kicked in the belly by a cop . . . or even," she added with a stretch of heroism, "to fall and slip in a snowstorm. But one thing I don't have to do. I don't have to *marry* guys like you just 'cause you done had your big ole prick in my little ole psyche."

"In your pussy, why don't you say? That's all you 'free' women know how to do. You cain't do nuthin' but talk dirty. . . . It's free speech I reckon, though, huh?"

Marilyn had her hand on the door. Outdoors, the snow flew under the lamplight as if it had gone mad. The pathway lay covered with silence.

"And I'll tell you another thing," she said, opening the door slightly. "The reason I was afraid of snow . . . am afraid of the snow," she faltered, "wasn't that it was my past life, my buried life. It was my *future* life I was afraid of. . . ."

He began putting on his shoes idly, as though scarcely listening: but she knew he was.

". . . the emptiness of a *future* life without schmucks like you. Because in our loneliness, we need even schmucks like you."

"Wa—el, leastaways you admit it. You admit you need us, even if you do call us names."

"We need you," she echoed, "though you call us names: slut, whore, pussy, clit, fallen woman. . . ."

"Wa—el. Enjoyed it," he said laconically, and turned to the mirror.

"Me too," she said, and hurried into the silence.

How I Saved Mickey
from the Bomb

My name is Gabriel de Mirabeau. I am six years old, weigh 5 lbs. 2 oz. and stand exactly nine inches high. Like Mickey, I am a native New Yorker by birth, but when for the sake of the sunny climate Mickey elected to go to the University of Florida, naturally, I went along. I will say at once that the decision was entirely my own. There has never been any force in our relationship; whatever the issue, Mickey and I have always discussed it together and arrived at a mutually satisfactory solution. The only matter on which Mickey and I disagree is that of personal expenditure. She has a tendency to be extravagant where I am concerned, although I assure her that the luxuries in which she indulges me are totally unnecessary—that I am not the kind of dog that needs material things in order to feel that he is loved. Take the matter of food. Mickey insists that I share whatever she herself eats, no better, no worse. Whereas I know for a fact that Tarquinius, a Korean K-9 veteran who lives on our floor, eats a wretched mixture of ground meat and wheat germ every day. Also, with regard to sleeping arrangements: I have always had my own wicker basket, thickly padded with foam rubber, and a blanket besides. So you see I have never had to struggle for survival, for which reason some people think Mickey has spoiled me.

I do not agree with them at all. Mickey, it is true, allows me the run of the neighborhood, but I prefer to remain in our apartment where she has provided me with endless resources for self-education. I must say here that Mickey has never treated me like a child, and has always allowed me the same intellectual prerogatives she claims for herself. She has made no distinction for me, for example, since as a very young pup I first learned to read, between Browning and Burroughs, Lamartine and Lennon. So you see I have enjoyed all the advantages of a companion who has encouraged my development without the snobbery of a mistress who lives with a dog for the sole purpose of improving his mind. She has never, for instance, so much as suggested that I read *Call of the Wild* or Virginia Woolf's *Flush*, as if books written by or about dogs were the only ones which might interest me.

Although for the most part I prefer to remain at home among our books and records and few fine prints, I do enjoy social gatherings and Mickey rarely goes any place without me to escort her. If by chance we find one of those anachronistic little signs on the door which discriminate against those of us who have furred skins, she simply tucks me under her coat, cautioning me not to say a word. And so we pass through the marketplaces of the world unharmed. The only shop at which we have real trouble is at the Poodle Parlor where Mickey is always taking me to try on collars. It's the one subject we quarrel about. Such frills are much too expensive for us, we can't afford them, and I try to explain to her they are just vanities—a dog like myself doesn't need his manly pride sustained by such gew-gaws.

Since Mickey and I do go everywhere together, it was natural for me to be present one evening when she attended a special discussion group on the Survival of Man. It is a question which interests me considerably. I am not one of these dogs who thinks a wholly canine world offers any real solution to intrapersonal relationships. Just because I tend to favor my own kind like Tarquinius (shepherd), Pablo (Chihuahua), Limey (English sheep), Sheba (Doberman pinscher), and even that spiteful little Peke, Nguyen, nevertheless I do feel convinced that this would be a much better world if we continued to have men in it. I find the variety of species a source of inexpressible delight: it would indeed be a very boring world if all dogs were alike. You will perhaps argue that I feel this way about people because I love Mickey, and it is quite true, we would not have the problems today—the car-chasing, the involuntary mongrelism, the street-fights, and the increased need for leash and lash if everybody were like Mickey. But that is another problem which, if you care to discuss it with me, I shall be glad to take up with you at a later date.

At any rate, we arrived together, Mickey and I, at this little discussion group made up mainly of a few very dedicated people who belonged to the Association for Hamlet-wide Protection Against Nuclear Attack, or something like that. When we entered the room they were all already seated in an informal way around one of the tables in a corner. There was to be a Guest Speaker whom I identified at once by the way he stood at the head of the table, casually putting everyone at ease so people would not feel awed by the presence of a famous man in their small if significant circle.

The room in which the meeting was being held was not large —it was in fact the teachers' section of the high school cafeteria— but it certainly was not crowded either, and there was no valid reason, in my opinion, why Mickey should not have been allowed to bring a guest like myself to the discussion table. I even took note of the fact that old Mr. Fierbaum who lives in our building was there, and I was fairly certain that he was not a member of their association (he is nearly eighty years old).

When we sat down, however, there was a sudden hush and one or two persons, The Speaker included, took exception to my presence. I think now that they realized Mickey was not a regular member of the Association but had come with a natural and perhaps feminine desire to hear The Speaker explain how men might go on surviving. With a glance in our direction, one of the gentlemen from the Association observed pointedly that the discussion group—for obvious reasons—was for adults only. Now Mickey herself was twenty-three on her last birthday and looks a year or two older than she actually is, so we both understood at once that this rude observation was not intended for *her*. To my immense satisfaction (though from past experience I would not have expected Mickey to behave otherwise) Mickey replied, with a faint

flush of anger in her otherwise pale face, that I, Count Gabriel
Honoré Riquetti de Mirabeau *was* an adult, and she offered on
the spot to show the gentleman my birth certificate and rabies-
immunization record. I hurriedly whispered to Mickey that we
had better not engage in any verbal arguments over my presence
there, but rather that the best strategy would be simply to remain
seated as if we belonged there—a *fait accompli*. I felt pretty certain that if we did not raise any sort of *éclat* from the start that we
would soon be swallowed up in respectable middle-class
anonymity (Mickey was on that occasion sedately dressed in a
black voile suit with a rhinestone clasp, and I myself had been
freshly clipped and shaved—certainly we were not looking the
vagrant hippie type with ambiguous intentions: we did indeed
look as if we wanted to survive.)

Yet in spite of my display of insouciance there was something in the atmosphere, the very rut and drain of fear, which
from the very beginning seemed to permeate my delicate nervous
system in an extremely unsettling manner. In spite of my air of
bravado, and expressed assurances to Mickey, their collective rude-
ness had injured my *amour propre*. Mickey caressed my ear affec-
tionately once or twice as if she sensed this, but nevertheless I
was experiencing a growing *malaise* which seemed to go to the
very root and haunch—beg pardon—root and branch, of my
primordial memories. To climax my discomfort, I don't know
what it was, a *je ne sais quoi*, something elemental, something
atavistic perhaps, but from the moment The Speaker's voice registered on my auricular system, I became as nervous as a cat.

Perhaps it was Jungian racial memory, but from the mere
overtones of his speech I began instantly to distrust the man.
I am, after all, French; he was, after all, German: perhaps the
explanation was as simple as that.* From the time of the Visigoths'
invasion of Gaul down to the present historical moment our two
nations have struggled against each other for either physical or

---

* Of course I realize that the Germans have tried to spread a rumor that
"the French poodle *so-called* (italics mine) is not French at all, but German,"
but personally, after exhaustive study of the genealogical sources, I place
absolutely no credence in this rumor.

cultural victory. And now here we were in a situation where I was going to have to be not only courteous but positively deferential. It was more than my Gallic *esprit* could take lying down.

Perhaps to distract me, Mickey began to read to me in a soft undertone the brief details of The Speaker's life—his crusade against the forces of evil, his personal contribution to the development of the Big Bomb, his present dedication to the concept that in spite of the fact that all men are created mortal they shall, nevertheless, survive. I was not sure I had grasped the scientific data concerning The Speaker's personal contribution during World War Two, so I asked Mickey to hand me the mimeographed page, but she would not allow it: she refuses to let me do things in public which might be considered the least bit unusual.

The Speaker started out, as it were, on the wrong paw with me at once by talking about the need for organization and *obedience* during a thermonuclear attack. If we don't have some Plan, he said, during the holocaust following the bombing, some Leader will take over who would *enforce* discipline. . . . What we needed was a codified instrument of *Order*.

Now the word *obedience*, I must explain, immediately triggered in me a chain of reactions, solely neurogenic in origin, which made me extremely restive. I tried to camouflage my reaction with a sudden seizure of asthmatic coughing, but it was useless. I could not conceal my feelings from Mickey who, moreover, realized at once what was touching off this syndrome. She was well aware that my psychological reaction was in part the consequences of her early errors in bringing me up. Because it was she who, having raised me from puppyhood on doctrines of permissive behavior, had suddenly despaired of Freedom and longed for Discipline; so she had sent me off to an obedience school to learn to sit and heel. I spent an entire week at that military base called a "school," *achtunging* it around with my tail between my legs, marching behind a pair of cleated boots that offered nothing but dog biscuit (*dog* biscuit!) for its archaic Watson-stimulus-response type reward. The experience had been devastatingly traumatic, creating in me such intense anxiety symptoms that—it is peculiarly embarrassing to relate—I regressed into nocturnal, and even diurnal, bed-wetting. . . . Mickey had then insisted that, whatever the cost,

I must go to the very best psychologist at once, that I simply would be unable to live with myself unless I did. The psychologist had been an excellent one; he had immediately recognized that the bed-wetting was simply a reaction against compulsory military service: it sometimes happened to ROTC boys, he said.

I am endeavoring to explain to you as objectively as possible why it was that on this memorable evening, right under the auspices as it were of the Association for the Hamlet-Wide Protection Against Nuclear Attack, my urinary system began to exhibit such ominous symptoms of regression. And although I was careful not to complain about it to Mickey, she immediately recognized the dangers of my situation for what they were, because she picked me up and held me in such a manner (I do believe it was deliberate) as to clamp my legs tightly together across the erring aperture.

The Speaker, who evidently did not relish these demonstrations of what must have seemed to him mere maudlin tenderness, glared at me. And in spite of my discomfort, I glared back at him, flicking my ear with distinct bravado. And just to express my attitude toward obedience schools in general, I bit at an imaginary flea at the base of my tail.

At last—with a sigh of what was, I imagine, supposed to express superhuman patience—The Speaker went on to explain that it was not, in point of fact, a question of *obedience* and organization, but a matter of Reasonable Capacity for Recovery.

For a few minutes, under the spell of this verbal sleight-of-hand, I allowed myself to relax; my muscles unclenched their apprehensive grip upon my prostate, and although I could still feel a distinct tremor of response from this repetition of the dread word, I managed to listen to The Speaker with what I felt was a genuine effort (on my part, at least) at peaceful coexistence. True, he was my historical enemy—as directly descended from Attila the Hun, perhaps, as I from the Pope of Avignon—but I have little doubt that, intellectually speaking, he was my peer. And so I was busily constructing tolerant democratic syllogisms (all men are created equal, therefore The Speaker etc.) when the specialized vocabulary The Speaker was employing finally penetrated my canine intelligence and I realized from *what* we were all going to show this Reasonable Capacity to Recover. At the realization I leaped up on Mickey's shoulder in excitement and, had it not been that she warningly placed her finger to her lips, I veritably believe I would have snarled at the guest in a most ungentlemanly manner. After all, seventeen million dead (The Speaker's figures), even if they are not your own kind, is a not-insignificant percentage. I am not one of these dogs who can sit idly by while bombs one thousand times the power of Hiroshima are dropped over cities with millions of people in them. To me, no matter what other dogs may say, people are not inferior. Although I realize that they do show a certain instability of temperament, I am not convinced that this instability is caused by the necessity they experience of standing upright, causing—some dogs have insisted —an unnatural strain on the central vertebra. I believe this instability is to a large extent environmental, not hereditary, though I know there are many dogs who would disagree with me.

Mickey managed to calm me somewhat by taking me in her arms and kissing me gently on the forehead—something she never, ordinarily, does in public. She assured me that the figures The Speaker was using were not *facts*, but merely an example of the mania for statistics which learned people employ when, during moments of supreme irrationality, they wish to appear sane. She's very clever, that Mickey, and although I admit now that I did not—even at the time—wholly credit her explanation (of The Speaker's state of mind, that is), I did perhaps allow myself to be persuaded out of a cowardly sense of decorum. She even told me —and in my infinite canine vanity I accepted the preposterous assurance—that The Speaker was just trying to impress me, though I might well have asked myself: why should an educated speaker like him want to impress an ignorant dog like me? It was not as if he were speaking to Tarquinius who has served in Korea and has been twice "rehabilitated" in the course of which, under the counsel and care of several dog psychologists, Tarquinius has acquired the equivalent of a college education. Whereas, I, Gabriel de Mirabeau have had no formal education at all; I am merely one of these autodidactic types so disdained by Mr. Pope. The little I know I have learned only by rigorous self-application; and, alas, you know the proverb: "Self-taught, ill-wrought." The problem of modern English usage, for instance, has been an inconquerable barrier to me, and not seldom have I felt that for all Mickey's encouragement (and one might almost say, uxorious admiration), I should have had more formal schooling in my early months. To this day Tarquinius, for example, has an admirable command of the language of logistics and *matériel*, while I, on the other hand, am barely able to grasp even the most elementary scientific details offered by NASA. I *will* say in self-defense that the influx of new words in our language has rendered Mickey's old Merriam-Webster obsolete. For instance: *stock-piling*. I had always had the vague philological impression that the movements of stock took place at Wall Street. Stock went Up or stock went Down, but either way it went, it was all part of an extremely complicated science of the invisible.

Now on this fatal evening The Speaker confused me by insisting that it would be necessary for our nation to maintain stockpiles if we were to continue to be Masters of our Fate. We must, he said, stockpile enough for two years following The War: food, water, medicine, oxygen, tools, trucks, cars, refined gas, nuclear power plants—whatever, in short, would be enough to sustain 200 million people (only deducting the 10% who would not survive the blast). And my confusion derived solely from the fact that I did not grasp the modern meaning of the verb: to stock-pile. Before I could extricate myself, however, from this semantic dilemma, The Speaker had gone on to assure us that it would not be at all difficult for us to stockpile enough food and so forth for these more or less 200 million people because we already have a stockpile of unskilled, unemployed labor in our cities; that indeed, it was a stockpile of which we had too much. We must, he said, begin by employing this stockpile of labor to produce a stockpile of products. And we must stockpile medical personnel —physicians, nurses, orderlies, etc. Then, though we would not have the survival of individuals (he said he was sorry about that), we would have the survival of the nation. We must build under-ground, he said. We must have everything underground. We must, he repeated with growing passion, have our mass shelters for the *people* under the ground. Only in that way shall we be able to save the *people*. . . .

I must confess I was so carried away by The Speaker's eloquence that I failed at first to grasp the full import of his omissions. . . . Also, I realized that it was only natural for him to value his own kind above all others; so I accepted his impassioned rhetorical plea for the *people*, and even justified to myself his Antony-like oratory on the basis of the emergency he himself propounded. I awaited with blind naiveté to hear what aid and comfort The Speaker would offer the canine world. But none was forthcoming. In fact, in what seemed to me a crudely cold-hearted manner, he went on to discuss the construction details of shelters for *people*, without so much as an apology to those of us who would be left behind in the crush of the catastrophe, to wit: Tarquinius, Pablo, Limey, Sheba, Nguyen, and me.

This time nothing Mickey said could calm me. Lowering my voice as much as I could in spite of my rising agitation, I expressed my deep chagrin to her, and she agreed to speak up for me—though personally, she said, she did not think it would do any good. Nevertheless she agreed with me that someone ought to point out The Speaker's glaring omission. So my dear Mickey stood up and, with a timid glance in my direction and following my cue, as it were, she tried to make it clear that our objections were not founded on internecine jealousies: that we were far from coveting the five billion dollars which The Speaker proposed to spend every year for the next ten years on shelters for *people*, but she . . . we were only deeply hurt to think that not one dollar, not one cent had so far been suggested by The Speaker for the construction of dog shelters. And in what home in our land, Mickey went on in what seemed to me a very poignant and appealing manner, in what home is there not a dog? Even at the White House—.

Here someone caustically interrupted with the observation that all dogs could sink into the China Sea so far as he was concerned but he had thirteen cats: what about *them?*

A murmur which rippled through the audience showed that the interrogator had made a telling point. But then someone else tried to divert the audience from a consideration of Mickey's serious proposal by extending the problem to irrelevant and unmanageable proportions: that is, if we had canine shelters, wouldn't we also need equine, bovine, ursine, vulpine, and porcine shelters? And what about birds? Thus was Mickey's very reasonable suggestion hustled right off the forum. When she sat down again, I climbed, exhausted, back into her lap.

But at least Mickey's question seemed to have stimulated further thinking on the problem of shelters, because at this point a young man, who identified himself as a student of architectural engineering, addressed a question to The Speaker with regard to the actual per capita cost of *mass* underground shelters. The word *mass* elicited from me a truly visceral shudder, evoking as it did the very scent and sinew of barracks life—the shared privies and opened laundry bags and all the vulgarities of obedience. By this time, I must confess I was feeling extremely bitter at what seemed to me their people-centered plans for survival of *their* masses, while totally ignoring what seemed to me, if not a more urgent problem, then at least one which warranted equal justification of time, energy and financial outlay: that of dog shelters. And even cat shelters. But since our previous efforts to express our dissatisfaction had proven so fruitless, I now watched the proceedings with a jaundiced eye, disdaining to take part.

In discussing the problems of concrete and steel insulation against heat blast, the young engineer seemed to be making the point, if I understood him correctly, that the cost of such shelters in all our cities would be prohibitive.

At the question of money, The Speaker raised both hands in the air beneficently.

"Hardly anything! Hardly anything! Only ten per cent of our military budget—exclusive of Vietnam—will do the trick. Nothing fancy, of course—" (with a derisive glance at me) "—let's say at a cost of $500 per *person*—" (another glance at me) "we can have simple underground shelters with steel protection for *people*. Actually, what it amounts to in our cities would be a system of underground tunnels in which people would live for not more than two weeks. Since of course they would be obliged to come out for short periods to clean up. . . ."

"But if everything has been levelled by the blast . . . ," hinted the engineer.

"*Levelled* but not *destroyed* . . . not incinerated! We must clean up the bodies, preserve order, prevent disease, avoid chaos. . . ."

The same young man now engaged The Speaker in a brief but confusing dialogue which I confess I was unable to follow very well, partly because I was nursing my own canine grievances, and partly because statistics is a subject which, even under the best of conditions, I find bewildering. In retrospect it seems to me there must have been some disagreement between The Speaker and the engineer as to how many people would be "lost." The engineer claimed that The Speaker had originally said 17 million people would be "lost" in the United States, but that 90% would be "saved." Now he, the engineer, had projected a population growth chart which showed that during the supposed ten-year grace period before The War should break out (during which time we would hypothetically be building our shelters), our population, at an annual increase of 1.7 million per year computed on the present base of 200 million would have increased by 36,719,-336—rounded off to the nearest person. Now—the engineer went on lucidly to explain—if we lost 10% of that projected population we would have lost (an odd smile of triumph appeared on the engineer's face as he raised all ten fingers reprovingly at The Speaker) *not* 17 million but 23,671,933.6 people. . . .

There was a mild rustle of shock at this attack on The Speaker's infallibility. It was plain that in matters mathematical The Speaker was regarded as speaking, always, *ex cathedra* and had never before been challenged.

But Our Speaker was imperturbable. He shook his head in the way I have seen old Tarquinius move away from pesky flies, without so much as a shake or a gnash of jaws—merely a massive self-removal: of body, of psyche, of personal involvement. Only The Speaker's hands were raised before us—solemn, unmoving, demanding reverence as he bestowed his benediction.

"Nobody can tell you exactly *when* there would be War," he said with equanimity. "In four years? In six years? In eight years? In ten? But I feel that with defensive warfare we would never have War. And with respect to the exact losses, I say this much: you will lose the forests, you will lose the cities, but how many people exactly that you will lose, that cannot be calculated exactly."

146

The young engineer, however, insisted on his peculiar brand of logic: "But if you lose the cities and the people are *in* the cities? . . ."

Again the broad hands waved their blessing.

"Ah, but what kind of cities are we talking about? In the big cities, you need only the blast shelters; in the smaller places what you will need is radiation shelters. Of course you need food, water, oxygen—but everything can be quite simple. If everything is done as I say, even in a sudden accidental war, we would save 90% of even," he smiled tenderly at the engineer, "a *projected* population."

"Accidental war? *Accidental?*" somebody was interrupting.

For several seconds I could not relate the strange piping voice to any of the people present, for the voice seemed to be that of a ten-year old child. I soon realized, however, that the voice belonged to a young man who now stood—in an heroic effort to imitate the deference of his predecessors who had all risen when they addressed The Speaker—gripping the table while he straightened himself slowly and painfully on his brace-heavy legs. In this neuter, piping voice he informed The Speaker that he had been reading an article which predicted that with the increase of nuclear weapons there was a 40 per cent chance of accidental war within the next generation.

The Speaker's eyes glowed prophetically. "*Nobody,*" he said, "absolutely nobody can predict the probability of accidental war. In the first place, the variables are immense. . . ." The Speaker then went on rationally to enumerate the variables: whether the "accidental" attack came from Russia or the "accidental" attack came from China or whether "accidental" attack killed one million people during its first strike or whether the "accidental" attack merely knocked over a kerosene lamp in a cowshed, or whether in an "accidental" attack we had adequate ABM or not. . . .

But at this point, just when my own confusion among the variables had become overwhelming, so that I was hiding my head under Mickey's arm in desperation, old Mr. Fierbaum suddenly rose to his feet. Mr. Fierbaum had lived in New York over twenty years since the Last War and knew Mickey's parents. She would sometimes stop to chat with him as we waited for the elevator, and he would ask her about her parents in Queens and how did she like the University here as compared with Queens, and other such human matters which old men apparently find an inexhaustible source of conversation. Mr. Fierbaum was homesick for New York and considered that he lived in exile under the Florida sun—the only compensation being, he used to say in his heavy Russian accent, that he continued to live. . . . Mr. Fierbaum had survived many horrors, and it was only of late, Mickey said, that his mind had become confused, so that the horrors he had actually suffered during the war had somehow merged with events which he had subsequently only read about: for instance, he believed that he had seen his own name carved in the Jewish mausoleum at Prague, which any dog, of course, will tell you is impossible.

When Mr. Fierbaum now stood up I scarcely recognized him. I had always thought of him as a melancholy but peaceful old man who wouldn't hurt a flea. But when he stood up to confront The Speaker, his face was livid, his hand gripped his cane as though it were a sabre; and when he finally overcame his emotion so that he was able to articulate his words, they came out in a high, weird treble, as if they had begun as a scream deep in his groin, slowly travelled upward, and finally emerged in this shrill, keening sound, something between a crackle and a groan. Mickey covered my ears caressingly as though to prevent me from hearing what old Mr. Fierbaum was saying. I sensed somehow that Mickey herself was more frightened of the old man than of The Speaker —as though The Speaker were only a phantom in a nightmare which she knew she was dreaming, but old Mr. Fierbaum was a genuine Rider of the Apocalypse.

"What you're saying, young man," Mr. Fierbaum managed at last to pronounce, "what you're saying, young man, is that in a thermonuclear war more than fifty million people will . . . ," the flaccid muscles of Mr. Fierbaum's face contorted convulsively ". . . millions of people will . . . simply . . . *die*. . . ."

The Speaker gave a patient philosophic shrug, smiling wearily.

"Not so simple. Not so simple. War is not a picnic. And this, *this*, will be total war. Because other countries have already spent ten times as much on civil defense as the United States. We, *we* are not ready. *We,* even if we start now, this very night, we would need at least four years to catch up. And we must start immediately: that is my message."

"Your message, sir," said the old man, "is fear and trembling and sickness unto death. . . . You know nothing what you speak about. You have not seen the bodies. I, *I* have seen the bodies, piled up. . . . I have seen them at Prague, I have seen them at Maidanek, at Treblinka, at Dachau. . . . People will die from the very stench of the bodies from the *stockpiling* of dead bodies. In my city alone, in New York City alone, where I lived for more than twenty years since the war, in one block maybe three thousand people live together, all my neighbors. . . . Old people, young people, children, cripples, people in hospitals, people high up—thousands of feet in the air—." The old man's voice broke; he looked as if he were about to begin sobbing in the harsh, dry hopeless tones of an old man.

There was a terrified hush among us. People began to collect notebooks, scarves, pocketbooks, any material thing to which they could cling and prepare to depart in peace and decorum. It was as if the old man had begun to toll some unanimous, subconscious alarum, signalling their common flight.

But The Speaker was more than equal to the situation; indeed, everyone calmed down at once as soon as they realized that The Speaker had only been waiting for this supreme moment to discuss his most persuasive points.

"Ah, I am so glad, so glad you have brought up this question of New York. New York is the *one* city, in my opinion, which will be . . . would be the most defended city against attack, not only here, but in *all the world.* . . . *If* we have ABM, *if* we have ballastic missile defense, no bomb can touch New York City. And, in fact, we *must* have ballastic missile defense, because actually, you know—," he smiled at the paradox of his argument, "the buildings there are so high the people wouldn't have time to get downstairs anyway. . . ."

At this whimsical *obiter dictum,* I felt a shudder go through Mickey's body and she burst into tears. Her parents, relatives, friends of her childhood, all still lived in New York, and, as she told me later, the mental image of her arthritic grandfather in the Bronx laboriously descending a six-flight walk-up to get to the bomb shelter (within a five-minute alert), and the idea of her own parents in Queens—the very soul of gentleness, they are—fighting with their neighbors in order to get into the only available elevator (to say nothing, as she afterwards told me, of the necessity of abandoning their dog who was *my* grandmother), had been altogether too much for her. She began weeping hysterically.

Now I will tell you, I felt that all along I had been a superbly patient dog. I had accepted the acrimonious insults upon my arrival concerning my age and maturity; I had listened to The Speaker ignore and ridicule millions of my own kind; I had witnessed the lame and the halt and the purblind jiggling their statistics and building their concrete fortresses over the very bones of my grandfathers, as it were, and I had sat quietly through it all, conscientiously concerned with the care and control of my urinary bladder, so as not to disturb their *danse macabre*.

But here was my Mickey, whom I loved this side of idolatry, reduced to tears by someone who represented himself in my Jungian memories as a heavy-booted Prussian rolling out the ballastic missiles like panzer divisions. *"Schweinhund,"* I growled in my throat . . . and then . . . and then (the very thought today makes me tremble with humiliation). I began *barking* at the Guest Speaker. It was no sham yakkety-yak-yak either. I was furious, and if I could have managed to get his gigantic Teutonic scrotum between my delicate Gallic jaws, I would have crunched a thing or two. But all I could do—due to limitations imposed by his height —was terrify him with the perfect simplicity of my violence. I barked. I barked and barked. Nothing anyone could do was able to stop me. Even Mickey was helpless before my savage onslaught. When they tried to catch me, with Darwinian precocity I made a survival tactic of my size and slipped under a chair or a desk, and then finally behind the wastebasket—from which invulnerable position I let fall a volley of insults which would have reduced any countryman of mine to a jellied nonentity.

It was Mickey who at last scooped me up with an all-embracing tenderness and, kissing me and scolding me both at once while the tears continued to flow down her cheeks, carried me back to the discussion table. Here, with caresses and blandishments did she beguile me. Here, my cup of humiliation was truly drunk to its dregs. Here, before I could protest, Mickey had opened my mouth and gently slid several valium pills down my throat (she licked them herself in order to deceive me—a fact which I have continued to hold against her). These pills acted at once as a total anesthesia upon my overcharged nervous system, and within a few minutes I not only dozed, I slept, and if Mickey's account of it is to be credited (which of course it must be: a home life in which Mickey and I could no longer believe each other would not be a life at all but something worse, even, than being the head of a political party) —if Mickey's account is to be credited, then, I even snored.* Which I give you my word as a French gentleman, I have never done before in my life—at least certainly not in public.

What occurred when my valor was rendered worse than useless by valium, may be explained by my dream. And the dream, of course, will be quite transparent to all who have heard what has gone before, including my own particular psychogenic syndrome.

I dreamed that Mickey and I were back in New York, spending the week-end with friends who lived near Columbia. For some reason the friends were not there, but Mr. Fierbaum was there looking, however, not like himself but very much like Mickey's grandfather living in the Bronx—only in the dream Mr. Fierbaum spoke with strange Prussian mannerisms and wore cleated boots. On the day in question Mickey was knitting a sweater for me, Mr. Fierbaum was reading the newspaper, and I was looking out the window at a pretty little thing who sat scratching herself in the sun on the steps of St. John the Divine.

Suddenly there was a sound as of a million howling dogs, and the building began to tremble with the sound of running feet.

"It's the Bomb," said Mickey quietly and, folding up her knitting, she took another bite of her apple. Then she said to me

---

* In self-defense, I have since made inquiries, and the dosage which Mickey slipped me is equivalent, in a canine body weighing approximately five pounds, to swigging down a fifth of bourbon.

in the tone she uses for our evening walks: "Let's go." Mr. Fierbaum followed, banging his cane angrily against the door.

We walked out to the hallway to the elevator in the center of the building. But it was full. In it were a cow, a bear, a wolf, a pig, and thirteen cats. The cats were curled around the inner cage like monkeys, and as they passed they hissed at me, crying out triumphantly: "No dogs! No dogs allowed!"

In protest, all the dogs of the building gathered around, including Tarquinius, Pablo, Limey, Sheba, and even Nguyen— all complaining that we were being discriminated against, that the elevator was being monopolized by the bovine, the ursine, the vulpine, the porcine—and, especially—the feline. As if in confirmation of our worst fears, The Speaker suddenly appeared in the hallway and repeated with authority: "No dogs! No dogs allowed!" At this moment the architectural engineer suddenly appeared.

"We have plenty of time," he said slowly. "This building will stand. It is built on the core principle. The core is ½ the base and ⅓ as high. . . . Only the outer part will be crushed. . . ."

"There are no such buildings in New York," said Mr. Fierbaum.

"I am not speaking of New York. I am speaking of Florida," said the engineer. "In Florida there is no way for people to go underground. Because of the sand and because of the 30,000 lakes."

"Damn your 30,000 lakes," said Mr. Fierbaum.

We glided soundlessly down the staircase. At every floor we stopped and buzzed for the elevator, waiting patiently to see if the porcines and felines would send the elevator up the well. But we heard only the yowling of cats. So we began walking again. At the sixth floor we stopped. There was the distinct smell of smoke.

"Fire storms," announced Mr. Fierbaum with a significant wink at me.

But The Speaker raised his hands in a *benedicite:* "Fire storms will occur only in California, New Mexico, Arizona, Texas and Colorado, where the forests will be lost. Last year the rainfall in New York City was 42.37 inches. Therefore there is no need to worry about the forests in New York City."

The smoke funneled up the staircase. Mr. Fierbaum leaned over the bannister, spit directly into the stairwell, and yelled: "Put out that cigarette down there!" Then he turned to me, grinning with the sharp, triumphant joy of a prophet.

Meanwhile I kept close to the wall for fear of being crushed by The Speaker whose great legs were sometimes beside me and sometimes over me. Mickey remained calm throughout. Only now and then she took a bite of her apple. When we reached the ground floor she deposited the core in the refuse can on which the sign *Beautify America: Deposit Litter Here* was slowly melting from the heat.

"We must go underground," said The Speaker. So we circled the ninth flight of stairs and came to the entrance of the basement. The smoke was now so thick that I could no longer see Mr. Fierbaum nor the engineer. Apparently they had been overcome by smoke. One by one, also, the dogs had stopped along the staircase, some exhausted from the descent and the heat, and others to scratch wildly at their fleas. The atmosphere did indeed seem conducive to the proliferation of fleas and I noticed that several had come to burrow under my collar for shelter.

From the mouth of the boiler room (our shelter) issued clouds of smoke, grey and symmetrical as umbrellas. There seemed at first to be no fire, only this choking, annihilating cloud of smoke.

"The shelter is on fire," said Mickey.

"There is no fire," said The Speaker. "It is only fallout."

"Oh," said Mickey. "Will it not contaminate the world?"

"Nonsense," said The Speaker. "It would take one Hiroshima-sized bomb on every square mile of the earth's surface to do that. Now who has time for such things? We have only five minutes to reach our shelter—so hurry."

"But there *is* a fire," said Mickey as the flames licked around our feet. "I cannot bear the heat. I cannot go in there. What shall I do?"

"You *must*," commanded The Speaker. "In the Year of the Holocaust we need *obedience*."

Then it was that at the word *obedience* I felt a surge of fire spread throughout my body. My bladder swelled like a great navigable balloon, and it was precisely at that instant that I experienced my greatest inspiration. In a flash I recalled how Lemuel Gulliver had saved the Emperor's Palace from the flames; and, arching my back like a bow, I lifted my hind leg in an arc *de triomphe.*

The next instant I was awake; The Speaker had seized me by the scruff of the neck and was trouncing me soundly. Like a drunk flung from a barroom, I was ejected from the discussion table in utter disgrace. And as I fell yelping to the sidewalk—you may imagine I was now fully awake—I saw from the corner of my eye that The Speaker, having removed his saturated shoe, was furiously engaged in shaking his trousers. . . .

In retrospect, in spite of the ignominiousness of my ejection, it seems to me that there was great glory in the manner in which I extinguished the blaze in the bomb shelter. In fact, I am secretly so pleased with my feat that I have taken up archery lessons, so to speak, and I can now hit a target dead-center at three feet. Since that evening I have also been doing research on Heroic Feats—on the age and species of the Hero, on the situation and manner in which the rescue is conducted, etc. And wherever I walk with Mickey I keep an eye out for even rudimentary escape hatches as well as for poolhall rallying corners where, in an emergency, one might receive voluntary assistance from street dogs; so that, when the emergency arises I will be in a position to fully realize what so far I have merely dreamed of: I will be able to put out real fires instead of imaginary ones, and I will be able soon, very soon, to show Mickey how I can be Dog of the Year in the Year of the Holocaust.

The End of The World

Kaethe Kluge—Kate to her friends—was blonde, chunky and loved a good laugh. She believed the end of the world was coming, not in any religious sense, but simply, casually, with no diabolical intent but just the way under-the-arms is the first place a dress rips. It was the sweat that did it, there was nothing one could do about it. Some of Kate's friends were joining communes, they foresaw the end of the nuclear family. Others were laughing or nodding themselves to death on grass or smack; but Kate stayed away from all that, preferring to go out neither grinning nor sleeping but in her right mind. When the time came she was going to stand on a mountain top (she imagined herself somewhere in Nevada), and watch the fire storms from L.A. shake the trees out of their roots.

In the meantime one had to survive, and one stayed clear of jobs that could be called commitments. Kate could have told her friends a dozen ways to survive besides selling their books. But the best way of all, the blood bank, she simply kept to herself, knowing that it took more stomach than most, and scorning any one-upsmanship with her friends.

The first time, she herself had keeled over. The sight of the cold-looking instruments and of her own blood welling into the plastic tube was what did it. But she had got used to it. All her friends knew of it was that twice a month Kate disappeared for the weekend, turned up with fifteen dollars which she promptly spent at the students' co-op for a bag of brown rice, a sack of pinto beans, three pounds of powdered milk and a can of soy bean oil. As to fresh vegetables, that kind of thing, it was rumored that Kate was often seen sauntering down Milford Avenue with an open shopping bag—out on maneuvers, they said.

But the fact was that Kate rarely found it necessary to use her shopping bag for edibles; she reserved it instead for such inarguable necessities as toothpaste, scotch tape and notepaper: she claimed she was keeping a journal for the time capsules, something she predicted would become a popular fad toward the end.

All this required no preparation and no regimen, she could let things slide. But when she met Jésus Quatre-vingts (was it his real name? her friends asked; but Kate only shrugged: if it was *his* name, it was real), she understood at once that he was a threat to her freedom. Waiting for the end of the world was a safe enough thing, she had discovered, but falling in love quite another. For the first time in her life she was seized by a desire to buy land, plant seeds, overcome popular prejudice by being a perfect example of something.

Quatre-vingts was very tall and lean, his pupils seemed ringed with iridescent shades of blue to light purple like the throat of a pigeon. And he had those corkscrew earlocks that, as a child, had made her weep when she had realized that they were nailing Him down to the cross. In the picture the sweat had run from His curls, just like Quatre-vingts' when she had met him at the blood bank.

She had had no supper that evening and was feeling woozy anyway. She was thinking, when she got the money she'd go out and blow a third of it on a steak at Masschio's. To-hell-with-it-you-only-live-once, you know, that sort of thing. Not far from her were a couple of winos, grumbling that it was taking so long today. One of them had come fifty miles, from over the state line and claimed he was dead tired: though he didn't stop talking for a minute. He was explaining the ropes to the younger guy alongside him, who didn't want to have a thing to do with it, but listened anyway, the TV set being out of order. The old guy sold his blood like apples: he was a professional; he said they didn't keep track of you if you travelled from one town to another; you could go in every week to a different one and they wouldn't notice. Only he wasn't feeling up to it any more. The wine built up your blood but it didn't do much else good. He went on to show a sore elbow that hadn't healed. Also some black-and-blue spots on his legs. "Bad sign," he said. "You're not usin' up the sugar fast's you're takin' it in." The other wino nodded indifferently. It was clear that he was fresher, newer at the trade and he was bored by stories of failure; he had his own row to hoe, all he needed was a gallon of Gallo, he said, and he'd be ready for the job in the morning. "Job? What job?" asked the older man. The younger seemed to reflect a moment, caressing his veins tenderly. "Clean-up man. A couple of churches over to the Hill district." "You gonna clean churches for the *colored?*" The older man's ruddy face turned beet-red with digust.

It was at this point Quatre-vingts had come in. He was bare-footed and that was all Kate could see, as she was lying down, waiting her turn. The attendant had directed him to a table beside hers. She had noticed how slowly he swung his body back onto the table, briefly balancing his weight on the palms of his hands, then with a great sigh he leaned his head back on the table as though he had come there to rest. He turned to look at Kate. His eyes were so deep in his head they seemed sculptured in a vein of stone, with the rings of the pupils shading chromatically outward from the dark pool at the center. As Kate lay there staring, she felt herself falling into his vision as soundlessly as a swimmer who knows his own power and the depth of the plunge. They lay there silently a few moments, then seized by her own comic demon, Kate had cried out with mock terror: "I'm innocent, innocent! Let me go, and I'll tell all...." Quatre-vingts had grinned and muttered under his breath in movie tones, pseudo-heroic: "Just stick with me, do exactly as I say, and we'll both get out of here alive—I promise you that." During the interval before the attendants return they plotted strategies of "escape." . . . Quatre-vingts had begun to laugh, his joy and recognition resounding through the blood bank.

When he laughed, Kate noticed that he had several teeth

missing. It had made her heart ache as though she herself had lost something precious, not having been there when he lost them. She would have said something to comfort him, perhaps: it was clear to her that at this rate, he'd never have money for new ones. Perhaps it was that she was already lightheaded and supperless, but the dark wounds in the laughing mouth had hit her like a bomb, her mood of merriment had suddenly vanished and, instead, a tear rolled down her cheek.

Quatre-vingts had risen from the table. Her eyes fell to the omega sign he wore around his throat; she could see the bones at his neck, thin as knives; and she continued to cry.

"Say, kid, why're you crying? Hey, don't do that. You'll be out of here in a minute. . . . It won't hurt. You won't feel a thing, I mean it."

She knew it was only hysteria and hypoglycemia (or whatever the damned word was) but she couldn't stop. "For a lousy fifteen bucks," she whimpered. "For a goddam lousy fifteen bucks," she sobbed, "they'd crucify Jesus himself."

"Say, kid, how'd you know my name?" he laughed.

And that's how they fell in love. On their way out of the place, the two winos stared at them, they were already holding hands. "Where those two think they're goin'?" demanded the younger sourly. "They're gettin' married," announced the older as if he'd known them all his life. "Oh yeah? And what the fuck they gonna live on?" "Blood," chortled the old wino. "They gonna live on blood."

When Kate had told her mother about Quatre-vingts, Mrs. Kluge had sighed and reminded Kate that she had already been through one marriage to a sweet-looking angel who hadn't made enough money to support his habit.

"But, Mother," Kate argued good-naturedly. "It was you taught me not to be money-minded—told me all about the Rich Man, the one who was going to get his fat stomach stuck in the eye of the needle."

"But that doesn't mean you have to go and marry every bleeding heart you see, does it?" said Mrs. Kluge.

"Well, all I can say is," Kate continued, "that you have only yourself to blame. All those pictures of Him you used to keep tacked all over the goddamned wall. So now naturally when I see anybody looks like him, I just fall all over myself to be in love first thing."

Mrs. Kluge had accepted the injustice blandly. "Well, when you get pregnant, be sure and tell 'em it was the Holy Ghost. . . ."

"Mother . . . people don't get pregnant anymore," Kate said.

Her mother raised an eyebrow. "They don't? . . ."

Kate hadn't answered: because regardless of mother-warnings Quatre-vingts was who Kate wanted, even if the end of the world were to be tomorrow. And on that subject, he and she were of one mind. They believed that People had had it, that Population and the Unthinkable were going to get them before too long. So they made love as though they were on a Sunday school picnic that was scheduled to last till the last megaton bomb. And theirs could have continued to be the savored joy of those who shut themselves off from the plague to tell each other stories, except that (of course, Quatre-vingts said) Kate became mysteriously pregnant. At first they couldn't dig it, and cursed the statistical warranty of the pill-makers who, they said, were probably also turning over a few shares in maternity hospitals. Then they laughed and said what the hell, why not? Having a kid wouldn't halt the apocalypse, but one slightly breathing child wouldn't pollute the air very much either.

But vitamins, iron pills, calcium tablets—these had never been among Kate's inarguable necessities. Such items strained the image of colossal indifference she had used to make as she strolled through the open-shelf drug stores: she was getting too big, in her sixth month, to look indifferent to anything. So Quatre-vingts decided they would swing it somehow with two blood bank visits a month (his), plus one night a week washing glasses at the local bar. And he brought home the entire ten bucks too; the owner of the bar didn't even bother to take out social security, health insurance, that kind of crap intended for when the world was young.

The baby was to be called Consuelo—their Consolation: what else had they found that distracted them so utterly from Armageddon? They found themselves considering unheard-of sacrifices for this generation they believed they'd never live to see. Quatre-vingts even started talking about going to school—they paid people to let themselves be taught how to teach other people, he explained. But Kate was not ready for such commitments. Besides, all her teachers had been a drag, she said: products working to produce products for the Establishment. So Quatre-vingts said, "O.K., Let's wait and see." Meanwhile he enrolled in a course in Hindi at the Free University. "Who knows? Maybe we'll go to India, learn how to be non-violent." Kate smiled and echoed dreamily: "Who knows?"

The seventh month, the eighth, and finally the ninth. Money was more and more tight, they wouldn't take Kate at the blood bank. She couldn't have swiped a hair pin without the Keystone cops coming after her, she was that big. Then towards the end of the last month she noticed for the first time a tremor in Quatre-vingts' hand as he poured their coffee; and he began falling asleep in his chair, his hand dropping silently to the floor. Kate suspected he was taking side trips, away from the inner city, to blood banks where they didn't know him. How many trips she couldn't know, but he brought things home regularly—safety pins, teething rings, calcium tablets. She began to be afraid for the first time in her life, but said nothing. It was too close to the last week of her time.

At last they thought her time had come, but it turned out to be false labor; then the doctor required x-rays, measurement of the pelvis and all that. The bastard just wants to scare me, Kate decided. Make it look like twins, quints, Caesarean sections and concomitant appendectomies. Make himself look like a big Herr Doktor. But finally the doctor simply directed Kate to take some pills and to sit with her feet propped up: what the hell, what Chinese peasant sat around with her feet propped up to have a baby? She ignored the doctor and her ankles swelled up like cotton candy.

Twelve days later the doctor was proved right. "O.K., O.K.," she was ready to admit she was wrong; it had been a bad scene, but now it was over and they had their Consuelo. Kate had been in the hospital over a week and they were going to release her as soon as they'd run a series of tests on Consuelo. The tests turned out O.K. Consuelo was a great kid, and that was lucky, at least. They had their future, their consolation.

160

But suddenly the future broke in two, leaving only Consuelo. Kate, who had been awaiting the end of the world for so long, was shocked but unastonished: it was a way for the world to end.

During the second week of her hospitalization—she'd been very sick, one bad scene after another, with fever and mastitis and freaky nurses—Quatre-vingts had been found slumped up against a fire hydrant along Second Avenue, not far from the blood bank—sound asleep. A friend who had picked him up knew instantly that he was not drunk, just wasn't getting enough oxygen in his brain to stay awake. "Christ," the friend had said, offended and grieved, "if you needed money that bad, why didn't you ask me?" "I need money that bad," Quatre-vingts had replied, "and now I'm askin'." The friend, however, didn't have any bread himself: what he had was a lead on a job. Not a nine to five, but something cool that would keep them together, Consuelo, Kate and Quatre-vingts. A job that paid real bread and they could put money in banks instead of blood, "ha ha," the friend had joked encouragingly. And he got Quatre-vingts a job at the check-out counter of the Shop 'n Save. Most of the night it was quiet, the friend said, you read or dozed by the counter. In the early morning the breakfast shoppers would hurry in, half-asleep, for a loaf of bread, a carton of milk, that sort of thing. On this particular morning, along with the silence, had appeared an armed robber— or rather two or perhaps three: nobody ever figured it out, nobody was ever really arrested, though a suspect was picked up in the desert in California and beaten up by the fuzz just for show. The killers had ordered Quatre-vingts into the food locker, filled his head full of holes and left him to freeze. He was found by the morning sweep-out man who was the first to open the cooler. Quatre-vingts lay in a pool of half-frozen blood.

He was shot up so badly they wouldn't even open the coffin. At least that's what they told her. The company had paid for the funeral. Plastic flower wreaths ringed the coffin, which seemed to Kate not much bigger than a shoe box: though Quatre-vingts was tall, very tall. At another time the cheap wreaths feigning melancholy affluence would have fired her with rage. But Kate was thinking hard and without amusement that the guy in the shoe box, whoever he was, certainly was not Quatre-vingts. The whole thing was a put-on. What it was: Quatre-vingts had wanted to go to India, that's all; and he and his friends had planned this hoax between them. The rest of the world might believe it, but not she, not she. Somewhere in India Quatre-vingts was meditating; so it was clear that the thing to do was to follow him there.

So as soon as the funeral was over, Kate returned to their room, packed a small duffel bag and strapped Consuelo across her bosom, hammock-fashion. She stopped off at the local Family Service long enough to pick up a check they had promised her "to help make her way in the world again," then she flew one-way to Amsterdam. From there she wrote her mother that she was going to walk to India, begging all the way. And she did.

Bye Bye Birdie

My job was to clean the cages. As a consequence of my love of adventure, I'd been forced back to work. Unfair: too high a price to pay for a little excitement. Every year, all during the nine months of school, I'd swear that I *would* manage better —eat less, walk more, save money, beat the rap. And every summer found me like Oedipus at Colonnus, tap-tapping my way in beggary. Reader, if I could give you a list of summer jobs I've had, you'd weep. If it's standing guard over tombstones in pet cemeteries, or washing bottles for urologists, or bobbing babies into bassinets, or bloodletting at bloodbanks: in short, any Augean stable avoided by the whole of civilized man, *me voilà*, Bernard Klein.

That summer it had been a whanging trip to Salt Lake City with my girl, Molly, and my good friend, Bob Bischoff. And why Salt Lake City? Why, to see something I hadn't seen before. Like the Mormon Temple. Latter-day Saints. The Dugway Proving Ground. Anything. I may as well confess, I'm hooked on novelty. What's new by me is good. Tell me there's an iceberg in the Gobi desert and I'll try to get there before it goes away. About ten years ago my grade school teacher announced there'd be a duck-billed platypus at the petting zoo; and I believed her: I walked all the way into town to see it. A schmuck.

But now I was paying for this tragic flaw—or, to bring

Tragedy up to date—what you might call a credibility gap. Pigeons and doves, doves and pigeons. As I slanted my spatula across the trays of frothy elixir (chemical changes), I tried to remind myself that such birds were romantic: that there were people who were known to be dovelike, that there was a novel by James known as *The Wings of the Dove;* and that Noah, when he wanted to see if the world was still out there sent a dove across the still waters. To no avail. The trays of the doves still stank. As I loaded the prodigious heaps into tubes, barrels, aqueducts—it was a veritable TVA project—I mournfully recalled what folly had sucked me into the pit.

It was like this. One afternoon dense with that tropical humidity that keeps east Texas in the Age of Reptiles, I was cramming for my geology exam when Bischoff flew in and perched on the bed opposite me.

"We're leaving! leaving! going! going!" he crowed, flapping his arms wide with anticipation. Then he pulled off his shoes and socks and began to cool his feet by spreading his toes like an aersol bomb onto the air.

"Would you turn those feet *off*, please?" I said. "I'm sensitive—."

"Sensitive! You're a goddam bloody E–63 Manpack Personnel Detector!" he exclaimed. Bob talks like that. He's just come back from doing his stint in Vietnam and he's full of these exotic references.

"Going where?" I added somewhat more politely, turning the fan so as to shift the wind in *his* direction.

"On a trip, man. To the lovely Anywhere & Anytime that'll get us out of this godawful town. There's a sign up in the student union—this guy needs drivers to Salt Lake City. And I tell you, Bernie, to get out of these tropics, I'd fly my 'copter over Hill 631, I would . . . ." Then he pointed his chin toward his navel in those special exercises he does to correct a spinal injury he got during one of those unpronounceable Viet battles.

"But what about my geology exam?" I whined.

"Well, what about it?" Bob challenged. "Will your rocks be gone when we get back?"

I felt, of course, that this was unanswerable: so I went. And we would have had a great time too—a graduate student in Classics had a party just for us—except that people at the party insisted on talking about their V-X gas.

"They bring that stuff into our city all the way from Denver," complained one woman, popping a mushroom into her mouth. "Then they cart it right through the center of town. Why don't they keep it in Denver where it belongs?"

"It doesn't mean a thing to me *personally*," said a cute little thing with a pair of wiggly buttocks that seemed to swell up right before my eyes, like clouds of pink bubble gum. "But with that kind of publicity, who'd want to visit Salt Lake City?"

"Who'd want to visit Salt Lake City anyway?" interposed my Classics friend, dreaming of Pompeii. "But gas is cleaner than magma. It doesn't mess up the artifacts."

"But I *like* Salt Lake City," said Bob. "It sure beats bombing the Cong."

Privately, however, I complained to Bob that the trip was a bust. "Salt Lake is a lovely place to visit, but who'd want to die here?"

"Who's talkin' about dyin'? It's a great party, isn't it? And that chick with the parachute blooming right out of her bum is about to come down on a land mine that'll explode right in her lap. Only she don't know it yet, of course. I ain't told her my plans. . . . So live it up, Bernie. It's a swinging party, and we've hit it damned lucky. Those VC in the hills 'll never dare come down to Main Street."

"Bob," I said sadly, realizing he'd missed a visit to his psychiatrist because of our trip. "There are *no* VC in Salt Lake City."

"Don't con me," said Bob. "VC are everywhere."

Anyway, before I knew it, the party was over, the trip was over, exams were over, summer was on me again, and I was making the pigeon scene. My job was to feed them, clean their cages as if they were about to inherit the earth, take notes on their diurnal, nocturnal, and sempiternal copulations, and finally, to put red metal bands around their feet—each one numbered as carefully as if they were God's sparrows, about to fall.

Now Reader, you well know, if you've cleaned one bird cage, you've cleaned them all, so you know what I mean when I say I was getting a turd's-eye view of life. Just multiply the waste-product of your ordinary homey-type pair of parakeets by five hundred. Five hundred Columbidae in the most gigantic cloacal conspiracy ever organized on this planet. Pure manna for the fertilizer factories, and I couldn't help asking myself after a week or so of incalculable ooze—was it fledglings we were after or chemical by-products? I mean, did we want more birds or more birdshit, as it were?

Cockbirds and henbirds created we them—by day and by night. By virtue of some fancy round-the-clock illumination they were kept in perpetual sexual excitement: wantonly they copulated, incubated, and multiplied like flies. In addition, we were feeding them an enriched grain raunchy with Vitamin E, hormones and (probably) gism. Naturally these overbred, overfed birds decanted a *merdre* as pungent as hookah fumes. By the end of the second week I felt I must find out just where my future lay amid all this offal. So when Schmutkoph, the Director of the Ag Program came in, as he did every day to check on a pair of starlings he kept in a circular glass cage, I strolled up to him and asked: "Really sir, could you tell me exactly—I mean: are we out for more squab—or more squish?"

Just like that I asked him. Dumbbell that I am—I'm the guy who, if the Industrial Revolution is on the way to strangle him anyway, rushes out to invent another machine to save himself a bit of work. He saves, he saves: sure enough, a month or two later—No More Work.

For what seemed a long time Schmut (as we refer to him informally) stared at me as if I were the best specimen he'd seen in years of a perfect idiot. Now I must tell you right now, at the very beginning, that Schmutkoph and I were bound to have trouble in our interpersonal relations. First of all, he was my boss, and that was enough to set my teeth on edge. But more importantly, I'd suspected him for some time to have a hot yen for my own little chick, Molly, ever since she'd been a student of his. Now Schmutkoph is not only a fairly successful guy with money jingling in his pockets, but he's also one of these ugly mesmorphic types with *charisma*: you know, the kind you'd never think *your* girl could possibly be attracted to, then you discover that all her life she's had this secret itch to be switched bare-assed with birch leaves: and who should turn up as the world's *top*most authority on birch leaves, but naturally, Some Schmutkoph.

Anyway, after my first naive question (see above), Professor Schmutkoph gave me one of those looks that always reminds me that I'm still only five feet five (as last measured when I was nineteen: since then, I've disdained to occupy myself with such matters. Who needs problems?)

"Klein," he said, glancing at me from between his corkscrew burnsides. "You don't deserve an answer to a smart alecky question like that. But out of respect for the *project*, I'll tell you, YES, we want birds—preferably all exactly the same size, same shape, same wing span, same oviductal and testicular enlargement. 'Cause what this country needs is good birds, strong birds, the healthiest. So make birds, Klein, make birds," he sang out, then paused and looked at me speculatively with his zinc-colored eyes.

I must admit that at this moment I grinned at Schmutkoph in a friendly sort of way. The fact is, I was so happy at the prospect of reducing the *dreck* that I became for a moment, quite manic with my vision of a shit-free universe.

"Oh, I'll breed you birds, Professor Schmutkoph. I'll breed you enough birds to invade Cuba. I'll make 'em big as Pteranodons, strong as B-52's with a built in roundtrip hijacker's communication system. Oh God," I cried joyously, "what a slogan: MAKE BIRDS, NOT TURDS!" I stopped aghast at the look Schmutkoph swivelled down on me.

"You think you're funny, don't you, Klein?"

"No sir, not funny. Oh me oh my no. But sir, I *am* pleased to be allowed a reduction in our stercoraceous Columbiforme deposits, sir. . . ."

When Molly came in, I was feeding the birds again.

"Why are you always feeding them?" she demanded, with her usual feminine illogic.

"I'm not always feeding them. It's *they* who're always eating."

She settled herself down on a garden bench to watch as first

I mixed the correct proportions of corn and wheat with a gravelly grit of ground bone meal, then poured over a bucketful of syrupy vitamins: A, E, D. B1, B2, B6, B12.

"What's all that for?" she so intelligently asked.

"Keeps 'em sexy. See that one over there? Name's Thaïs. She's the pin-up girl of the colony and a real tart if ever I saw one. One look at her and a hundred cockbirds start clawing for straw. . . ."

Molly looked enviously at the dove-eyed bird. "Straw. . . ."

"Nesting instinct. With the cocks it's each one reach one—a straw, that is."

Molly moistened her lips and I could see an ague of competition go shuddering through her. "*I* have a nesting instinct, too," she cooed.

"Look, I'll take care of *you* soon as I'm sure these birds are copulating."

"Coo-coo roo-coo me-too," she sighed, swelling her bosom sweetly.

"Aw, cut it out, Molly. Go lie under the starlings' cage. I'll be there in a minute." (Molly liked to make love under the starlings' cage: she claimed it excited her to see the birds experiencing their so-called "migration restlessness," as Schmut referred to it.)

Obediently Molly walked out to the small adjoining patio where Schmutkoph kept the starlings and began throwing bits of rock, straw, sand and fallen tail feathers into a heap under the glass cage.

"Hey, what're you doing?" I demanded. But I knew already.

"I'm nesting . . . nesting," she cooed and arranged herself like a sitting hen. "Bernie baby—what do you think it'll be: a boy or a girl? Or multiple births, maybe?"

At first I refused to believe it; but I thought to myself: with girls like Molly you have to resign yourself to accidents. It's *a priori*: the first thing they do is get pregnant. Natural breeders.

"How do I know it's not Schmutkoph's?" I said at last, glumly.

For several long seconds she was silent, then she gave me what her mother calls "Molly's radiant smile." "Do you think he'd be a good father? Genetically, I mean? A strong survival-type? . . ."

"In the war-of-the-worlds, Schmut will survive us all," I snapped. "He has the heart of a roach."

"Hmmm . . . ," said Molly thoughfully, and raised her thighs. She always claimed she could think better that way.

When Schmutkoph came in the next day, I told him I needed a raise, that I was going to get married.

"Oh? Pregnant, is she?" he announced with satisfaction.

Later I remember asking myself: how did *he* know? But at the time I parried my reply, deeming it—in my old-fashioned way—indiscreet to betray Molly's innocence. So I aimed a faltering poke in the ribs at Schmutkoph, adding a roo-coo-coo of ribald laughter, as though we were both a pair of pro's who really knew how to breed; "Well, if not now, she soon *will* be—haw! haw!"

"Well," said Schmutkoph drily, "just be sure to put the right number on her ring-band, so if she migrates, whoever gets her will know where she's come from. . . . Funny thing about migration," pursued Schmut, off on his favorite obsession, ". . . a bird'll go eight thousand miles just to get to a nesting place, how about that? You know what I saw down on the beach last year?—an Arctic tern, and she could have been on her way to the Indian Ocean for all I know. . . ."

I wanted to interrupt Schmut with serious talk about inflation, money-power, research assistants, pregnant wives: but once Schmut flies off on this migration stuff he's like a guy driving from New York to San Francisco: all he wants to know, how many miles did they do today?

"Now a migrating bird can go as fast as sixty miles an hour— not all the way, of course, she's got to stop and eat. . . . It's where she stops we're not sure of. . . . It's those *routes*, those migration itineraries we got to find out about. There's a guy I know does work with turtles. Those turtles *radio* back their migratory paths, y'see? Telemetry's the thing, Bernie, and that's why we want big birds. We could wire 'em up on their legs, see?"

Why don't you and the FBI and the CIA just hop into a plane and *follow* them?"

Schmutkoph looked at me with a certain respect. "Not a bad idea, Klein. Not a bad idea at all. And you know—pigeons don't scare near so fast as your pelagic bird when they see a plane coming up alongside them. . . ."

I was hoping Schmut would clear out and leave me to my own devices (I figured I owed myself a nap before lunch), but instead he began explaining to me that the trucks would be coming by that afternoon for a shipment of birds, so I'd better get hopping. "Just be sure to get the same number of cocks and hens: the computer prefers standardized sex characteristics." Then he was off again on one of his favorite topics, how birds cohabit: how they billed and cooed and displayed and mounted and charged and jumped and got jealous; how they were usually faithful to one another but "sometimes, you know, you get a hen bird that'll let anything mount her that even *acts* like a male. . . ." Sounded to me just like the crowd I ran around with—I figured I wasn't learning anything. So while Schmut followed after me—alternately clucking and crowing—I got the birds ready for shipment. I soon began to feel that the only way I would ever get shut of Schmut (to coin a slogan) was to excuse myself on the pretext that I'd planned to meet my friend Bob at the local Fish House (those days I ate nothing but fish). Ordinarily Molly brought our lunch in a paper bag and we shared our sandwiches and thermos under the starlings' cage. But this afternoon, in order to get away from Schmut and his transatlantic terns, I left Molly a note (taped to the bottom of the starlings' cage) and sneaked off to meet Bob at his place.

"I think the man's a Mad Scientist," I complained to Bob. "Now he wants to chase pigeons in airplanes."

"*Clay* pigeons?" he mumbled, tearing through the daily newspaper as usual to check on how many VC had got killed today.

"Does he need a pilot?" asked Bob eagerly; then as I shook my head: "Did you get the raise?"

"No, I never got around to it. He went off on one of his bird-dealies. Say, did you know an Arctic tern can travel eight thousand miles?"

"Forty VC today," said Bob.

On my way back to work I decided absolutely I should get a research assistant's pay. I was no mere shit-shoveller; I was a scientist. So I was gratified when I arrived at the Ag. Bldg. to see that Schmut was still there, standing beside the starlings' cage and contemplating the Heavens—wondering, perhaps, how he could assault it with giant birds. He looked as if he'd scarcely moved since I saw him an hour ago, but there was a lecherous disarray about the place, a frenzied, scrabbling look amongst feathers and sand. . . . With extraordinary disingenuousness (as it seemed to me) I wandered around the starlings' cage, tapping at the birds in their pre-migratory glass prison, while I waited for the moment when Schmut was not watching me; then I doubled quickly under the cage to hunt for my note: there it was, still taped to the cage, and at that moment I noticed, right in bird's eye view as it were—Molly's handkerchief. How long had it been lying there? I wondered. More important, under just what circumstances had she let it fall from her grasp? Tenderly, but with my pulse beginning to quicken with suspicion, I held the handkerchief to my face: sure enough, it was the familiar pungent odor of Molly's *La Penne Brulante.*

". . . Molly been by?" I asked with enormous casualness.

Schmutkoph adjusted the screen which surrounded the starlings: they were shut off from their Real Environment and were only supposed to know when it was time to split when they got to feeling randy.

"Who been by?"

"Molly. Molly. *Molly.*" I spoke soothingly to myself: it doesn't pay to get irritable, Klein. Play it cool. Don't blow your stack. Be a big-time operator. . . . "Molly, Molly, Molly," I babbled. "Has Molly been here?"

He stared. "Haven't seen her. No, not a bit of her."

Now if your boss says he *hasn't* been screwing your girl, what do you do? Call him a liar? ("You have!" "I haven't!" "You have!" "I haven't," etc.) No, you just get back to cleaning the cages. Which I did.

"Let's see those breeding graphs," said Schmutkoph. I handed him the sheets and he stood there beside the cages, moaning over them with a voyeur's vicarious satisfaction. "Good.

Good," he repeated with pleasure. (In a minute he'll have an emission, I thought savagely.) "If they keep on like this, we should have *thousands* of 'em. . . ."

It was an apocalyptic vision. "What in God's name will we do with thousands of pigeons?" I gasped. "We'll lose our tourist trade. We won't have a hotel left on the beach at Galveston. No one will insure us——."

"Don't be an idiot," interrupted Schmut. (It seemed to be his favorite phrase with me.) "Nobody in his right mind breeds birds just to keep 'em. We goin' to ship 'em all *over* the U.S. And to the rain forests too. And the Pacific *Theayter*, maybe."

I wasn't at all sure what his reference to the rain forests meant but that bit about the Pacific Theater roused bravura echoes of heroic action from my father's war: Pearl Harbor, Okinawa, Iwo Jima, Bataan and General Wainwright and nuclear testing on the Atolls. . . .

"But the war's over," I remembered just in the nick of time. "We're pals with the Japs now. They got Avante Garde Art, and Kinetic Films and the World's Fair and Sony Television. They're our strongest bastion against the Yellow Peril of Communism—aren't they? I mean, we wouldn't . . . would we . . . not again?"

I guess my knowing even a little bit about *his* war made him mad, because he really insulted me then—I mean considering my job and everything, he called me the worst thing he could think of. "Klein, you should keep your *shiteating* head out of military matters and keep it down with the rocks—a fossil. You're so ignorant you'd make a molecule look educated. Look, Klein, I was in the Pacific Theater during that war." (Like I hadn't guessed.) "And those little skirmishes we had are gonna look *historically* like we were fighting with jawbones, compared to what we got now." Suddenly Schmut cupped his hand into a toucan's bill and preened himself under the armpit. "Klein, you know what we can do now?"—he lashed out the sharp profile of his hand—"we got an anthrax, for example. . . ." He paused dramatically, rightly figuring I wouldn't know Anthrax from Borax, Ajax, or Tampax.

"We got an anthrax germ *concentrate* what one *teaspoon* carries ten million germs. Only trouble is," he sighed, "You can't use it. You can't get it out. Stays in the ground over a hundred years. . . . Like, say, you were to invade an anthrax field that'd been seeded a hundred years back. You wouldn't hardly be ready to start living there. Wouldn't anything *grow*."

Now for the life of me I couldn't see what the fifth plague of Egypt had to do with birds; but at the same time I was not in a hurry to go back to dropping droppings. If Schmutkoph wanted to pat himself on the back on company time, who was I to complain? So I laid down my spatula and grinned encouragingly at him—a grin as wide and treacherous as the San Andreas fault.

He looked real gratified, as if it were a sacrifice on my part to give up *merdrolatry* to listen to him: "What we're gonna do," he said, "and of course it's just between you, me and the compost pile—is to use birds to see how far they can carry combat-diseases."

Sleepily I nodded approval of the project's humanitarian aim. ". . . 'to combat diseases . . .' Naturally. Animals have always been used in experiments. Dogs in heart transplants—monkeys in orbit. . . ." My voice faded away and I nodded contentedly, hoping he would continue while I rested my weary legs. I presumed, even, to sit down on a packing case: I wondered if he would accept a piece of the chocolate bar I hadn't had time for at lunch.

But instead of continuing with one of his bird-jive solos, he looked at me with passionate disgust, as if I had just confessed to being a twenty-one year old virgin. He waved me back to work and turned to his birds who were fluttering nervously against their glass walls: they were showing real migration restlessness, Schmut said.

During the afternoon the phone rang twice and each time, when I answered it, the same slow, hot breathing incubated silently on the other end: I could have sworn that I detected Molly's *La Penne Brulante*. My misgivings were intensified by the sight of a typewritten note in Schmut's *IN* basket, with the word *psychiatrist* misspelled as only Molly, in her female obstinacy, could continue to do over and over again. . . . Altogether, I was in such a bad mood by closing time that I couldn't face going home to Molly; instead I stopped in to talk to Bob Bischoff at his place.

173

Bob had just returned from his psychiatrist. Poor Bob was seeing his doc every day now (he'd started boasting about how he was "Puff the Magic Dragon" which could shoot 5,000 machine gun bullets a minute: but his psychiatrist was trying to bring him around to admitting that he'd never flown a DC-3 in his life). Completely hung up about his own life, and living only to see his psychiatrist (he claimed to be passionately in love with her, though she looked to me like what a Russian wolfhound would look like if it lived to be seventy years old), Bob nevertheless showed great lucidity in discussing Affairs of the Heart.

"I think she's doing me dirt, Bob," I said. "I think she's screwing that Schmutkoph!"

"Schmutkoph! But how can that be? He doesn't have any balls. I've seen him at the *shvitz*. I swear to you, Bernie, he's as sterile as a mule's stool. I've seen him naked as a jaybird a dozen times and it isn't even big enough to pee with."

I thought bitterly of the hen birds in their perpetually illuminated ardor, worshipping the divine Phallos—running after the cockbird as though he were a blooming dildo. "Doesn't matter," I said. "When it's nesting time, a lipstick'll do. . . ."

Bob started doing exercises for his back—his way of thinking out loud. Finally he came to an abrupt halt. "Bernie," he said. "It's all clear to me now. It's that Molly. You can't trust her. . . ."

"You're telling *me*," I said, and quoted something about Centaurs from the waist down.

"She uses the pill?" stated Bob rhetorically, adding up the facts like an attorney.

"No. She's scared of it. All four of her grandparents died of embolism."

I was quite unprepared for Bob's fury. "You don't use the pill?" he roared. "What are you, a holy roller or something? The whole fuckin' world's gone chemical-biological, and *your* chick won't even swallow a hormone tablet! Get her on the pill," he commanded.

I shrugged. I knew Molly. "What good would that do? Schmutkoph's got her knocked up, and *I'm* the one she's picked to marry herself off to. Myself I use only the best prophylactics— but can I prove it? Only the starlings know for sure. . . ."

"Listen to me Bernie, and I'll explain. You're only a child —you didn't fight in no war—not a single war. War learns you things. Man, listen. The whole thing is a plot for Molly to get— not *you*, dumbkoph, but Schmutkoph. Who'd want to marry *you*, anyway? Have you got a dime? Have you ever been in a war? Have you ever killed any VC? You're a terrible risk to an ambitious 20 year old girl. Maybe you're a good lay, Bernie, but Schmut's the guy with the degrees—a B.S. and a M.S. and some other 'esses too, but I don't remember what. And schmutcock, he'd like a good steady hen too. . . . But he's scared to death she'll find out the *one thing* about him he wants kept top secret. Now *what* in a Big Corporation like his, could be the most important thing to know? Just this, Bernie. He ain't got no worm in his sperm. You're staring, Bernie. You don't believe it. Listen, I *know*. I got a private access to that kind of information (210 VC today, by the way) . . . ."

"Bob, do you mean to say they're *both* trying to marry her off—and to *me*? Awjeez, Bob, you ought to go see a psychiatrist— in fact, see two or three of them. Go 'way, Bob, you make me feel about that low. . . ." In despair I raised my finger about a centimeter from the floor.

"You're not just low, Bernie, you're pretty near lost in them hills! But listen—I'm flyin' down to get you!" Bob exclaimed, and went on to explain in his own occult way what Molly was up to: how, what it was that Molly really wanted, was for me to knock her up—because Schmut couldn't get a pigeon pregnant if his life depended on it: how in his pride, Schmut would never admit his spermlessness, however, and would be delighted in fact to have this visible proof of his powers. . . . "Then she'd get the guy with the twenty-thousand-a-year job, not *you*, you schmuck," concluded Bob philosophically.

If true, 'twas fantastic. But why shouldn't it be true, after all? Why should Molly want me, a mere Merdre-loader, a dreamer: What confused me was why she should be telling me she was already pregnant? . . . But Ole Puff-the-Magic-Dragon had an answer to that too. . . .

"Aah . . . it's an old game, Bernie. Every married woman knows that if she tells her husband she's going to have a baby, he's only too happy to stop wearing those damned condoms. . . ."

"Oi. Oi. And then she *would* get pregnant. That bitch. That slut. That tramp. Using *my* good sperm to trap a Schmut!"

"Cut the larking around. Those VC aren't going to wait all day. This is no time to take cover—it's time to *attack*." And Bob flew up on the table, his priapal weapon in hand, yelling: "Five thousand bullets a minute, man—you can do it too!"

When he had calmed down, he outlined our "attack." Unbeknownst to herself, Molly was to be put on the pill. "You eat together, don't you? Sleep together? . . . A pill is just like a grenade. You slip it up on them while they're unaware. Put it in her milk, in her ice cream, in her tea, coffee, Metrecal, in her crunchy peanut butter, in her thermos. Just remember, One-a-day keeps Junior away. . . ."

Dear Reader, during the weeks that followed (true to Bischoff's diagnosis and prediction), Molly gave me no peace. She coddled and cozened, lapped and diddled; yet my ejaculations of joy gave her no pleasure. More persevering than ever in her attacks, she remained an unhappy wanton with a scowl on her brow as of a worker who is forced to work longer hours for less pay. . . . Secretly I sympathized with her even while I continued to jettison my pleasures like the Tivoli fountains.

Meanwhile, with every passing week Molly became more tense and worried. On two occasions she had paused *in medio cunnilingus* to take issue with my Dionysian mode as being decadent and *sterile* (italics mine), and had ended up by hitting me across the head as if I had debauched *her*, when, as the Reader is well aware, it was quite the other way around. Anyway, it could not have gone on much longer without a physical collapse on my part. I was beginning to feel like D. H. Lawrence with saltpeter in his carafe.

Then at last one afternoon, after weeks of lubricity, I spotted her in Wise's drug store, stashing away a package of tampons. She was trying to thrust the box deep into her poke when I approached her with what seemed to me an irresistibly engaging grin.

"Can I help you, lady?" I said.

She flushed, looked up from her work, her hand trying in vain to shield the box from view.

"What are you doing here? What do you *mean* by spying on me?" she demanded hotly, the color singeing her pouter-like cheeks.

"Spying? Who's spying? I just came in to see if I could be of any assistance. Maybe help you carry something or something."

"See? What did I tell you? You're following me. You've been following me for three weeks now."

I shrugged, trying to look indifferent to my own triumph: "G'wan. Don't be paranoid," I murmured.

For a moment Molly glared; then she curved her small fist into a carnivore's beak and sank a hook into my shoulder that sent me plunging into a Modess display: blue boxes flew like tail plumes across the floor. Sobbing, Molly pursued her prey (me), into the very center of the heap, till suddenly, with an exclamation of helpless rage, she vanished down an invisible labyrinth. . . . From the corner of my eye I could see a store detective lighting out after her.

There I sat, like Ruth amid the alien corn. There seemed no way I could explain to the manager of the store that my girl was angry with me because she was *not* pregnant; so I sat there meditating among the baby-blue boxes for a while, till at last, with what now seems to me enormous presence of mind, I strolled up to the counter and asked in a deep voice—calm, untroubled, conscience-free—for an economy-size pack of prophylactics.

After that Molly wouldn't even answer the phone when I called. So I hadn't seen her for several weeks (I want to emphasize that) when one day as I was cleaning the cages, Schmut came in—preening himself as usual.

"How we doing?" he asked in one of his friendliest, most democratic tones.

"What you mean we?" I demanded. "*I'm* the one doing it."

"Well, how's their over-all size what I mean?" amended Schmut in the most placatory manner I'd ever seen him assume.

"I'm in charge of laying, not weighing," I said.

"O.K. So I see you're not in a good mood today," said Schmut, with the gentleness of a conqueror. "But let's get a report sheet from the lab, eh? I want to see what's been happening. Just give 'em a call and tell 'em to send it on over. . . ."

Now it may have been my imagination, but it seemed to me that as we waited for the reports, Schmut became increasingly nervous (showing, one might have said, almost a migratory restlessness). He began opening the cages needlessly, peering into their depths at the faces of the birds. . . . He counted the females, then the males twice over. Then he gave them all fresh water and added an extra dose of vitamins to their feed as though he were anticipating an outbreak of deficiency symptoms. And although he never got so far carried away as to clean the cages, Schmut hovered around those birds all afternoon with something bordering on human concern.

Finally, toward the end of the day a messenger-type flunky arrived and handed Schmut two reports—one computerized, and another neatly typewritten in five columns. With scarcely a glance at me, and with something like creative pride in his voice, Schmut read aloud:

"Autopsies on reproductive organs over a period of . . . months. Desanguination made the computerization of weights possible since the removal of blood from oviducts, gonads, spleens and livers rendered data fairly stable. First the intestine was removed. . . . The mesenteric folds opened. . . . Intestines were measured to the centimeter. All thyroids were taken out. Increases in size of ovaries and testes are indicated on enclosed graph."

"All hearts were measured."

As he read, Schmut bore down from time to time on an item, savoring the succulent syllable like a scavenger—*au*topsy, *blood, go*-nads—and then he would blink a single vulturous eye in my direction as if to share with me his necrophilic joy: while I, dear Reader, began to tremble in every nerve as the whole truth, the unthinkable truth slowly dawned on me.

"Schmut," I managed at last to protest. "I thought we were going to breed birds—not have this . . . this purge, this blood bath." I shuddered. ". . . this—*desanguination*. It's no use denying it to me any longer, Schmut. Those birds I've so carefully bred and fed for you, those thousands of billing and cooing sex-intoxicated birds are *dead*."

Schmut denied this with a promptness which temporarily derailed me and allayed my fears.

"Of course not, boy. You always want to jump to conclusions. Jump first, think later, that's your style, Klein. Just hang on a minute while I explain a few things. Sure we had to have autopsies . . . and a bird has to be dead before you can perform an autopsy on it. . . . But the others, we're sending to labs all over the country. They're the new army, Klein. We're on a big Disease Offensive and birds are going to fly where even herbicides can't reach. We could use birds for aerosol bombers, boy—don't you see the genius of it? . . ."

I shook my head.

"Birds can carry living vectors—get it? Let's say you vaccinate a whole entire indigenous population—the Good Guys, that's *our* guys—and then suppose the yellow hordes (the Bad Guys) come swooping down from the North—they haven't even *heard* of vaccination, much less living vectors. What might they get? Just imagine, Bernie, What might they catch?"

I struggled with the passion tearing at my throat. At last I managed to sob: "A bad cold?"

"Always the punch-and-judy guy eh? Well, we'll see how far that'll get you in the Next War. But guess again: *What do birds carry?*"

"Straw," I said. "Each-one-reach-one." (Oh Molly, could you really marry a Dachau doctor?) "Also: birdshit," I managed as an afterthought.

He put his arm around my shoulder (he did, he actually did!) and led me in a comradely way to a map of the world he kept on the wall. He started sticking in pins—orange pins, blue pins, white pins, black pins—my flesh prickled as with a Lilliputian plague of pins.

"Look here and see. Just follow my finger. . . . See that migration pattern?" He slashed his finger across the latitudes from Venezuela to Peking. "Down here we got VEE. Up here we got *no* VEE.* A transportation problem, pure and simple. And

---

* Author's note: Schmut explained to me that VEE is short shrift for Venezuelan Equine Encephalitis.

birds are our ultimate weapon. We can use 'em in the war. . . ."

"War? What war?" My mouth tasted bitter as muck. I made a vow to call the Texas Naturalist Society about this as soon as I got home. Or write to *The New York Times*.

"Any war. The next war. The 'Meta-war' as somebody's called it. You just can't conceive of the real potential of birds for a humane war. Just think of it. Suppose you had an enemy with a growing army—you wouldn't have to drop napalm on the whole civilian population. And then look what happened in Saigon, in Da Nang, in Hué. Destruction. Terrible destruction. Some of the most beautiful buildings in the world and hardly a one left standing. . . . Why, with birds, you could achieve a 30 per cent mortality and not destroy a thing. . . ."

"*How?*" I demanded, backing away from him. But I had already divined the purpose of our great breeding experiment. Nevertheless, I repeated: "*How. Tell me how?*" as if the short, fat one-syllable plosives were all that were left to me.

"*Psittacosis,*" he said, and winked like a mischievous Santa Claus. "Encephalitis," he exclaimed, and stuck a shiny black pin into the red heart of Peking. "Tularemia—," and stuck two missile-bright heads into the industrial complex of Russia. "And a teensy bit of bubonic plague." He bowed funereally as he furrowed a black pin into the peak of Albania.

"Schmutkoph, you monster, you're going to make all my beautiful birds *sick*. Damn you, I'll get you Schmut. I'll tell the Audubon Society. I'll tell the Animal Rescue League. I'll report you to U.S. Wildlife. I'll tell *Molly!*" Spluttering furiously, I threw down my trowel, picked up my book (*How to Raise Squab*), and slammed my way out of the Ag building. At my last sight of Schmut he was standing with one hand spanning the United Arab Republic while sticking a pin into the polar peaks of the Arctic.

I was so upset by the time I got back to my room that it was all I could do to control a convulsive case of hiccoughs. Nevertheless, true to my threats I sat down and began phoning the Texas Naturalist Society, the Audubon Society, the Humane Society and the U.S. Wildlife. But to no avail. The abandonment of a Fourth of July weekend had set in like the plague; there was not a soul in the offices to answer the phones. To me it was a day of national mourning.

When Bob came in, he found me lying on my bed—mute, dry-eyed, exhausted, awaiting the apocalypse.

"So what's new?" he said. I noticed (in spite of my misery) that he'd had a haircut since I last saw him. It seemed but a part of the perversity of the universe that everyone should begin to *look* so civilized.

Falteringly I explained to him how I had been exploited as an unwitting accomplice in the biggest birdicide of the century.

Bob stood up restively, looked into the mirror and patted his once grassy poll with satisfaction: "How you like my defoliation job?" he asked. "By the way, forty-two VC today. Pretty clean, eh?" Then he turned toward me, hunched over, eyes gleaming: "Fight fire with fire. We'll get every one of them. If our first attack fails, we'll try another, but always remember: Only You Can Prevent Birds. . . ."

Unheeding, I buried my face in the pillow. "Oh, my pretty ones. . . . Think of it—Thaïs, that lovebird, that trollope, that sexpot—nothing but a sink of psittacosis—a carrier of not even venereal disease!"

"Hold on a minute, Bernie. You caterwaul like a burning village. Listen to ole Poppa Bischoff. While I was in the barber shop, I saw this item pasted up on Whimpy's mirror. You know how he keeps his mirrors—like a bulletin board: anything *he* wants to talk about is scheduled right there in front of our nose as he clips you. Well, first there was this big ad for pigs. You know, they get the scours. . . ."

"Hell, I thought you were going to help me. It's pig-eons, not pigs I love. P-i-g—."

In calm, cold-blooded mime Bob took an automatic pistol from his cartridge belt and shot me through my head into silence.

"Well right alongside this item about the pigs was this other thing—and I thought of how it might be useful for Molly, you know?"

"*Molly!* Don't talk to me about Molly! What do I care about that slut! Thousands of pigeons are doomed to die—don't you realize that? I'm dropping out of school, Bob. I can't take this atmosphere of violence. I'm going into a Buddhist monastery. . . ." I believed every word I said.

"We'll save 'em," said Lt. Bob crisply. "Straighten up. Fix your tie. Why don't you ever wear a tie? You need a haircut. Get out of that bed. Read your orders. . . ." He paced up and down as he spoke, and suddenly became so nervous that he broke out into a sweat. "*Read*," he commanded, in a voice cold with heroism.

I read aloud:

City Manager P—— F—— is pondering the pill as a panacea for prolific pigeons. . . . The City Council proposal involves the use of a new chemical which is mixed with wheat, then fed to the unsuspecting birds. . . .*

Reader, I stared a long while in unbelief at this deus ex machina, then threw myself, whooping with joy onto Bishchoff. For several minutes we struggled together on the floor, snorting, moaning and roaring with laughter—and just at the climax of this orgiastic laughter (as it were) Molly stuck her head in the door.

She didn't even bother to come in. "Oh!" she jeered. "*Homosexuals! That* explains it." And she waved her left hand at us in airy contempt: "Just stopped by to show you my ring." And to be sure, on the third finger, left hand Schmutkoph (who else?) had lavishly banded her with a diamond as big as an egg. Then, without waiting for our exclamations of mock congratulations, Molly walked off, leaving us agape on the floor.

Bob turned to me at once with the obvious question: "*Whose is it?*"

"Damned if I know," I retorted, then I rose and began flapping my wings, crowing, strutting and treading my arched claws above an imaginary hen: till I remembered I'd seen a scene like that in Blue Angel, and that what it had meant was that the

_____

* Author's note: This news story is reproduced as it appeared in Whimpy's Barber Shop. I have tried to get Whimpy to give me the source (I'm a scholar at heart), but he claims he can no longer remember.

guy was cracking up. So I just lay back on the floor instead and laughed till the tears came.

"That's women for you, Bernie old pal," said Bob consolingly. "I suggest you reenlist."

"Bob," I asked, "How many VC today?"

Reader, you know the rest. Schmutkoph ran off with his bride to the rain forests of Brazil (since then I've heard that Molly had multiple births: how many is evidently a tightly guarded secret). Determined to save us all from birddoom I began, with the bitter dedication of a celibate, to feed my birds their Pill (called Nix-Nest, if you'd like to get some and assist in a good cause). Daily I have noticed a decline in their statistical birthrate: their natural instincts, however, seem not to have been stifled; if anything, they copulate more wantonly than ever, billing and cooing with the mournful intensity of unrequited love. I make no attempt to assist or impede them in their coupling. I let them screw—it's the kindest thing I can do.

The Festival

T hose of you who have been following the other events sponsored by Vita Company will at once understand the need for our Annual Spring Festival, for which celebration the Company selects a qualified person to act as Festival Man. This event is an important historical occasion in the Vita Community, and the selection of the Festival Man is a matter of the utmost seriousness and responsibility.

In the past the Festival Man had been selected by a Committee, a procedure which had come under sharp criticism from the news media. Although I can sympathize with some of their objections, yet in all fairness to Vita Company, I feel that a large share of this criticism derived from the fact that these young journalists had little or no knowledge of Vita traditions and tended to criticize what they could not relate to in terms of contemporary issues. A frequently heard charge, for instance, was that the appointment of the Festival Man was made by an elitist committee which only solemnized the entrenchment of an oligarchic society. But I assure you—those of you who are presently policy-holders with the Company as well as all other interested citizens—that this charge was quite untrue. Our Festival Men have always been taken from the common people: one of our Festival Men, for instance, spent the first ten years of his life on a quiet island off the coast of South Carolina. He did not learn to read and write until he was twelve years of age. At fourteen he engaged in his first sexual experience, and at eighteen he considered himself a member of our community. But this man had the one most important qualification: never had he been known to have expressed a view which was not in harmony with the precepts on which the Company was founded. I stress this fact because even reputable historians and scholars engaged by the Company to preserve community records have, by their "explanations" for the choice of our Festival Men, created an atmosphere of illusion and romanticism surrounding the Festival. This Biographical Series, instead of illuminating the role of the Festival Man in our Company, has consequently reinforced the popular notion that the Festival Man is chosen for his remarkable character—or even that some hierarchical power in the community inheres to the Festival Man himself, as if Vita Company were some sort of synod of presbyters instead of an insurance company.

But perhaps I have belabored this point. You have only to consult the Historical Archives for the records of the past twenty-five years to see at once that all our Festival Men have been ordinary men. The only difference between the Festival Man and the usual policy-holder is that the former, upon being informed of his selection, is offered the option of insuring himself, his family, his worldly goods, and even his future historic reputation against any discovery of Deviation on his part, either moral or intellectual. This Option-to-Insure is one of the marginal rewards of his position. It is offered to him at a below-cost premium, and rarely does a Festival Man not see the advantage of it.

It was my good fortune, after the adjustment of several large Grievance Claims for Vita Insurance to be appointed Festival Director. It was I who made certain radical changes in the manner in which the Festival Man was chosen. For instance, the choice had previously been arrived at during an annual meeting at which all the Grievance Adjusters presented their favorite candidates; the candidates were argued over endlessly and these annual meetings frequently ended in factionalism and injured feelings which lasted a lifetime, with the resultant claims under Vita's Slander, Innuendo and Allegations Policy for which the Company paid full compensation. In concern over this costly divisiveness, the Committee decided to dissolve itself and appoint instead a single Director. The unanimous vote in my favor was the highest honor which had ever been conferred on a rank and file Grievance Adjuster. I had been with the Company only six years and it was a gratifying experience. Besides the high honor of the position itself, the promotion entailed marginal emoluments such as: the use of the Company limousine; a reduction in my own insurance premiums (at the time of my promotion, nearly 35 per cent of my gross income was being paid for a Fealty Policy with Catastrophic Liability Clause covering Despair, Suicide, etc.); and above all, automatic exemption from service as Bathhouse Adjuster or as Rape and Resuscitation Adjuster. You can imagine with what joy my wife, Moira, greeted me on the day that Vita Insurance announced that I alone would be organizing the next Annual Spring Festival, attended every year by thousands of people from the Vita Community. I will always be grateful to Mr. Cormoran, our Vice President, for the few well-placed words by which he recommended me to the Committee. "*This* is the man," he said, placing his hand on my shoulder, at which moment the few dissenters voted to make their election unanimous.

During the first few months of my appointment I considered making the Festival a bi-annual affair; but in order to maintain Vita's high standard for the event, I subordinated this aim to the more important one, it seemed to me, of selecting the best possible Festival Man. After all, thousands of Vita policy-holders would have their annual premiums affected by my choice. A flaw in the performance at the festival—some breach of decorum, some unpredictable break—could, because of Vita's long-accredited practice of sharing dividends with their policy-holders, cause a severe economic crisis in the community. If, for example, the Festival Man should for any reason cast doubt on the historical authenticity of the festival itself, then the loyalty of our policy-holders could significantly waver: there would be an immediate rush of claims by Fealty policy-holders. One year when the Festival Man who had been carefully screened and chosen for his office died of a stroke (it is not true, as some malicious persons reported, that he took his own life), the Company was obliged to mail out Supplementary Validations to all policy-holders. These

Validations assured the bearer that, while all Vita Fealty Policies were noncancellable, nevertheless, in order to forestall the remotest possibility of economic fluctuation, all Fealty policy-holders with Vita Company were advised to refrain from making claims for sixty days until a replacement for the Festival Man could be found. It was the only occasion in the history of the Company in which two Festival Men were selected for a single year.

My own method for determining the qualifications of a Festival Man is a simple one. Since all actuarial records of Vita Company are available to me, I pick a man who is *Devoted to His Family, Hard-Working, Trustworthy, Idealistic,* and *Under Severe Economic Stress.* Actually, *Economic Stress* and *Devotion to His Family* are more important than abstract moral qualities. And more important than any of these, as I have suggested, the Festival Man must never have shown any Deviation. This is because he embodies the perfect acceptance of those communal beliefs without which the Vita Insurance Company would cease to operate. These beliefs are affirmed by all policy-holders and upheld by the Company; any loss is fully compensated for by us, as guaranteed in our Fealty Policy; therefore all loss-of-faith suits are estimated to the nearest one-thousandth, a calculation which can be made only in a society which is perfectly stable.

There have been persons who have been critical of my inflexible position on this matter of Deviation, arguing that it could lead to "Mediocrity" in the Festival Man. In my opinion these definers of excellence are self-serving philosophers who hardly deserve the privileges and rewards of our Vita Community. Since no person who criticizes "Mediocrity" in this manner believes himself to be "Mediocre," but rather imagines himself to be "Superior," it is clear to me that they are only inflating their personal vanity at the expense of the public good. My usual procedure with such critics is simply to cancel their P & E Policy (Pride & Esteem), leaving them to float on the wreck of their own definition. Such policy-cancellations, combined with several months of shunning by the rest of the community, and they are only too happy to concede that "Mediocrity" is a concept derived from their own arrogance.

After this critical period I am happy to say that these people usually become our most solid citizens. This is because Vita's motives are not punitive but rehabilitative: proof of this is that we rarely, if ever, lose a client permanently. Within a year after cancellation, the client's eligibility for another P & E Policy is impartially reviewed, he is usually advised to reapply and is again accepted in good standing with only a small charge added to the premium for the damage done to the Vita Company public image.

The truth is that no one understands your average man better than Vita Company, but we are far from seeking those qualities in a Festival Man which go by the concept of *l'homme moyen sensuel*. Such a candidate would be overly preoccupied with physical sensation (Comfort, Gourmandism, Lust) whereas, the Festival Man (such as the one I selected for this year) should be motivated by a natural and even "Unselfish" desire for his children to have a better life than he has had.

With this in mind I selected for this year's Festival Man, one Miles Kennig, who subsequently chose as festival title "Hrothgar."*

This Miles Kennig is a fifty-four year old laborer from the potato fields—a man in perfect health, with a winning smile, and with no pretensions to learning except that he claimed to have read some Socratic dialogues years ago before the increasing burdens of his family allowed him no further leisure. Such a claim is a venial sort of vanity, I feel. It hurts no one, least of all, the Festival Man, to believe that he has been influenced by some philosopher: a Cervantes, a Plato, a Jesus. At any rate, it was not until after I had selected Kennig that he confessed to me his harmless philosophic delusion: that the "Soul" (as he termed it), was involved in some sort of Natural Selection which struggled through successive reincarnations to achieve spiritual perfection —or perhaps he meant that it (the "Soul"), simply stopped being

---

* Once the Festival Man is selected he is permitted to choose a pseudonym from a company-prepared list. This custom renders his role anonymous except to qualified historians and scholars, and also protects him from the malice and envy of the people.

reincarnated: I forget how his system worked. But since Kennig had a profound sense of community welfare and understood by his candidacy that he was helping to maintain belief in "Good and Evil," "Reward and Retribution," "Grace and Redemption" —all those illusions, in short, by means of which the people of Vita Community define their happiness—I did not feel that this bit of intellectual dilettantism disqualified him for his role. Moreover, Kennig's* income for several years had been well below the National Poverty level for a family of six. (Although his wife was seasonally employed by the growers nearby, she was usually paid in surplus produce or bruised fruit, so it would have been impossible to calculate their true income.)

Part of Vita's guarantee to Hrothgar was that his children would never do what he referred to as "stoop labor." Since most of this work would be automated by the time his children grew up, I was willing to write up a contract for him and his family which would doubtless have little relevance to social conditions fifteen years from now. Vita Company, for instance, is considering expanding into related industries such as produce and cattle —on the premise that if we think enough of our people to insure their lives, we ought also to insure their livelihood. Thus Vita Company is looking forward to the time when there will be a slot in our multinational systems for everyone.

Thus, Hrothgar's concern for his children was more "Idealistic" than real. Nevertheless, at his request, full educational benefits were included in the contract. His wife was to receive 100 per cent compensation, regardless of her physical condition or whether she ever remarried: I considered his attitude toward his wife "Romantic" in the extreme; but as I say, it is precisely this that we prefer for our Festival Man: such "Idealism" is the very substance of the event. In addition, he (Hrothgar) was to be given personally fifty thousand dollars in cash to distribute as he liked, or to gratify whatever ambitions, dreams, etc., he might wish to fulfill up to and including that figure, and so long as his desires could be directed from the compound.

---

* So as to avoid confusion in the Historical Archives, I will hereafter refer to the candidate as *Hrothgar*.

I was rather annoyed to have Hrothgar ask that a small library be built with the money, adjacent to the compound. At first I argued that this was impossible, the compound itself was only fifteen feet in diameter, and there would be no means of entry for him from the compound to the library structure. He said he did not intend to enter it, but he wished it to be built.

You will understand the reason for my annoyance when I explain that after his selection as Festival Man, for a period of about one year, the candidate is installed in a compound about fifteen feet in diameter. This allows him adequate space for perambulation, but not so much as to give him a delusive sense of being allowed to go wherever he likes. We have found that the illusion of freedom is counter-productive; on some occasion the Festival Man, particularly toward Spring, will feel himself seduced by the sunlight and air of the walking area: instead of spending his time in meditation and prayer for the happiness of the commuity, he tends to look forward instead to the end of his time in the compound. This attitude on his part is regarded by the people as a kind of spiritual defection: to concentrate on the happiness of others is the primary responsibility of the Festival Man.

For the purpose of the Festival the compound is constructed of wooden laths, the surface of which has been sculptured out into small concave units, like a bee hive or wasp's nest. This surface is then loosely ornamented with thousands of colorful pebbles or sea shells which Vita Company has been at great pains to select precisely for this architectural effect, sparing themselves no expense in time, energy or money. Several amethysts are set in a triangular hieroglyph above the lintel. On a sunny day the colorful spectacle of the geodesic dome spanning the compound is an impressive sight: the beauty of this structure has brought visitors from as far away as Alaska and the Keys to see the Annual Festival. Although it is regarded as a temporary edifice, the Company nevertheless takes great pride in constructing this dome annually.

Within the shelter of this geodesic dome the Festival Man most of the time remains standing. He prefers to do so even though his is a decent-sized cell, not constrictive: he is able to walk around and reach out with considerable ease to the delicacies so many visitors are happy to offer him. I should perhaps emphasize that it is not only the pleasure of every man, woman and child in the Vita Community to share the delicacies of his table with the Festival Man, it is their civic duty. The happiness of the Festival Man at this time is a prerequisite to the joy and conscience of the community. For this reason I personally brought to Hrothgar's cell a fine new stereo with the best obtainable recording of Mahler's *Das Lied von Der Erde* (Moira's favorite). Also, under my Directorship, Festival Men have been permitted to have pets, although of course they must be removed from the compound at night: we cannot allow the Festival Man's cell to smell of animals; the people would be repelled by such odors and would neglect their visitations.

These visitations, I never fail to remind them, are obligatory and must be rendered in the proper spirit. Thus when I visited Hrothgar several weeks before the Festival I was not at all pleased to find a shambling group of people behaving in a manner which seemed to me inappropriate and disrespectful to the Festival Man. They had brought nothing for Hrothgar to eat and were, moreover, laughing and joking with him as if this great annual event were a mere carnival.

Nothing is more likely to arouse my indignation than to see normal respectability dissolve into antic behavior. In no uncertain terms, therefore, I ordered these persons out of the compound. "You are worse than the money changers in the temple," I said. Upon which they had the grace to look ashamed, and after a brief catechism from me by which I believe they were well-edified, I instructed the gatekeeper to conduct them single file out through the front entrance (which has an extremely low lintel at the threshold). Then I thoughtfully turned to Hrothgar.

I handed in to him the food I had brought him, carefully sliding in one package at a time so that the cakes and cookies Moira had prepared for him would not be crushed by the bars. Some of the packages were too wide. "I'll tell the guard to open your cell," I assured Hrothgar, "and he'll bring the rest of these in for you after I go."

But he seemed not to have much interest in the delicacies

which Moira had personally prepared for him. Instead, he addressed me in a faltering tone which I had never heard before (he had, in fact, a rather powerful baritone): "How much longer, Mr. Derwenter?" he asked.

I pretended not to know, though I am very exact in these matters.

"A month? Two months? Tell me in days."

"About a month," I finally said, and I vowed at that moment that in the performance of my duties as Director I would visit Hrothgar daily, sacrificing all personal engagements in order to assist and instruct him during the next few weeks.

"I'll come by to see you and we'll have a drink together," I promised. "A celebration before the celebration, as it were." I spoke as lightly as I could, but I was deeply concerned.

He looked gratified. He must certainly have known that I was making more personal concessions that I had made to any other candidate: the idea of any conviviality between us in the confines of the compound, with perhaps a comradely embrace or two while we discoursed meaningfully on Hrothgar's selection as Festival Man made me feel faint. I quickly left the compound to get a breath of fresh air.

But I kept my word to Hrothgar. During the next few weeks I visited him every single day except those days on which I went to the Sauna Room—which is not only a form of relaxation for me from the heavy duties I bear with Vita Company, but permits me to make a bi-weekly check on the events transpiring in the Bathhouse. True, I am exempted from Bathhouse Service during my Directorship, but it is always a good idea to note what is happening in the Vita Community. It is over-all interest of this kind in the total community which leads to positions on the Board of Directors and to positions of responsibility such as are now held by Mr. Cormoran, our Vice President.

In spite of my distaste for the atmosphere, I visited Hrothgar regularly. We sat together in his cell for hours at a time, Hrothgar's huge arms weighing down the table at which we sat playing chess, drinking, and discoursing. Sometimes my boredom would become so acute that I would ask Hrothgar some existential question which I knew he would enjoy answering for half an hour at a time; then, while seeming to take notes on his discourse for the Archives, I would think about other matters. I soon found I could concentrate on entrepreneurial ventures and, in fact, two recommendations to Vita Company which the Company later incorporated into the Desert Real Estate & Development Project as well as Chemical Toilets for Public Events were conceived under these adverse circumstances.

This is not to say that these visitations became easy. Day after day it was necessary to conceal my fatigue and boredom, my disgust. I began to feel that when Hrothgar's imprisonment would end, mine would end too, and I longed for the day. I went home to Moira exhausted. And now that I have fulfilled my obligations to Vita Company I can admit that there were moments when I thought Moira might be turning away from me: I went so far as to take out insurance against Adultery and Loss-of-Confidence. Nevertheless, although the responsibilities of my position as Director of the Festival threatened the very security of my marriage, if I had done less I could not have respected myself. Since that time several people have suggested to me that insurance compensation for the Director of the Festival, as well as for other High Officers in the Company should be higher than for Suicide, etc., because of the risks to personal happiness which these officers are obliged to incur.

At any rate I know that I sacrificed many hours to Hrothgar in order to maintain in him a state of mind which would be most beneficial to him on the day of the Festival. And I am pleased to say that when the day arrived, Hrothgar appeared to be in a cheerful mood—self-confident and alert. He had chosen to wear a white jacket with dark pants. I myself had ordered for him a smart-looking pair of shoes in the newest fashion and had sent to him a white carnation for his lapel. Altogether he looked like the best man on his way to a wedding and it gave me immense satisfaction to think of the role I had played in achieving this impression.

The only question which still disturbed Hrothgar was the matter of excommunication. Six days before the Festival Hrothgar was informed that he had been excommunicated from all established churches, irrespective of creed, and Hrothgar was made uneasy by this prospect of eternal damnation. But by means of what seemed to me to be a very sound philosophical proposition, I managed to make him see that damnation for a worthy cause must be a kind of apotheosis after all. I am not sure whether he wholly understood me, but a smile of acceptance moved across his face and I felt that the Festival had been saved.

The day before the Festival I sent all Vita policy-holders a memorandum reminding them to come to the Festival costumed in a manner reflecting their Vocation, Special Interest or Means-of-Livelihood. Then on the following day, when the hour of the Festival approached, as one of the principal representatives of Vita Company, I took care to dress in a conservative dark suit with appropriate shirt. I decided at the last minute to wear my best leather gloves, although it was entirely too warm for gloves. Then Moira and I walked together toward the Plaza, where already hundreds of people had gathered around Hrothgar's compound. For the past twenty-four hours he had been bound in chains, but in a few minutes he would be brought out into the Plaza and released.

The area around the compound (referred to in the Historical Archives as Alegría Plaza) presented a colorful view, fit for a Breughel or a Titian. Surgeons had come in their white suits, their surgical masks on their foreheads, judges in black gowns; dozens of nurses in uniforms, housewives in aprons; teachers carrying books, plumbers with tools, butchers with their aprons still flecked with blood. There were many children carrying small flags and with pennants attached to their chest identifying their school.

After about twenty minutes the sun suddenly clouded over and people became restless, they complained that the Festival ought to begin at once, that it might begin to rain and their day would be spoiled. Several persons approached to ask me if we might begin, but I replied that I had no wish to expropriate authority which rightfully belonged to others; I added that I thought we ought at least to wait until the Vice President, Mr. Cormoran, arrived; and then, even if not all other officials (members of the Board of Directors, etc.,) were present, we could in all fairness to the policy-holders who had gathered there, begin the Festival.

I was pleased to hear Mr. Cormoran, upon his arrival, echo my sentiments. He looked up at the sky which had become more clouded than ever and announced that we would begin. He ordered that the masks be distributed. This was done in a matter of minutes: the children shrieked with delight at their ingenious disguises—some of gargoyles, some of witches and wizards, some of devils. With considerable deliberation I selected masks of a pair of mourning doves, and after fitting mine securely into place, I handed the other to Moira. Although she did not seem so pleased with my choice as I would have hoped, she made, at the time, no objection.

The blowing of an antique horn (one of my innovations) announced the freeing of Hrothgar. The crowd stood breathless. The silence was so complete we could hear the chains clanking as they were removed from Hrothgar's arms and legs and dropped to the concrete floor. Many women stood expectant, hopeful, their eyes behind their masks filled with tears; and I was pleased that I had chosen well: the Festival was sure to be a success.

As they led Hrothgar to the outer door of the compound he lowered his head so as not to strike it against the stone lintel. Then he stood quietly blinking at the strong sunlight and smiling at the people who had been awaiting him. The guards began a procession directly through the center of the crowd, down an improvised path strewn with rushes, while Hrothgar moved slowly behind them. Hrothgar's holiday attire, his superb form, his warm smile—all were more than the people could bear; his very beauty made waiting any longer impossible.

According to the rule, the first stone, usually an amethyst, is the honored prerogative of the highest man in authority at the Festival, which in this case should have been Mr. Cormoran. But so enthralled was the crowd by Hrothgar's elegance that three bright stones, shining with mica (these had been expressly shipped from the Arizona desert area) were tossed at him from the crowd, all three striking him in the forehead. Blood came freely to his brow as if waiting for just this moment to rush forth. The crowd followed Hrothgar while he ran (as he was required to do) toward the outskirts of the city. For a while, in their zeal, there were so many shells and pebbles in the air that the atmosphere seemed to explode into color, the crowd was in danger of striking each other. Hrothgar ran just far enough ahead of the crowd so that even the most biassed journalists afterwards reported that he ran only in accordance with the rules of the Festival and not through cowardice. From the crowd came repeated cries:

"My sins on your head, Hrothgar!"

"Eternal damnation to you!"

"May all my enemies prosper if I do not hate you, Hrothgar, above all mankind!"

"Murderer!"

"Traitor! Liar! Heretic!"

"Child-beater!"

"Sodomist!"

"Filth-eater!"

"Adulterer!"

The list was endless, the freedom and joy of it dazzling. Hrothgar waved his hands, involuntarily shielding his eyes, he beckoned toward them, then began running again at a measured pace.

"Forgive us, Hrothgar! Love us, Hrothgar!" they wept. They pursued him to the ditch where in the past all Festival Men had stumbled or prepared to stumble. Should the Festival Man's own determination weaken, there were entangling vines and winding creeks which would easily slow him up. But Hrothgar's will was strong, I noted with pride: I felt that the investment of my time with him had been worthwhile. He fell into the ravine like a liege lord from his horse. Quickly the people gathered on either side of the ravine, each one tossing his pebble till the water on each side of the creek ceased to flow and they had created a dam with the body of Hrothgar: one could see all the little creek animals fleeing from the watering place.

Later his body was removed from under the pile of stones and he was given a full military burial, but without sacrament, since his excommunication is irreversible: it is a necessary prerequisite for the renewal of all Vita Fealty Policies that the Festival Man's damnation be perpetual. In the weeks following the Festival, dividends were paid as usual to those policy-holders who had been with the Company at least eighteen months. Others will be obliged to wait until their policy matures, which under a new ruling initiated by Mr. Cormoran requires a waiting period of two years.

Natalie L. M. Petesch was born in Detroit of Russian parents who settled in the black ghetto. She received a B.S. degree from Boston University, an M.A. from Brandeis University, and a Ph.D. from the University of Texas at Austin. She has taught at the University of Texas, Southwest Texas State College, and at San Francisco State College. Her stories have appeared in a number of literary quarterlies and in two anthologies. She is the author of two unpublished novels, and a third, *The Odyssey of Katinou Kalokovich*, is to be published this year. The mother of two children, she presently lives in Pittsburgh, where her husband is a professor of English.

Book and jacket designs are by Dermot McGuinne. The text type is Linotype Palatino, with display lines in Typoscript elongated Roman shaded.